Follow the Infinity

BOOK ONE DAWN

WRITTEN BY

ROSIE ARIANNA

ISBN 978-1-957220-48-2 (paperback)
ISBN 978-1-957220-49-9 (digital)

Image Credit: Mariah Ulrich

Rushmore Press LLC
1 800 460 9188
www.rushmorepress.com

Printed in the United States of America

This is a collection of the madness inside my head. So, mark my words when I say:

Nobody deserves these secrets.

INTRODUCTION

Light. Darkness. Healing. Poison. Ice. Fire. Sky. Earth. These are the eight known types of magic in the world of Wonderland. The wielders of these magic types include elves, fairies, unicorns, fallen angels, changelings, dragons, and other exotic creatures, all of which fall into one of two categories: creatures of light or creatures of darkness. Beings of light tend to be considered 'good' or non-hostile, such as unicorns. Creatures of darkness are thought of as being the complete opposite, or even *evil* in some cases, specifically the dragons.

But in truth, *none* of these creatures are what humans consider to be 'good.' None of them are truly good. Some are just merely *not evil*.

Many of these creatures appear to be very human-like on the outside with exotic features. Others, such as dragons, have humanoid avatars that they can shapeshift in and out of.

Each of these creatures can wield one type of magic, or even be magic-less, determined by their species and nation of origin. Magical creatures can wield *only one type* of magic. Persay, sometimes two types, depending on the creature, but never more . . . never more.

The exceptions to this rule are the Light Spirit and the Dark Spirit. The spirits can be easily identified by the unique silver or black markings on their faces. These two individual beings can wield *all* types of magic between them. The spirits have been protectors of Wonderland since the beginning of time itself. It has always been their duty to keep peace and balance in the world.

To keep Wonderland in a state of balance, the Light and Dark Spirit live in a reincarnation cycle. When they die, they are reborn as someone new. They master the eight types of magic, bring peace to the world, die, and then do it all over again in the next generation of lifetimes.

Wonderland has always consisted of nine nations, each with its own distinct culture and population. There was the Etaellaca Empire, the land of diversity, the Underworld, the realm of eternal night, Luzia, the clown territory, Kuistion Keep, the land of the centaurs, the Piniel Dynasty of the skinwalkers, and the four elemental territories: the Ice Nation, the Fire Kingdom, the Sky Kingdom, and the Earth Nation.

But this world of wonders is a thing of the past. Times have changed and centuries have passed.

The most recent set of spirits lived nearly one thousand years ago. They were Light Spirit Lexa and Dark Spirit Akaos. The two of them never played by the rules. Rather than protect the world from harm, they lived a life of outlaws, running from their duties.

Lexa truly believed it was not fair to be forced to sacrifice over and over again in every lifetime to protect others. She fought her responsibilities at every opportunity—that is until those responsibilities became unavoidable.

A new era was drawing near. The world they lived in was drastically changing, and a new disaster was quickly approaching. At the time, this disaster was referred to as *Nightfall*. But now, it's simply called the end of Wonderland and the start of Infinity.

A massive asteroid was hurtling towards the planet, full-scale destruction of the world would be brought with it. The only ones who could stop it would be the spirits.

When it came down to Nightfall, Akaos was prepared to make his sacrifice, and he wanted it to mean something. Using his immense power, Akaos stopped the asteroid from destroying Wonderland and reflected it into space. However, Akaos had to abandon his life to do so.

With Akaos gone, Lexa became infuriated. She displayed a horrible outrage of her magical capabilities and had turned many of the nations into rubble. Akaos' death had been in vain; the world was destroyed anyways.

Afterward, Lexa had decided that the cause of all her suffering was due to darkness, just like Akaos himself. And she took it upon herself to kill every creature of darkness in the world, wiping them all out into extinction, that is, except for the dragons. The dragons were nearly unkillable, so Lexa did the only other thing she could.

Using the land that was formerly known as the Underworld, Lexa created a new nation, or rather a prison. She forced every dragon from all corners of the globe into this territory and had it named Dragonia, the land of the dragons.

Using her influential abilities as a superpower, Lexa made a statement declaring that if a single dragon were to step claw, wing, or tail out of their territory, it would be constituted as an act of war—a war in which all other nations would engage, essentially, a war the dragons could not win.

And then came an even greater change—Lexa declared the reign of Wonderland over. The world had now entered a new age, an era to be named in honor of what Lexa hoped would last forever. And she named the world *Infinity,* a world without darkness. With this, Lexa's life was over, and she died a year later.

After the tragedy of Lexa and Akaos, neither of them was reborn. Centuries passed while the world eagerly awaited the birth of the next Light and Dark Spirit, but they never came. The cycle was broken. And without the spirits to keep order, the world tumbled into a state of chaos.

But finally, almost seven hundred years after the death of Lexa and Akaos, a spirit was born, a single spirit. In the year 1729, the Dark Spirit had returned to the world in the form of a boy named Zaszage Arazeiros. This new incarnation of the late Dark Spirit Akaos was especially untrustworthy because he was the son of the Dragon King. Zaszage was the Dragon Prince.

Zaszage was furious with the state of the world, furious that his freedom had been stolen from him since birth. He was wicked evil, and at the tender age of thirteen, he killed his mother, the Dragon Queen, before leaving Dragonia.

Once word had gotten out that the new Dark Spirit, a dragon, had left his territory, the other nations were quick to keep their promise. And in the year 1745, they had declared war on Dragonia.

However, one nation didn't attack Dragonia but sided with them. It was the Fire Kingdom. The Fire Kingdom had betrayed its alliance with the rest of the world, and standing beside Dragonia, prepared to take over the other nations.

At the lead of the rebels was the now fifteen-year-old Dragon Prince and Dark Spirit, Zaszage. Standing beside him was the sixteen-year-old newly crowned Firelord, Ash Levitt.

The two of them, working side by side, had caused extreme amounts 0f damage to the other nations in only the first few months of the war. But then, with no warning at all, during one of the larger battles, Zaszage disappeared never to be seen or heard from again.

With Zaszage gone, the rebels lost their greatest asset in this fight, and at this point, the world had gone more than seven hundred years without a Light Spirit, but yet, the war persisted.

And to this day, nearly three hundred years later, with the Light Spirit still gone and the war as inflamed as ever, Zaszage has failed to resurface. If asked, most people would tell you he must be dead and the cycle is broken once more. But the alternative is still a very real possibility.

Dark Spirit Zaszage could still be out there somewhere, hiding and planning his return as the world's greatest threat . . . the Dragon Prince.

PROLOGUE

Year 2053

"It's all ready!" Wesley called from the port. He and the others had already boarded the ship. Alice could make out his silhouette against the setting sun. She had decided to take an extra moment before heading over to the ship, to walk the beach one last time.

Tonight was her last night. Her last night to walk the sands of her homeland one last time. Her last night to say goodbye to everything. Her last chance to set things right. After her twenty-one years of life, it would all end tomorrow with the return of Nightfall. Tonight would be the last time any of them saw daylight.

Alice looked out at the ocean. She let the waves wash up and down over her feet. The sun was casting orange rays over the water as it got ready to retire for the evening.

She felt the presence of someone behind her and turned to see Jack and Fawn. Their expressions were unreadable, but they walked to stand next to Alice with purpose in their stride.

Calmly, the three of them stood next to each other, staring out at the sea and not saying anything. They didn't need to say anything; everything that needed to be said already had been.

But still, there was something Alice had yet to admit. She had been avoiding it, just like she had avoided everything else in her life. If this was truly the end, she might as well face the fact that this would be their last one.

"This is our last adventure," Alice said. "Isn't it?"

Fawn and Jack regarded her with saddened expressions. It was the one thing they never thought they'd hear her say.

"I'm afraid so," Jack said quietly.

"We had a good run," Fawn added, with her eyes glossy.

Now that their time was coming to an end, Alice had been wondering recently how the others felt about those days from the past. Was their time together saving the world with the rest of the Eternals real or just a mantle to be cast off to the future generation? Would they embrace the time they spent together, or would they pretend their adventures had never existed? Would Alice? Their journey certainly hadn't lasted long in the grand scheme of things.

Alice reached into her pocket to hold the crystal that she had stored in there. She wrapped her palm tightly around it. That crystal was the last thing she had of him, the one who she had loved the most in this life. But he was gone now. He had seemed invincible. War would change many, but not him. However, just like so many of the others, the strife of their world had claimed him and he was gone now too.

Alice rubbed her thumb along the smooth side of the crystal. She was careful not to take it out of her pocket for she couldn't let the others see it, at least not yet. That was the crystal made from her own horn and infused with his black blood. Her life was still alive, and his was now gone. Some of his life was inside that crystal, but now Alice would have to let that go too. It was the last thing she had of him, and she'd lose him all over again.

For a moment, an image of his green eyes and chestnut hair flashed across the back of her mind. It was an eccentric time of her life, romantic and uncertain. But that had all died with him.

"To be honest," Alice began. "For once in my life, to be honest, I never thought it would ever end. I always thought we'd live a life full of adventures, until the very end."

"We did," Jack said, turning to face Alice. "Just like my mother always said we would. Up until the end, we experienced a life rich in adventure. Ever since we were those kids traveling to Etaellaca."

"And now," Alice said, "it's up to us to leave the rest for them. All the things we couldn't do will be left for them to experience. For Astrid, and Kimba, and Koda."

Huh? Jack and Fawn thought. Astrid? Kimba? Koda? They knew no one of these names . . . *wait.*

Jack and Fawn looked at each other at the same moment. They were both thinking of the same thing. *Two* people had once mentioned those names to them before. Specifically, the names Kimba and Koda. But who were they? And besides, that was all the way back at the beginning, when they had heard the names. What did it mean for them now?

The thought of the beginning saddened Jack. What he wouldn't give to go back and experience everything all over again. Despite the pain, despite the sadness, in the end, it was worth it all. It was all more than worth it, to have been able to have those good times.

Jack almost forgot what he had come over here for. He held a book in his hands, a scrapbook he had pieced together over the years, filled with treasures from all of their adventures.

"I just don't get it," Alice continued. "Why does it have to end like this, *for us?*"

"We had our chance with saving the world," Fawn began. "But we couldn't stop any of this when we had the chance. And we had a lot of chances. The spirits. The artifacts. Now we're out of chances. I guess the Red Isle is better than nothing. It will be better to die bravely among our friends than to die hiding."

"To understand the ending," Jack said, "we'd have to go back to the beginning. Catch." He tossed Alice the scrapbook. She had never seen it before, so at first, she looked at it, confused. Alice opened it to the first page and almost broke down into tears right on the spot.

It was a picture of her, Jack, and Fawn, a picture that had been taken ages ago. It had been taken on her thirteenth birthday, eight years ago, the day when their adventures had first begun.

"This is from—" Alice's eyes glossed over before she could finish.

"From when it all began," Jack concluded.

Alice touched the picture. She traced the faces of those kids who were now unrecognizable from their former selves.

Alice whispered the words that she thought she'd never hear again. The words that she thought she'd never relive.

"Our very first adventure."

CHAPTER ONE

The Adventure Begins

Elkmire, Capital of Earth Nation, eight years earlier, April 2045

"It's not getting away from me this time," whispered Fawn as she crouched along the tree branch. She peered down at the wolf cub on the ground in front of her. It was all black with blue eyes. She crept further along the wide branch, the leaves of the tree hiding her. The wolf pawed at a puddle in the ground. It hadn't noticed her yet.

From above, Fawn looked down at the cub and caught her reflection rippling in the water of the puddle. She had long orange hair that was always rather messy and had lighter undertones, green cat-like eyes, and freckles that looked like paint splatters on her nose and cheeks. As a wolfwalker, she also had black fluffy ears with a matching tail and a few black stripes on her tan skin.

Fawn was ready to pounce on the cub and claim it as her pet. She peered over her shoulder, her hair drifting in the wind.

"Watch and learn, Alice. This is how you catch a wolf," she quietly exclaimed to the girl who was hiding up in the tree next to her.

Alice snickered. Fawn had underestimated how much faster she had gotten these past couple of months. Fast enough to even outrun a wolfwalker.

However, she miscalculated where she was resting her foot on the branch and accidentally kicked a few leaves off, sending them floating down. The wolf immediately noticed Alice in the tree. It stared directly at her with wide eyes.

Alice was caught off guard. She had expected the cub to run as soon as it saw her. She found herself staring back at the wolf, mesmerized by its curiosity in her.

She had short blonde hair that was tied into ponytails, blue eyes, and silver markings on her face. Alice was a unicorn, with the magical abilities to heal and create light. However, she had lost her horn that was once attached to her head right on the hairline. She had no memory of how it happened or who she was before then. It had always seemed her life didn't exist before her memories did, which started when she met Fawn. Alice was eight then.

Over in the other tree, Fawn prepared to jump down. The cub was still looking at Alice. This was her chance. "Just a little closer." She started sliding off the branch. "It's okay, little wolf, you're gonna be my new pet!"

At that moment, Alice sprung onto the branch Fawn was standing on. "Not if I get it first!" she shouted as she passed Fawn.

The sudden movement of the branch caused Fawn to fall off, and she hit the grassy ground with a thud. "Hey!" she yelled.

Alice ran along the branch and jumped off when she got to the end. Naturally being very athletic, she landed lightly before instantly giving chase to the cub that had already darted off.

Fawn quickly got up and ran after Alice, her long legs gaining fast.

The forest was covered in thick undergrowth, the trees had to be ten or twelve stories tall, and because the land had frequent rain, everything was damp and squishy.

The rainforest was a maze of endless trees, but the girls knew the lay of the land well. After all, they had grown up here, hadn't they?

Alice ran after the cub. She was right behind it. She ducked under low tree branches and hopped over logs in pursuit, and then something bumped into her from behind. Fawn had caught up. She smirked at Alice.

Alice hadn't expected Fawn to catch up so quickly, but it didn't matter. They had spent weeks tracking down the baby wolf. She wasn't about to let it slip away again.

The pair ran side by side. The wolf was slowing down as it ran out of energy. Fawn and Alice were closing in on it with each step. Racing neck and neck, they got closer. . . and closer. . . and closer. . . and then they were right on top of it!

Alice and Fawn dove in at the same time, ready to pounce on the wolf, but it jumped out of the way just in time. And instead, the two girls were left piled on top of each other.

The wolf scurried away in the undergrowth, disappearing.

Alice and Fawn laid there on top of each other, laughing. Surely, they would catch the cub next time.

The girls quieted down as the sound of shoes crunching on leaves got louder. Someone was approaching.

"I see that you two are having fun without me again," came a soft voice from above.

From her upside-down position, Alice looked up to see Jack towering over her. She scrambled off of Fawn and onto her feet.

"Jack!" she shouted as she threw her arms around the boy in a hug. Alice was so eager to see her other friend that she almost caused him to topple onto the ground.

After she let go, Jack helped Fawn up. She dusted herself off. "What are you doing here? I thought you had to go to that important war meeting with the queen," Fawn asked him.

Jack was the son of the queen of the Earth Nation and the only prince. He was fourteen, with silver hair, blue eyes, and pale skin. He was a unicorn, with a long pearly white horn sticking out of his head.

"It's not until late this evening," Jack responded. "I wasn't supposed to leave the palace today, but I managed to pull some strings. After all, today is a special day . . ."

At that moment, Fawn and Jack shouted in unison, "Happy birthday, Alice!"

All of their giddy excitement made Alice smile. She had almost forgotten it was her birthday today, although she was reminded this morning when she checked the calendar. It was April eleventh. Alice was thirteen now. She was several inches shorter than Jack and Fawn and more immature by a long shot, which always happened to make her feel a lot younger than them. However, now that she was thirteen like Fawn, she seemed to be catching up. Fawn would be quickly approaching fourteen.

Fawn and Jack hugged Alice.

"Aw, you guys remembered," she said.

"Of course, we did. What kind of friends would we be if we didn't?" Fawn exclaimed.

Jack reached into his pocket and held out a small wooden device to Alice. "For you," he said.

Alice took the device and looked at it. It was a hand-crafted camera. She knew what it was from pictures she'd seen in books. They were expensive objects that only the rich in places like the Etaellaca Empire and the Piniel Dynasty could afford.

"A camera!" she exclaimed. "I've never seen one in real life before."

"It was *my* idea," Fawn boasted. "Took me months to collect all the pieces."

"Ahem," Jack stated. "Where's *my* credit?"

"Oh right, sorry. *Jack* assembled it. He was the mastermind behind its composition."

"I love it!" Alice squealed. "How does it work?"

"Give it here," Jack said, reaching for the camera.

He ran over to a nearby tree and placed the camera on a low branch. He clicked a button and ran back over to Fawn and Alice.

After a moment, the lens of the camera let out a sudden flash of light. And then a paper was released from the back; it drifted to the ground. Jack went and picked it up.

"Haha! Look at your faces!" he said to the others.

Fawn and Alice looked at the image. The two of them looked stunned by the light as if they had seen a ghost. Jack, on the other hand, smiled at them.

"Guess I have to work on my reactions . . ." Alice said with a tight smile.

"Practice makes perfect!" Fawn exclaimed. "Now, let's go have some fun before the sun goes down!" She skipped away into the trees. Jack and Alice trotted after her.

The trio ran through the rainforest, occasionally swinging on vines or jumping over ravines hidden in the undergrowth.

Before long, they came to the river. The water was crystal clear, and there were colorful fish swimming around in it. Alice stopped and peered into the water at a fish. Her eyes were wide with curiosity.

She reached a hand in to touch the fish, but of course, it darted away. Instead of giving up, Alice jumped into the river and began splashing about it, trying to touch the fish.

From the bank, Jack and Fawn laughed. "No way am I getting wet," Fawn exclaimed as she climbed a nearby tree.

Once a good distance up, she caught hold of a vine and swung across the river. "Woohoo!" she shouted on the way to the other side.

Jack walked a little way down the bank to stepping stones that went across the water and used them as a bridge.

Once over the river, the forest began to thin out. There wasn't as much undergrowth and the trees were slightly further apart. They were nearly back in town. Alice took off running faster and faster in the direction of the city.

"Hey, wait up!" Fawn shouted from behind. But Alice didn't slow. The trees were thinning out even more, and Alice picked up her pace. She was almost there. Just a little further until the cliffside. . .

And there it was. The forest came to an abrupt stop. The ground was far below at the bottom of the cliff, but it was beautiful. On the ground was the Earth Nation capital city of Elkmire. Almost the entire city was in view from this height. Alice could never get enough of this view.

She peered down at the wooden network of shops and houses, all built in the middle of the mountainous rainforest. And just beyond that, she could make out the palace. It was late afternoon, so the sun was reflecting off of the palace's silver sheen.

Fawn and Jack came to stand beside her. They too looked out at the city below.

"This view never gets old," Alice said to them.

"How could it?" Jack started. "This is our home, after all."

Alice thought about the word for a second. "Home," she whispered.

Jack looked out at the city. "Yeah, our home. Where the sun sets behind the mountains every evening and rises above the treetops each morning. Where the wind always carries the scent of rain. This is where we laugh, where we dream, where we love."

"I want to stay here, just like this, with you guys forever," Alice said.

"And we will, won't we?" Fawn asked. Alice looked at Fawn. Fawn was calm with a hopeful expression, but Alice's was unreadable to her.

"I hope so," Jack finally said.

Although she didn't say it, Alice knew deep down that they wouldn't stay there for much longer because they wouldn't get the chance to.

Just outside of Elkmire, in the mountains to the west, was a Fire Kingdom military base. There were several of them throughout the nation dating back to when the war first started. More of these bases had popped up in recent years near Elkmire as the Fire Kingdom prepared to take the last Earth Nation city still standing.

The base had a large wall encircling it, with a gate at the front. In the center of the wall was a large open area, with red flooring that served as a fireproof training ground. The vehicles and weapons were stored on the right-hand side of the base, and on the left were the housing dorms built inside the wall.

Sitting on the top of the wall with her feet dangling off was the Fire Kingdom Force Captain, Wildfire Amulet. She looked down at the city of Elkmire in the distance with a stern expression on her face.

Wildfire was only fifteen, one of the youngest to ever be appointed Force Captain. She had long red hair that had orange and yellow streaks through it, with matching amber eyes. Her skin was tan and because she was a Fire Blood Elf, her ears were pointed. A pink scar stretched over the bridge of her nose.

Seated on the wall next to her was Wildfire's pet supernova, a giant red cat that she had named Nova.

Two Fire Kingdom soldiers walked up to Wildfire. She did not acknowledge their presence, either because she didn't notice or didn't care. One of the soldiers was a Lieutenant, the rank below Force Captain.

"We don't mean to interrupt you, Force Captain," the Lieutenant began cautiously. "But it's been over three hours and you haven't given the troops any orders."

Wildfire was quick to shoot a response. "I don't care what they do!" she exclaimed. The Lieutenant looked at the soldier next to him. They were treading on thin ice.

"I don't need to remind you of the deadline approaching," he went on.

Wildfire shook her head, looking weary. "What deadline? What are you talking about?" she asked.

"The deadline Firelord Ash set for you a year ago when he promoted you to Force Captain and tasked you with conquering the rest of the Earth Nation." The Lieutenant replied.

Wildfire laid down along the wall lazily. She had always been somewhat oblivious to her role in this war.

The Lieutenant continued. "If you don't conquer Elkmire by the spring's end, Firelord Ash will almost certainly denote you from Force Captain, and the rest of us-" Wildfire cut him off with a threatening stare. He had gone too far.

Wildfire stood up, a new sense of fire burning behind her eyes. "You better watch your mouth, Lieutenant. I am your Force Captain. Show some respect, or *I'll* teach it to you."

The Lieutenant looked away. He and the other soldier stood completely still, afraid of aggravating Wildfire any further. She turned around to face away from them.

After a moment, the Lieutenant went on, choosing his next words carefully. "My apologies, Force Captain. I did not mean to disrespect you. As one of your serving Lieutenants, I only wish to inform you of your duties. The Earth Nation is in ruins, Elkmire is the only stronghold left. Why don't we attack now while they are still vulnerable?"

Wildfire whipped back around to face him again. "Because I don't want to!" she yelled. Her eyes were blazing, and a piece of her hair came undone to dangle in front of her face.

The giant cat, Nova, flinched at Wildfire's sudden outburst and sat up. Wildfire suddenly became more aware of herself. She turned around, smoothed back her hair, and collected her composure.

She began to speak without turning around, more calmly now. "The Earth Nation capital is a strong and powerful city, I don't want to attack until we are fully prepared. If we launch an attack and fail, Firelord Ash will be disappointed with me, and I *cannot* let that happen. Tell the troops to continue their training, we will attack Elkmire when the opportunity to do so arises."

At this, the supernova laid its head back down and resumed its calm composure. The Lieutenant and the soldier saluted to Wildfire and then marched off.

Although it seemed as if she had cooled down, the thought of Firelord Ash ever being disappointed with her scared Wildfire out of her mind. What would she do then? More than anything, she needed the young Firelord's approval of her.

But yet, here she was, on the other side of the world. He wasn't around to tell her what she should be doing, and it's not like he cared about her that way anyhow.

Wildfire gave an angry "tsk." and then stormed off.

Alice, Jack, and Fawn ran through the streets of Elkmire. The city was mystical. It had wooden buildings built amongst the trees and hills, and paved stone boardwalks. It was twilight out, so lanterns illuminated the streets.

Alice breathed in the familiar smell. Out there, freely running around those streets, had a certain aura to it. That aura took the form of the smell of a fresh breeze carrying the scent of rain. It had to be her favorite scent in the whole world.

The trio approached a small stand in front of a shop selling rose moose pudding: a dessert similar to flavored whipped cream that had rose petals sprinkled on top.

Alice asked for banana flavor, Jack settled on blueberry, and Fawn wanted strawberry.

The seller turned away to prepare the dish, and while he wasn't looking, Fawn snatched a few snacks from the stand, hastily pocketing them away. At this, Alice gave Fawn a stern glare. Fawn had a habit of taking what wasn't hers, something that stemmed from not having enough as a kid.

Jack stepped in front of Alice, and, taking Fawn's hand in his, he placed a few coins in her hand to pay for the items she had stolen. Fawn looked at the money, and then looked up at Jack, his blue eyes filled with kindness. With her cheeks a rosy red, Fawn placed the coins inside the seller's jar.

After a few minutes, Alice and Fawn stepped away from the stand, eating spoonfuls of their pudding. When they realized Jack wasn't behind them, they turned around to see a group of older girls who had encircled him, begging for his attention. They must have recognized Jack as the beloved prince of the nation.

Jack's cheeks were bright pink as he tried his best to amuse the fans. From where they stood watching, Alice laughed at the sight, but Fawn just blew the hair out of her face with a heavy sign. After a moment, Fawn smirked and then flicked some of her pudding onto Alice's face.

"Ah!" Alice shouted out. Fawn skipped away and Alice took off after her, the two of them flicking pudding on each other as they went.

As the sun began to set, the three kids made their way to the palace. The Earth Nation palace was a solid silver color and towered about thirty stories high in the air.

The guards opened the large doors for them, and in they went. Jack had mentioned there was something he wanted to give Alice, so they walked swiftly through the many corridors.

As they walked, guards, servants, and any other staff would all nod at Jack as he passed, or even salute. Jack would always smile in response or casually nod back.

Eventually, they made their way to a floor high up in the palace. The long corridor had massive windows that overlooked the city. Standing in front of one of the windows was Queen Rosenia.

She had long brown hair and brown eyes. Rosenia was a middle-aged Earth Blood Elf.

"Hey, mom!" Jack exclaimed as he ran up to hug his mother. Jack looked nothing like Rosenia. Not only was he a unicorn unlike her, but with his silver hair and blue eyes, he was definitely his father's son.

"There you are, Jack," Rosenia said with a voice as smooth as honey. "I've been looking for you." She switched her gaze to Alice. "Alice, happy birthday, dear child."

"Thank you!" Alice said, smiling.

Jack shifted closer to his mom, quietly saying, "So, uh . . . mom, do you have the . . . uh . . . well the thing?" he asked.

Rosenia laughed and said, "Yes, actually I do."

She reached into her pocket and pulled out a glowing pink crystal attached to a chain. Fawn's eyes widened and Alice's sparkled.

Rosenia began to explain the breathtaking object. "This is the Crystal of Life. It has immense healing abilities. However, it can only be used once before its life energy depletes. It's a very rare relic that has been passed down in my family for generations."

Rosenia handed the crystal to Alice. "It was given to me by my mother, and now, I want you to have it."

Alice could hardly believe what a precious gift it was. Sure, she had personally known Rosenia for a while, but the queen had many children she could have chosen to give the crystal to, but she chose Alice.

"What an honor! Thank you so much," Alice said. She held the crystal up above her face, the pink light emitting out of it brightly.

"Use it wisely," Rosenia said quietly. The queen gently touched each of the kids' shoulders before walking away, out of sight.

Alice thought about the crystal. If it could only be used once, she would have to save it for something extremely important, but what? Use it wisely, Rosenia had said . . . Alice slowly turned her head to look at Jack. He was looking up at the crystal. The pink light softly illuminated his face.

Alice looked into Jack's eyes. For a moment, *she could have sworn she saw a splatter of blood and an image of death in the reflection of his blue eyes.* This is what Jack wanted her to have . . . but why?

At that moment, two guards approached from the direction Rosenia had gone in. The guards bowed their heads to Jack and one of them said, "Prince Jack, the queen has requested an audience with you."

"Y-yes. Tell her I'll be right there," Jack responded. After the guards marched off, Jack turned to face Alice and Fawn. "Well, that's my cue. Time for the meeting."

"We'll catch up with you later," Alice said. And then Jack left, walking quickly down the hall. Alice watched him go, looking on as his shadow dissipated beyond the corridor.

The sun had set behind the mountains of the military base, casting an orange glow through the sky. Force Captain Wildfire stood on the red flooring of the base practicing her fire magic as she sparred with a soldier.

She blasted a fiery kick at her opponent, exerting flames from her foot. The soldier stumbled out of the way. He was not able to keep up with her.

Satisfied, Wildfire looked over to an older man sitting next to the red flooring who was casually sipping tea. Without looking up, the man said, "Again," before taking another sip of his tea.

He was Master Yagatsu, a Fire Blood Elf and a retired Admiral of the Fire Kingdom military. He had long black hair, a matching beard, and pointed ears.

Wildfire snarled at Yagatsu and then whipped around and hit the soldier with the same fiery kicks as before. This time, he fell over, but Wildfire also fell in the process.

"Do it again!" Yagatsu yelled at Wildfire.

She stood up and stormed over to the master. "Enough. I've been practicing the same move all day! Teach me the Skyfire move. I'm more than ready!" she demanded.

Yagatsu looked up from his tea to meet her gaze, "No, you are impatient. You are strong, but you lack restraint. Do the kicks again! And get it right this time, would you?"

Wildfire angrily whipped back around and launched a huge fire blast at the soldier who had not yet recovered from her previous attack. He was sent flying backward and hit the wall with a grunt.

Wildfire turned back around and marched up to Master Yagatsu. "You're a pathetic old man. Do you know that?" she began. "You've been teaching me fire magic since I was a toddler, and you've never been any good at it! All I ever wanted to learn from you was the Skyfire move, and you never taught me anything! The Earth Nation is on the brink of rebelling. They have an army filled with elves whose earth magic alone can take us out! Not to mention they have unicorns who can heal their wounded faster than we can take them out! If Firelord Ash will only be satisfied with me once I've taken this city in his name, then so be it!" She was breathing heavily and was wildly out of control, which normally happened when she talked about Ash.

Master Yagatsu sat there, unfazed, and calmly sipped his tea, as Wildfire continued to shout, "You *will* teach me the Skyfire move!"

Yagatsu stood up and set down his tea to walk onto the mat. "Very well," he began. "You can have it your way, but don't say I didn't warn you."

He walked out to the middle of the mat and took a few deep breaths. He then began to create a huge ball of fire with his hands. He positioned himself into a lunge position, all the while continuing to keep the fireball going. In a single motion, he sent the fireball shooting up high into the sky. It continued to go higher and higher, absorbing air and growing larger. And then, all at once, it began its descent. With alarming speed, the fireball crashed onto the ground on the other side of the gate, lighting the area on fire.

The master walked over to the gate, opened it, and stepped outside. With a wave of his hand, the flames dispersed into nothing to reveal a crater the explosion had made.

Walking back over to Wildfire, he explained, "The Skyfire move is a rare fire magic skill that can only be performed by highly trained Fire Blood Elves. This move requires not only great skill but also strength and concentration. If one does not have the willpower to send the ball of fire high enough into the air, it will come crashing back down on you."

Wildfire's eyes grew wide with her own inner fire. "I'm ready to try it!" she exclaimed.

As she walked further onto the mat, Yagatsu said, "Remember what I told you about control," but Wildfire ignored this comment.

She proceeded to create a ball of fire just as Yagatsu did. Wildfire had a raw talent for fire magic. Her fireball had to be twice the size of Yagatsu's, and it continued to increase in size because of her lack of restraint.

Wildfire sent the ball of fire into the sky with perfect form, but she deserted her stance too soon. The fireball ended up shooting only half as high as Yagatsu's example had, and in an instant, the ball came crashing back toward her.

She yelped and covered her face with her hands. A moment before the ball would have scorched her and the surrounding area, Yagatsu stepped in and pointed his hands at the fireball. In an instant, the heat, the fire, and everything the ball was made of vaporized into thin air.

Wildfire was now on the ground. Yagatsu stepped over her, picked up his tea, and began heading indoors. Without looking back, he said, "I told you, you were not ready."

Alice and Fawn walked through the empty streets toward the outskirts of the city where Alice's house was. The sun had almost completely set and everyone had gone home for the evening.

Eventually, they made their way to the Liddell family house. This was where Alice lived with her adoptive family. The house was at the forest's edge, built high up in the treetops with many bridges and structures dangling in the trees.

Alice and Fawn walked up a spiral staircase built among a tree, up to one of the bridges. From there, they entered the main structure of the treehouse.

Inside was a man with a sturdy build and brown hair. He put on a silver and green uniform in front of a mirror. He was Nickoli Liddell, an Earth Blood Elf who had adopted Alice when she appeared in Elkmire when she was eight.

"Daddy!" Alice shouted as she ran up to hug Nickoli. He hugged her back "There's my girl! I was hoping you'd make it back before I had to leave."

Alice looked up at him. "You have to go to the war meeting too?" she asked.

"Yes, all the commanders and high-ranking soldiers are required to attend."

"But I just got home!" Alice complained.

"I know," Nickoli began. "But there is something I have that might cheer you up . . ." he walked over to an open window and shouted, "Lizzie?"

At that moment, a high-pitched voice shouted from somewhere outside. "Is it time? Is it time? Oh, please tell me it's time yet!" and then crashing through the window came the ten-year-old Earth Fairy, Lizzie.

Lizzie had long brown hair, tan skin, green eyes, and a freckle on her cheek. Her wings were green and looked as delicate as glass. Lizzie was Nickoli's biological daughter.

Lizzie zipped over to Alice and hugged her with such force the two of them ended up on the ground.

"Alice!" Lizzie shouted. "Oh, I'm glad you're here! I've been waiting for you to come home all day!"

Alice stood up. "Well, it's good to see you too, Lizzie."

Lizzie held up a pot of yellow flowers she had been holding. "It's for you! Do you like it? Do you? Do you! Do you!" she asked eagerly.

Alice's eyes grew wide as she held the pot of flowers. They were yellow dragon tulips, a very rare specimen of flower that Nickoli had given her every year on her birthday since he found her those five years ago. Alice treasured these flowers more than any other thing she had ever owned.

"How did you find these again!" Alice exclaimed. "They don't come into season for another two months!"

"I know, your sister and I spent weeks scouring the forest for these bad boys. Each time, we were practically almost captured by the Fire Kingdom!" Nickoli said. He walked closer and hugged both of his daughters. "But it was worth it," he said.

Alice and Lizzie walked back down to the ground with Nickoli to tell him goodbye before he left for the palace. He hopped onto a gigantic blue bird and shouted, "Reezu, Fly! Fly! Fly!" With that, the giant bird flapped its enormous wings and took off.

Back on one of the bridges of the treehouse, Fawn paced around. She hopped about from tree to tree with her nose pointed up in the air and her tail slashing from side to side.

"Is something wrong?" Alice asked.

Fawn replied quickly, "Just fine." She hopped onto the ground beside Alice and Lizzie and then snapped her head toward the forest.

"There's that baby wolf again!" she shouted.

"What?" Alice exclaimed. The two of them took off into the forest at full speed. Lizzie followed them from above.

Once the ten-year-old got a look at the cub, she shouted, "Aww, it's so cute!"

From the ground, Fawn replied, "Yeah, and I'm gonna catch it."

Before long, the girls had traveled deep into the forest outside the city. Alice was in the lead. She ran along a large log after the wolf. In an instant, Fawn appeared beside Alice on the log and shouldered her off.

She tumbled into a shallow ravine nearby and scratched her lip on a tree branch. She laid there for a second trying to catch her breath. By the sound of Fawn in the distance saying, "Finally!" Alice assumed she had caught the cub.

Alice sat up after a moment, and the sound of someone behind her whispering *"Alice. . ."* startled her. She did not recognize the voice, nor did it sound particularly male or female.

She turned around, but there was no one there.

"Alice. . ." the voice said again. After hearing the call a second time, Alice noticed something strange coming from underneath the vines in the ravine next to her.

She saw a small spark of something hiding in the undergrowth that caught her eye. She crawled over there to find a scroll hidden in the plants. The spark had come from the golden writing of a name on the side of the scroll. Alice was surprised to find that the name read ALICE in bold sparkly letters.

The sound of Lizzie shouting, "Alice!" and "Are you okay?" gradually got louder as she flew into the ravine with Fawn close behind. And the little cub was at Fawn's feet.

They came to sit by Alice as she peered at the scroll. "What is that?" Fawn asked.

"I don't know," Alice said. "It has my name on it."

Lizzie and Fawn looked at the gold writing. "Maybe it belongs to another Alice?" Lizzie suggested.

Fawn traced the letters with her fingertip. Her eyes were very wide and she looked absolutely shocked.

Alice quickly noticed Fawn's sudden change in behavior. "Fawn," she began. "Do you know what this is?"

Fawn quickly shook her head from side to side and stepped back. From the way her eyes darted around and the pounding of her pulse, Alice knew Fawn was lying.

Alice opened the scroll up, but there was no writing. The only thing on the paper was a strange black symbol.

Instinctively, Alice lifted her finger to touch the symbol. Immediately after the touch, the paper of the scroll began to ripple like water.

"Woah!" Fawn exclaimed. Once the paper cleared, it revealed a few sentences written in golden letters imitating a cursive font. Alice read the writing aloud:

"Greetings, Light Spirit Alice. You have been away for a long time. Infinity is in danger! Complete the tasks to return the world to a state of peace and balance once more. Lexa's time is over, and now it is your turn, your chance, so do not waste it! Touch the paper again to receive your very first task. Let us forever rejoice in your return, Light Spirit! And so, the adventure begins!"

Alice sat there completely still. What did this mean? Why was her name on the scroll? What Light Spirit? Who was it talking about?

Fawn and Lizzie, strangely, did not share Alice's state of confusion. Alice pretended not to notice. She lifted her finger to touch the paper again, but Fawn pulled her hand back. "No!" she shouted. "Don't touch it again, you don't want to mess it up!"

Alice stared at Fawn in disbelief. So, she did know what the scroll was, but how?

"But I want to know what it says!" Alice said. "It has my name on it. So, it must be meant for me." She hesitated for a second, remembering how it also used "Alice" and "Light Spirit" in the same sentence.

"It called me, the Light Spirit? But why, I mean the Light Spirit hasn't been seen for a thousand years, so—" Alice half expected either Lizzie or Fawn to finish her sentence and admit the scroll was talking about some other Alice or was just wrong, but they didn't.

In an instant, an eruption of thunder sounded from the sky and lightning struck the ground somewhere in the distance. Lizzie shrieked, and the wolf cub yelped at the sudden outburst. All at once, rain began to pour.

Fawn picked up the baby wolf. "Let's get out of here!" she shouted to them. Lizzie and Fawn headed for the exit of the ravine, but Alice sat there on the ground a second longer.

She slowly lifted her head to the sky and let the rain hit her face. It reminded her of the night when Queen Rosenia first found her. A lot of things had changed since then and would continue to change.

Alice sat there in a daze. She knew something like this was coming. All along, she had known but refused to accept it. And now, she would face the consequences.

Fawn raced back to Alice and pulled her to her feet. She snatched the scroll from Alice and tucked it into her pocket. Strangely, instead of being damaged by the water, the rain slid off the paper of the scroll easily. It was waterproof.

Alice and Fawn climbed out of the ravine to meet Lizzie and the cub at the top. The team raced through the forest, using their hands as shields from the rain. The rainforest was dark. There was almost no light coming off the moon. To suffice, Alice stretched her arm out in front of her and began emitting white light from the palm of her hand. As a unicorn, creating light was her specialty.

Lizzie struggled to keep up with Fawn and Alice. She squealed with each bolt of lightning or clap of thunder. "Can't fly in rain! Can't fly in rain! Can't fly in rain!" she shouted. Alice doubled back, and, taking Lizzie's hand in hers, continued to race through the rain until they had caught up with Fawn.

Jack sat perfectly upright on his throne in the war room. On the throne to his left was Queen Rosenia. To his right was his elder sister by one year, Princess Gaia, an Earth Blood Elf. Gaia had tan skin, blue eyes, and short brown hair.

On the throne beside Rosenia was Jack's other elder sister by three years, Princess Aurora. Aurora was also an Earth Blood Elf. She had long braided brown hair and brown eyes. The throne she sat in was designated for the leader of the military, a role typically taken by the King or eldest Prince of the nation. It had once belonged to their father, but seeing Aurora was the oldest child, the role of military leader had been passed down to her after him. As a natural-born leader, Aurora had always been a perfect fit for the job.

In front of the royal family was a long table that had a map of all of the Infinity built into it. Sitting around the table were the Earth Nation military's highest-ranking officers, including Commander Nickoli.

"Commander Shyo, give your report," Rosenia asked one of the officers.

The man at the head of the table stood. "Yes, ma'am." He walked over to the portion of the map labeled EARTH NATION. Almost the entire portion had been colored red as new Fire Kingdom territory.

The Commander spoke loudly for everyone to hear. "Almost four years ago, the Fire Kingdom launched a full-scale attack on the city of Ekasas, in which they conquered it, leaving our capital, Elkmire, as the only city still standing. The battle was a blood frenzy, leaving both sides with heavy losses . . . very heavy losses."

As Rosenia listened to the Commander speak, she began to look very pained. The battle of Ekasas, the battle that had stolen their King . . . had it really been four years ago?

"Since then, the Fire Kingdom has been regrouping and has not made any further advancements on our territory," Commander Shyo finished.

"What are your suggestions?" the queen asked him.

"I suggest we use this time to deploy all our troops to Ekasas, in which we will potentially drive the Fire Kingdom out of the region, and reclaim it for the Earth Nation."

Nickoli spoke up at this. "And leave our entire capital vulnerable? It's not going to happen," he argued.

Aurora sat up straighter. "I agree with Commander Shyo. If we don't start trying to reclaim our land now, we won't ever get the chance to," she said.

Jack wanted to pitch in his ideas and opinions, but he knew it wasn't his place yet. He and Gaia were only fourteen and fifteen.

They were allowed to be present at the war meetings, but would not be allowed to speak in them until they were at least sixteen.

"No. Nickoli is right," Rosenia began. "We can't afford to lose Elkmire too. Right now, our top priority should be keeping our forces here, to protect our capital."

"Then what would you have us do?" Shyo asked.

Rosenia got up and walked closer to the table. She studied the map, intently taking in the red-colored Earth Nation.

"I don't know if we can still win this war," she said quietly.

Before anyone could say another word, the double doors to the war room flung open, creating a booming noise that echoed throughout. In the doorway stood Alice, Fawn, and Lizzie. All of them were soaking wet and looking weary.

Jack's eyes grew wide with distress and his cheeks grew warm with embarrassment. He ran over to the girls. "You guys, now isn't the time for games! You have to leave! We're in the middle of important stuff!"

Fawn rushed up to Jack, and putting a hand on his shoulder, she whispered something into his ear that Alice could not hear. The two of them proceeded to rush over to Queen Rosenia, and the three of them began talking quietly in a hushed conversation.

Alice stood there idly. She kept her eyes on the ground. The whole way to the palace, Fawn had led them and insisted they speak with Rosenia immediately. What were they all hiding from her? Alice wanted to know, but she was not about to ask any questions. She didn't want to believe what was happening—what was about to happen.

Maybe this was all just a bad dream. . . perhaps, she'll wake up soon. . . and then life could go back to being carefree, just like it was this afternoon—adventures through the forest and snacking on rose moose pudding. Yes, Alice thought. That was it. It must be a dream. There was no way she was about to live through this nightmare again, no way would she allow herself to be preyed upon by him again.

Alice awoke from her thoughts to Jack shaking her shoulder vigorously.

She looked at her surroundings. She was still in the war room although all the soldiers had been dismissed. Now it was only Jack, Fawn, Lizzie, Nickoli, Rosenia, and the two princesses who sat in the room with her.

Everyone stared at Alice. Jack walked her over to the table and they sat down with the others. Queen Rosenia now held the scroll Alice had found.

From across the table, Jack whispered, "A-are you okay?" to Alice.

She looked at him. His eyes displayed all sorts of concern. "Yeah, why?"

"Well, um, you were mumbling something, and I was just a little concerned, that's all," he stammered. *Poor Jack,* Alice thought. *Always so concerned with others. He always has been. Sometimes, it ends up being his greatest downfall, but he's true to himself . . . and that's why I—*

"This is all happening just as I had expected," Rosenia interrupted Alice's thoughts. "We tried for five years to find the scrolls ourselves. But in the end, it was Alice, just as I had expected."

Alice didn't know what to do. Should she ask about whatever Rosenia was talking about, maintaining her naive act? Or should she just stay quiet because she knew what was coming? *No,* she thought. *I have to know more about the scroll and what they had to do with its appearance if I hope to get out of this.*

"What's going on? Why is this scroll so important? And why do you guys even know what it is?" she asked hesitantly.

Rosenia stood up. The room was quiet. She walked to the head of the table. "In our greatest hour of need, the legendary warrior has returned to us. After a thousand years of chaos, it is time for you to bring the world back into balance, Light Spirit Alice," she said.

Alice froze. It had been many years since she had been called that. Sure, she read it on the scroll a half-hour ago, but hearing it for the first time again, *Light Spirit,* was triggering. For a moment, she thought hearing the name would bring back all the memories she had fought so hard to forget. The way she had lost her horn, how she ended up in the Earth Nation, and who she was before would all be trickling back.

But by some miracle, the memories continued to distance themselves from Alice.

If she continued to play coy about being the Light Spirit, it would be easier on the others. They hadn't suspected she already knew, and she didn't want to hurt them with all the truth . . . at least not yet. And this single truth would lead to all the rest.

"Wh-what are you talking about? I'm not the L-light . . . the spirits are gone," she mustered to say.

"We have known you were the Light Spirit for some time now," Rosenia said. "Ever since I found you out in that storm, I knew."

A sudden bolt of lightning struck outside and lit up the room for a split second. In that second, Alice thought back to that night.

She was eight years old, stumbling through the forest just outside Elkmire in the night. She had a massive gouge on her hairline where her unicorn horn used to be. The blood poured down her face and mixed with the rain from the storm. She tripped and fell. Staring up at the sky, she thought this would be her end. This is how she would die. But then, a face appeared, a woman. She picked up Alice and carried her to a nearby structure. Alice caught a glimpse of a little unicorn boy with silver hair and bright blue eyes, a young Jack, standing near the structure, and then it all went black.

Alice's thoughts came back to the present. This was all happening too fast. She never wanted to be the Light Spirit. It had only ever caused her pain. She wasn't the one who could save the world, and she didn't want to. Her only hope would be to deny it further.

"That doesn't prove anything! The Light Spirit has been gone for a thousand years, and the Dark Spirit has been missing for three hundred! Just because some scroll says I'm the Light Spirit doesn't mean it's true! Do you guys even hear yourselves?" she shouted, grasping at straws.

Nickoli reached his hand across the table toward Alice. "Alice, honey, that night when Rosenia found you, she recognized the markings on your face, and so did I. The markings that hadn't been seen in a thousand years served as proof. *You* are the Light Spirit, a being many of us had thought vanished from the world long ago."

"But now you have returned to us," Rosenia said quietly. "And you have found one of the Sacred Scrolls."

Sacred Scrolls, Alice thought. *So that's what they're called.* She had heard of the scrolls before. She knew they were made of powerful time-warping magic, and they were supposed to help the spirits bring peace to the world during times of turmoil. But how did the others know about it? Fawn and Jack too? They were looking for it and never thought to tell her?

"Sacred Scrolls?" Alice asked, trying to sound as confused as possible. Rosenia nodded.

"Three hundred years ago, just before the war began, a skinwalker by the name of Karma Everday created two scrolls. This was a few years after the long-awaited rebirth of the Dark Spirit. Karma believed the world was tumbling into a state of chaos without the spirits protecting it, and he was right, you see, as the war was in the making. He created one scroll for the Dark Spirit, and one for the Light Spirit. The scrolls were rich in magic, and could only be accessed by the spirits themselves. The scrolls would tell the spirits step by step what they needed to do to bring balance back to the world.

"But Karma was a butterflywalker. When he made the scrolls, he was in the caterpillar stage of his life, and before he could help more, his transformation began, or so I heard. While he was wrapped up in his cocoon, the new Dark Spirit, a wicked and chaotic dragon, stole the scrolls to try and obtain the fruitful magic within. Not much longer after that, the war began. The Dark Spirit mysteriously disappeared, never to be seen or heard from again, and the scrolls were lost with him.

"I have heard many rumors about possible locations for the scrolls' whereabouts. Places like the dragon palace up in Windbourne, or hidden in the dragon temple, or even with the Dark Spirit himself, wherever he is. But one thing was always clear, the magic inside the scrolls is connected to the spirits. One way or another, the scroll would find its way back home. After we met you, Alice, I sent out undercover teams scouring the world for the Light Spirit's Sacred Scroll. That way, we'd be able to use it to help us in this fight. Fawn and Jack have undergone years of special training and went on several expeditions of their own in search of the scrolls. I thought that since they were close to you, they would have a better chance of finding the scroll."

Alice could not believe what she was hearing. This whole time, everyone had been dancing around her, pretending they didn't know anything about who she was, but all along, they were preparing to send her down the same path she had tried so hard to run away from.

"Now that we finally have the scroll, what's our next move?" asked Nickoli.

"We figure out how it works, and we do as it says. Alice will have to begin training as well," Rosenia responded. She looked over at Alice. "We had originally hoped to tell you of your fate once you turned sixteen, but I don't think we can afford to wait that long anymore."

Rosenia walked over to one of the large windows that overlooked the city. "The day has come when the spirits will roam Infinity once more. This era of chaos is coming to an end. In order to win this war, and restore balance to the world, Alice must follow the steps of the Sacred Scroll. She is our hope and our future," she said with the smallest glimmer of hope.

Alice stood up, and for the first time in five years, she let down her act. For the first time since she'd met the people in this room, she wasn't acting, she wasn't pretending to be a sweet naive little girl who didn't know anything.

Alice walked over to the window next to Rosenia. She opened the door to a balcony and stepped out into the cool night air. Jack and Fawn followed her out.

Alice looked out at the softly illuminated city. After everything she had done to ensure she wouldn't have to have the world's strife put on her shoulders, it was happening again. Everything had been for nothing. She thought back to something someone once told her. *No matter which way you try to run, you'll get caught in the end.* Sega had once told her that . . . wait a minute. . . who's Sega?

Alice couldn't seem to remember, but it didn't matter. The thought of everything that was coming weighed down on her. The dawn of this hour seemed to prey upon her. The realization of everything struck her deeper than ever. *She* was the Light Spirit, and she would have to save the world. She didn't have a choice. It was all too much to handle. Alice felt herself slipping.

As she looked out at the city, she felt a white glow seep out of her eyes. She could sense Jack and Fawn around her but couldn't hear what they were saying.

Alice's eyes had gone completely white. They were glowing like white fire. The markings on her face had lit up too. More white light seeped out of her and swirled around her body. And then, with no warning at all, the light gathered and shot up into the air creating a huge beam of light.

Jack and Fawn jumped back at the sight. After the beam shot up, Alice stopped glowing, and she collapsed. Jack caught her. The white beam of light had dissipated into the sky and left ripples of its white light dancing in the sky, like the celestial lights.

Jack looked up at the lights, and then back at Alice. She was unconscious, but even so, tears flowed down her cheeks.

Wildfire walked along the top of the military base's wall with Master Yagatsu at her side. It was late, and they had a long day. It was time for some rest.

But then, out of nowhere, a huge beam of light shot up into the sky from somewhere in Elkmire.

"What is that?" Wildfire shouted. She and Yagatsu stopped dead in their tracks to look at the light. After a moment, the beam dissipated and left celestial lights dancing in the sky.

"That . . . light . . ." Yagatsu whispered. "It has to be . . . it has to be," he was in too much awe to finish.

Wildfire finished for him. "The Light Spirit," she said. Wildfire stared up at the white lights in the sky. No being in all of Infinity could create a light of that magnitude. This was an omen from the gods, a sign that their world was changing.

If the Light Spirit has returned to the world, of course she'd be in Elkmire. She's probably trying to stop the Fire Kingdom from taking it, Wildfire thought.

"For a thousand years, the Light Spirit has been gone," Yagatsu said in astonishment. "I never thought I'd live to see the day of her return."

"Firelord Ash's deadline is approaching soon," Wildfire began. "I won't be denoted from Force Captain. I refuse to be a failure in his eyes. And I'm in luck because this is just the opportunity I've been waiting for."

"Wildfire," Yagatsu said. "What are you saying?"

She looked at him with a fire burning behind her eyes. "It's time for us to follow through with our plans," she said. "Elkmire can try and resist the inevitable, but their city will fall. Go and tell the troops." Master Yagatsu turned and walked away swiftly.

Wildfire looked at the glowing city of Elkmire in the distance. "Tomorrow . . . we wage war."

CHAPTER TWO

Fire in the Sky

The sun had not yet risen, but Wildfire was already awake, storming about the military base. Despite it still being dark out, the base was buzzing with life. Wildfire had given the order for an attack at daybreak. Today, they would invade Elkmire, taking the only remaining free Earth Nation land in the name of the Firelord.

For a task this large, she would normally have to consult with Admiral Aeros, the highest-ranking soldier in the Warrior Regiment who oversaw this portion of the military. However, Admiral Aeros was close friends with the Firelord and almost impossible to get a hold of, so Wildfire would just have to do this on her own.

As a Force Captain of the Warrior Regiment, Wildfire had about two hundred soldiers under her command. She could easily team up with one of the other Force Captains to double her forces, but Wildfire wanted this to be done solely in her name. This way, Firelord Ash would have no choice but to recognize her.

Wildfire walked swiftly over to where soldiers were preparing the vehicles for move out. They had the advantage of surprise on their side. This battle would be easily won. At the end of today, she'd have the Light Spirit captured and readied to hand over to Firelord Ash.

Alice laid unconscious on the large map table in the war room. Jack and Fawn stood near her, waiting for her to wake up. Rosenia had said the huge beam of light had been caused by Alice's sudden realization and that it had most likely drawn lots of attention from unwanted sources.

They had to be on edge, ready for anything. Now, most of the people living in the northeastern hemisphere of the planet had suspected the Light Spirit's return.

Alice suddenly awoke to a bright light striking her in the face. She sat up, startled.

"Sorry . . ." Fawn said, taking a step back. It took Alice a second, but she realized Fawn had been forcing her eyelids open as she was unconscious.

"What happened?" Alice asked wearily. Out of the corner of her eye, she noticed Jack and Fawn look at each other. They didn't know what to say.

"Well . . . um . . . there was a beam of light . . ." Fawn began. "And then, um . . ."

"Oh," Alice said. "Right." She knew exactly what had happened. She didn't know whether or not to keep up her act, the sweet, naive little girl who Jack and Fawn knew. It just wasn't her . . . but it was the only Alice they had ever known. Alice sympathized with them and put on a brave face.

"I can't *believe* we let this happen," Jack exclaimed. "We should have told you the truth a long time ago."

"It's alright," Alice said. She decided she would reveal to them a single truth. They were her friends and only family. This one truth would be okay.

"I've known I was the Light Spirit. I'm not *that* stupid," she said, trying to sound as innocent as possible.

"What!" Fawn exclaimed. Jack also looked shocked. "Why didn't you ever say anything?" he asked.

"I didn't know the rest of you guys knew," Alice began. "I was scared because I thought it would make me a target. I was scared of the responsibilities that came along with being a Spirit, especially one who hasn't been seen in a thousand years. And because I didn't remember anything else about my past, I thought it would be easy to rope the whole Light Spirit thing in with the rest of my forgotten memories. It's my fault. If I hadn't ignored this part of my life, I could've been training this whole time . . . I'm sorry." Alice was surprised she had just admitted all of that. It was the truth, something she had even lied to herself about.

Jack took one of Alice's hands in his. "It's not your fault. You had every right to be afraid," he said. "And even so, we shouldn't have kept everything so secretive from you. This all has to do with you and your life, and that's not something we should have kept locked away."

"Thank you," Alice said. "I wonder, why didn't you guys ever tell me I was the Light Spirit if you thought I didn't know? I'm not mad about it, just curious."

"My dad said it would be dangerous," Jack began. "Not just for you, but the whole Nation. The last Light Spirit wasn't exactly a person who was respected. If the dragons found out, they'd want revenge for what Light Spirit Lexa did to them and their kind. And not only that, but he wasn't sure how the general public would take the Light Spirit's return either. They might be upset with how Lexa's actions caused this war. And besides, you had no memory of anything before the night my mom found you, so I guess, it was just more convenient."

Jack looked away from Fawn and Alice. Talking about his dad was always a rather touchy subject for him.

"And as I said, it was my dad who had told us this. He told me you were so special, Alice. He said we had to do whatever it took to protect you. So, he sent us out after the scroll, hoping we'd find it. But the magic in the scroll didn't take to me or Fawn, so it didn't show itself to us."

That makes sense, Alice thought. The scroll wasn't always just randomly hidden in the forest. It was magically hidden and would eventually track down its target.

As Jack continued, his eyes turned glossy. "One of the last things he said to me was to *always* stay with you. To be there for you, Alice. Not long after that was when he died. It's like the last thing he asked of me, you know? To keep Alice safe, and our nation. And that's all I've ever tried to do since then. I've tried so hard to be everything my dad was."

A tear slid down his cheek. Fawn had no words that could comfort him, so she placed her hand on his lap instead.

Alice stood up and walked closer to Jack. "King Aeolus would be so proud of you, Jack," she began. "You may not be exactly like him, but that's okay. In time, you will grow to be all the things your nation needs."

Jack smiled and brushed off his face.

"This is just the beginning," Fawn said. "For all of us."

"Everything is going to be different now, isn't it?" Alice remarked. Everything she had hoped to avoid was happening. This was the end of all those fun and carefree days.

At that moment, the doors to the room opened. Rosenia, Nickoli, Lizzie, Aurora, and Gaia came in.

"Good, she's awake," Rosenia said as she took a seat at the table. The others sat down as well.

"Alright, Alice," she began. "I know it's late, but if you could just do one thing for us, it would help out a lot." Rosenia pulled the scroll out of her dress pocket.

"All you have to do is touch the scroll and then it should reveal your first task that will help bring balance back to the world. And don't worry, we're not taking action just yet. We just want to know what the task is so we can begin preparing for it and give you the proper training. Is that okay?" she asked.

Alice nodded and walked over to Rosenia. She held open the scroll. It still said the same thing as before at the bottom of the paper: *Touch the paper again to receive your very first task.*

Alice gently touched the paper, and immediately upon contact, the paper began to ripple like water, just as it did before.

Once the paper had cleared, there was new golden writing beside a drawing. The drawing looked like the outline of a girl wearing a crown.

Alice placed the scroll down on the table for everyone to see. At once, the drawing of the girl began to move. The crown on the girl's head lifted, and then sat back on her head. The motion repeated over and over again.

"Incredible," Rosenia whispered.

"What does it say?" Nickoli asked.

Alice leaned forward to read the gold print, it said: *Light Spirit Alice, your very first adventure begins here. Find the lost princess of the Etaellaca Empire to bring further balance to the world. The truth will clear the path and what you seek shall be found. But beware! Danger lurks in those shadows. Beware! And be forewarned! Slay the beast of the past. The princess waits . . .*

Alice read the words aloud for everyone to hear. After she had finished, there was a moment of silence while everyone pondered on what the task was.

Rosenia was the first to speak. "Find the lost princess of the Etaellaca Empire," she repeated.

"To find the truth and clear the path," Nickoli added. "What do you think that means?" he asked.

"I wouldn't know," Rosenia began. "But the lost princess of the Etaellaca Empire is infamous. She disappeared, what is it? Five years ago now? I don't know how this helps us in our current predicament, but we'll get right on it."

Rosenia turned to look at Alice. "Thank you, dear. You're going to save us all," she said with a hopeful expression.

Alice had nothing to say, so she smiled instead. She smiled the most real-looking smile she could muster. These people had no idea what they were getting themselves into. The lost princess of the Etaellaca Empire? Alice knew very well who it was. She had met that princess once when she was a . . . different person.

"The sun will be up very soon. Let us all retire for the night," Rosenia said. She stood, and taking the scroll with her, exited the room. Gaia and Aurora followed after her.

Nickoli picked up Lizzie who was visibly very tired. "Come on, Ali-bear," he said to Alice. "I know you got to be exhausted."

"Actually, I'm going to stay the night here, with Jack," Alice responded. She and Fawn often slept over at the palace, and she wasn't ready to go home just yet.

"You sure? Well okay, I'll see you tomorrow." He began walking toward the doors. "Fawn, you coming?" he asked.

"No, I'll stay here," she responded. Nickoli nodded and left.

Alice, Jack, and Fawn stood out on the balcony of the palace. They looked out at the city as it bathed in the grey light of the early morning hours. Alice felt like she should go to sleep since they had been awake all night, but she wasn't tired yet. Even so, there was no way her mind would calm itself enough to sleep. She had a lot to think about.

Fawn had brought the wolf cub out with them. It was official. The little cub was now her pet.

"So, what did you end up naming this little one?" Alice asked.

Before Fawn could respond, shouting sounded from somewhere on the ground below them.

An Earth Nation soldier raced on his horse to the palace yelling, "Mayday! Mayday!" he disappeared as he reached the castle.

"We could name her Mayday," Fawn suggested. But Alice and Jack didn't hear her. They were too busy peering over the balcony from where the soldier had come from.

"That soldier," Alice began. "Why would he be shouting Mayday? Isn't that a—"

Jack finished for her. "A distress signal," he said. Something wasn't right.

The three kids peered over the balcony railing, and then all at once, the ground began to rumble. In unison with the rumbling, a flash of light sparked over the treetops, temporarily blinding them.

The sun had just risen, creating the light. But the rumbling, what could that be?

"What's going on?" Fawn shouted over the chaos. Before Alice or Jack could answer, a huge fireball blasted into the sky from somewhere outside the city.

The three kids screamed as it shot up higher and higher. As it went up, it gained mass. They cowered on the balcony as the fireball crashed right into the heart of Elkmire.

Force Captain Wildfire stood on one of the war vehicles right outside of Elkmire. Her entire portion of the Warrior Regiment stood before her, ready to attack the city as soon as she gave the signal.

"We'll be approaching the target soon," she said loudly. "The Earth Nation capital known as Elkmire is just a mere stone's throw away from our present location."

Wildfire gathered up her strength. This day would go down in history. By the end of today, she'd capture the Light Spirit and take over the rest of the Earth Nation. She would finally have the level of Firelord Ash's attention that she so desired.

"We are the warriors of our superior nation. The blood of fire runs through us. Let them know how menacing we are. We are fire!" Wildfire shouted. The soldiers cheered in response.

"Only one thing stands in our path to victory, the Light Spirit! I am here today to tell you that this foul being is in Elkmire plotting to destroy us as we speak! This is the day the Fire Kingdom takes the Earth Nation in the name of the Firelord and burns the capital to the ground!"

The soldiers cheered even louder. They had been preparing for this for nearly a year. They were ready.

Wildfire turned around as they prepared to move out. Master Yagatsu stood next to her. "Fire when ready," she told him.

On command, Yagatsu began to create a huge ball of fire. The vehicles and soldiers on horseback all began racing into the city.

And when the sun cleared the horizon, Yagatsu sent the ball of fire high into the sky: the Skyfire move.

Lizzie and Nickoli sat in the saddle of their gigantic bird, Reezu, as they flew home. Out of nowhere, a rumbling began to sound.

Lizzie sat up. "What is that?" she asked.

And then she saw it, the huge ball of fire. It was coming right for them.

"Get down!" Nickoli shouted as he tackled Lizzie into the saddle. But he was too late, the fireball crashed into the ground right below them, immediately setting the ground, trees, and houses on fire.

The explosion knocked Reezu out of the sky, Nickoli, and Lizzie with him.

Princess Gaia and Aurora saw the explosion from a window on the twenty-fifth floor of the palace. They had suspected an attack and immediately went to get their younger sisters out of their rooms.

Now, the two girls headed downstairs with their ten-year-old sister, Talula, and four-year-old sister, Bella Didi.

Talula was a unicorn like her father and Jack. Her hair was half white and half brown, and she had large blue eyes. Bella Didi was an Earth Blood Elf like her mother. The toddler had short brown hair, brown eyes, and pointed ears.

The four girls finally made their way to the first floor of the palace. Near the entry, standing on the steps, was Queen Rosenia with Jack, Fawn, and Alice. Rosenia picked up Bella Didi.

"Mom, what's going on?" Aurora asked. She was panicking on the inside but remained calm on the outside for the others' sake.

"It's the Fire Kingdom," Rosenia said. "They're here to take Elkmire."

Gaia immediately started freaking out. Aurora grabbed her hand to keep her steady.

"What do we do?" Aurora asked.

Rosenia walked toward the entrance doors of the palace, with Aurora, Gaia, and Jack following close behind. "The three of you, get your horses and get out there. You've been in plenty of battles before so this will be nothing new. Those soldiers are counting on you three to lead this defense."

Aurora and Gaia nodded and then left. Someone grabbed ahold of Jack's arm before he could leave. He turned to see Fawn and Alice standing beside him.

"Please don't go." Alice pleaded.

"Don't worry about me," Jack said calmly. "I'm not sixteen yet which means I'm not allowed to actually engage in the fight. All I'm doing is healing the wounded and directing forces. You guys stay safe, alright?"

"You too," Fawn said.

Jack rushed out the door. For the split second the door was open, Alice could see the extent of the damage outside. It looked like the aftermath of a huge fight, not the start of an attack. This battle would be over quickly.

Nickoli and Lizzie laid unconscious in the rubble leftover from the explosion of the fireball, Reezu beside them. Flames burned brightly all around the huge crater left in the ground.

Nickoli slowly opened his eyes as he came to. He sat up, still dizzy. Everything was hazy and he couldn't hear a thing. Had the explosion ruptured his hearing?

He looked around, and then all at once, his senses came back to him. It was loud, people were screaming, flames were cracking, and explosions went off.

Nickoli's first instinct was to rush over to Lizzie. She was still unconscious and was bleeding from a cut across her temple.

"Lizzie?" he shouted. "Lizzie, wake up!"

Lizzie gradually opened her eyes. She sat up and stretched her wings. They had gotten crinkled in the fall. She looked up at Nickoli. "Daddy? I can't hear you," she whispered hoarsely.

"It's okay, honey," Nickoli said as he scooped her up. "Daddy's going to get you out of this."

Reezu had already stood up. Nickoli used earth magic to shoot himself and Lizzie off the ground and into the saddle.

"Reezu, fly! Fly! Fly!" he shouted. On command, the giant bird flapped its enormous wings and flew away from the scene.

Wildfire winded through what was left of the houses of Elkmire. She blasted away anyone who stood in her way. These Earth Nation soldiers were no match for her or her army. Fighting the Light Spirit could be troublesome, but there was no way a single person could destroy an entire army.

Wildfire turned a corner onto the main street, a few Earth Nation soldiers stood blocking the path. Surely, they had to be hiding the Light Spirit somewhere.

Wildfire blasted a fiery kick at one of the soldiers, flipped, and kicked two more at the others. Immediately, they had been knocked out. This was almost too easy.

Once the smoke from the fireblast cleared, standing in the middle of the path wasn't the Light Spirit Wildfire had been hoping for, but rather a girl. An Earth Blood Elf girl who couldn't be more than a couple of years older than Wildfire herself.

"You must be one of the pretty princesses," Wildfire teased. "Aurora, is it?"

Aurora didn't respond. Instead, she looked across to where the Earth Nation soldiers laid either unconscious or dead. The entire city was nearly destroyed. Aurora could hardly bear it, but now wasn't the time to show weakness.

"You've destroyed my home," Aurora began. "The trees have been set ablaze alongside family homes. People are dying, innocent people. Women and children. What did they do to deserve this?"

"They didn't do anything," Wildfire said calmly. "But they are an inconvenience. I won't let anything get in my way. After all, *you* have something I want."

"Is that so?"

"I saw the beam of light. I know she's here. The one who you're hoping to use to destroy the rebellion." Wildfire decided to lay her cards on the table. She wasn't getting anywhere by beating around the bush.

Aurora had already figured that much out. She knew this attack was not planned. Of course, they were here for the Light Spirit. She could tell because of the lack of dragons. If the Fire Kingdom had been planning to take Elkmire on this date, they would have consulted with the dragons and enlisted their help to ensure a clean takeover. But there were none. This attack had nothing to do with the war. It was solely because of one girl's desire to end whatever advantage the Earth Nation had over them.

Aurora instantly attacked. She used her earth magic to send the ground Wildfire was standing on upward. The act caused Wildfire to shoot up into the sky, but she flipped and landed easily.

A smirk spread across her face. The fight had begun.

Wildfire kicked and punched flame after flame out of her hands and feet, at her opponent. Aurora dodged them all, but Wildfire was very fast and extremely agile. With each flame that came out, more smoke filled the area. And before she knew it, Aurora had lost sight of Wildfire.

"How about we make a deal?" Wildfire's voice sounded from somewhere in the smoke. "*You* hand over the Light Spirit, and I'll let this pathetic village live another day."

"You have nothing to gain by lying, Force Captain," Aurora began. She turned around in circles, looking for Wildfire. "I know you might've come for the Light Spirit today, but you're here for Elkmire too. I won't fall into your trap."

Wildfire laughed wickedly. "So, you've got a good head on your shoulders, princess. That's a relief because I hear burn wounds don't heal very well."

At that instant, the smoke behind Aurora parted and Wildfire appeared. She sent a spiral of fire tumbling right at Aurora.

Aurora looked over her shoulder just in time. She dove out of the way and before she could stand up, Wildfire shouted, "Nova! Flames out!"

On command, a giant red cat leaped out of the shadows and breathed fire all over Aurora. She hadn't expected a surprise attack.

Right before the fire would have scorched her, she brought earth up from the ground to create a wall for her to cower behind. The earth wall crumbled a bit as the fire burned past it on either side. The heat was too close for comfort, but the wall held.

As soon as the fire stopped, Aurora dove out from behind the wall and sent several kicks toward Wildfire. Each kick lifted boulder-sized portions of earth from the ground and launched them at her opponent.

Wildfire blasted through the boulders with fire bursts, and once the smoke cleared, Aurora was gone.

"See you later, princess." Wildfire laughed wickedly.

Jack and Gaia sat on their horses at the front of the palace. A line of Earth Nation soldiers stood behind them in a last-ditch effort to protect the palace.

The Fire Kingdom military was the strongest and most advanced in the world. This battle had proven that to be true.

Jack wanted to be up on the front steps of the palace, helping to heal the wounded, but he didn't want to leave Gaia alone, especially since Aurora was out there in the battle fighting.

As if on command, Aurora appeared down the path. She raced toward the palace on her horse, and about a dozen Earth Nation soldiers came with her. Was that all that was left of their army? Those twelve with Aurora, and the fifty or so behind Jack? How could this be happening?

Aurora had reached them now. She wavered the soldiers who had come with her into position alongside the others.

"Jack, Gaia," she said as she marched her horse into place next to them. "Get inside. It's too dangerous for you to stay out here."

"No," Jack replied. "I won't leave you out here alone."

Aurora moved her horse closer to Jack. She looked him in the eyes sternly. "*Go* inside. It isn't your place to disregard an order from your elder. The city is going to fall. Alice needs to leave with the scroll now. Go and try to get mom and the others to safety."

Jack pleaded with his eyes, but he knew Aurora would not waiver on this. He felt his horse walking away as Gaia pulled its reins, but Jack didn't take his gaze from Aurora until the horse turned him around.

Alice placed her hand onto Lizzie's bleeding forehead. Moments ago, she and Nickoli came rushing into the palace. The explosion had nearly killed them.

White light emitted out of Alice's palm and the blood from the wound evaporated. When she lifted her hand, the cut was gone. The cut was only on the surface so it could be easily healed. Lizzie immediately looked more refreshed.

Talula examined Lizzie's left ear. The ten-year-old unicorn was unusually talented at healing, so Alice let her help.

"The eardrum has ruptured," Talula said uneasily. "I healed the damage, but from here on out, you'll be completely deaf in that ear. I'm sorry, but there's nothing else we can do."

Lizzie looked a little disheartened, but her eyes displayed strength. "That's okay," she said. "It'll be fine."

Down the hall, Rosenia and Nickoli conversed quietly away from the children.

"Nickoli," Rosenia began. "I'm not sure how much longer we can hold out for. Alice needs to leave now to avoid getting captured. She'll head for the safety of the Etaellaca Empire and begin the first task."

"Understood," Nickoli said, already walking away. "I'll ready my bird and get my squad prepared for departure."

Rosenia grabbed his arm before he could leave. "That won't be necessary," she said. "There's been a change of plans."

Jack and Gaia rushed into the palace. Gaia ran over to the steps to sit with Talula and Bella Didi. Jack turned a corner and walked right past Fawn and Alice down the hall to where he could see his mother. Fawn followed Jack down the hall.

As they approached, Rosenia didn't make any mention of their presence. Instead, she stared up a massive painting on the wall. It was a family portrait of the Everharts, the Earth Nation royal family.

Depicted in the portrait was Queen Rosenia holding a baby, two young girls, a toddler, and a ten-year-old Jack. There was one other person in the portrait, a tall unicorn man with long silver hair and blue eyes: King Aeolus. In the corner of the painting, the date read: *Spring 2041.* Exactly four years ago.

"Mom," Jack said. "We can't hold them off. The city will fall. Alice needs to leave!"

Rosenia slowly took her gaze from the portrait to look at Jack. "Jack, you look so much like him," she whispered.

"What?"

"Your father," Rosenia said. "I can't bear to let everything go like this. First, I lost my husband, the nation's greatest asset, four years ago. I will lose my city today . . . *his* city. Jack, you are all I have left to remember him by, and now I will lose you too."

"What are you talking about? I'm not going anywhere!" Jack shouted.

"You're just like your father," Rosenia smiled. "I wonder what he would have me do."

Fawn walked up to Rosenia and shouted, "Your majesty, I'm sorry about your husband, and even though it's been a while, I know you're still grieving. I've been through the same thing, ever since my family abandoned me, but that doesn't mean you can just shut down like this! Focusing on the past isn't going to help you solve the present. Alice and whoever is going with her have to leave immediately . . . before it's too late. With all due respect, your majesty, you need to get your head in the game!"

If there was one thing Fawn was good at, it was getting through to people.

"I know," Rosenia said. "Thank you, Fawn."

"Alright," Jack began, relieved that Fawn had been there to help. "Now, tell me who's in Nickoli's squad leaving with Alice, and I'll go get them."

"That won't be needed," Rosenia said. "I've decided not to send the Nickoli Squad with Alice after all. I need them here, as my most trusted and skilled soldiers, to help deal with the aftermath."

"What?" Jack and Fawn shouted at the same time. Who could possibly be more qualified to take the Light Spirit on a mission than the Nickoli Squad?

"This mission requires great skill and strategy," Jack said. "Alice can't go alone!"

Rosenia turned to directly face the kids. She looked right at Jack and said, "She won't be alone. With her, I will send the nation's bravest soldier." She turned to face Fawn now. "And our most courageous warrior."

What? Jack thought. Rosenia was sending him and Fawn?

"Us? But why?"

"Because it is your destiny," Rosenia said, sounding surer than she had during any other part of the conversation. "This quest has been written in your future ever since the day you were born."

How could she possibly know this? Jack thought. At the very least, how could she be this sure about something?

"But Fawn and I don't have any qualifications or skills that make us remotely useful to the Light Spirit, even if it's only Alice."

"I've known that this was coming for years," Rosenia said. "Long before you were born, Jack. I knew this day would come."

Rosenia thought back to a time many years before she had met King Aeolus and become queen. She was a young girl who lived on a poor farm outside of Elkmire. She peered into a pond that was filled with coy fish and that's where she saw it. A little unicorn boy with silver hair and blue eyes who would live a life full of adventures. That was Rosenia's destiny—to bring life to this boy and then send him on his way.

"And then, when you met Alice, it became even more apparent," Rosenia continued. "I could see it in your eyes, all the adventures you would have, the lives your kids would live."

It almost pained Rosenia to admit these things. Part of her had always secretly hoped it would be her who lived a life full of adventures, but if it couldn't be her, she was happy it was them.

"You really think this is what we were meant to do?" Fawn asked. "To go with Alice, to leave Elkmire?"

"I always thought my destiny was here in the city," Jack added. "Helping my people and being a good prince to them."

"You've already done that, Jack," Rosenia said. "For the past fourteen years in fact. *This* quest is the beginning. Your very first adventure."

Rosenia pondered in her thoughts for a moment. There were other things she saw in the water of that pond, but she didn't quite understand those visions. Still, she should try and warn them.

"The two of you," Rosenia said. She took Jack's hand and Fawn's hand and placed them together so that they were holding each other's hand. "The two of you must stay together, alright? Please, for Kimba and Koda's sake, stay together."

Kimba and Koda? Jack and Fawn thought. "Who's Ki—" Jack began, but Rosenia cut him off.

"I-I don't know," she said. What was she thinking? They didn't know anyone by those names, but that was beside the point. They hadn't the time to fool around.

Rosenia reached into her pocket and pulled out the Sacred Scroll, handing it to Jack.

"Take this," she said. "Keep it close. Alice will know how to use the scroll in order to bring peace. Follow her to the end of Infinity. Be brave and be strong. On your journeys, you will encounter many foes, but you will also make many friends. *The forces of light and darkness will collide.* This is all just part of your story. Alice is the Light Spirit, she's the world's only hope. You two bonded with her for a reason. Now your destinies are intertwined with hers."

Fawn and Jack looked at each other. Was this all actually happening?

Before they could say anything else, Nickoli came rushing down the hall. "Everything is ready for our team's departure. Supplies, transport, food, and water, it's all ready," he said.

"Thank you, Commander," Rosenia said happily. "You were a big help." Rosenia turned to face the kids once more, and with all the happiness she could muster, said, "Alright then. Time to leave."

Alice, Jack, and Fawn stood in the quart yard of the palace. The large bird, Reezu, was there with his saddle packed, ready for take-off.

Jack was saying goodbye to his mom and sisters when all of a sudden, a huge boom sounded from somewhere inside the palace.

A few moments later, Aurora ran into the courtyard. She was pretty banged up but seemed to be moving fine. "You guys have to leave!" she shouted. "They made it into the palace!"

That was it. It was over now.

Nickoli lifted Alice into the saddle. "Time to go, Ali-bear," he said with a sad smile. For her sake, he wouldn't dare cry. He reached up to hold onto her hand.

"You're not coming with me, are you?" Alice realized.

"No," Nickoli said. "But it's okay. You don't need me."

"I do need you! I can't do this alone!" Alice pleaded.

"You're never alone, Ali. I'm always with you . . . *always*."

Beside them, Jack and Fawn said their last goodbyes. "Any last words of wisdom?" he asked his mother.

"Take care of each other," she said.

"We will," Fawn replied before hopping into the saddle to sit with Alice.

"I have one more token to send with you, Jack," Rosenia mentioned. At this, Aurora handed her what looked like a sword tucked into its sheath. Rosenia handed the sword to Jack.

"This sword belonged to your father," she said to him. "I believe you will recognize the engraving."

Jack unsheathed the sword. He had seen it many times before, but not since his dad died. He pulled out the sword to reveal a long silver blade. The metal was so clear and perfect that its surface was reflective like a mirror.

Jack caught a glimpse of his eyes in the reflection. For a moment, he thought he saw his dad's eyes looking back at him.

He looked at the engraving. Carved into the metal of the blade were the words: *Never let fear decide your fate.* Something King Aeolus had said a time or two before.

Jack immediately teared up as he thought of his father who always carried this sword at his waist. The brave and beloved King Aeolus.

Jack hugged his mother. And he felt his sisters all hug him too.

"Jack!" Talula began. "Don't go, I'll miss you!"

"I'll miss you too, Talula," he said. "I'm going to miss all of you so much."

He hugged them one last time before getting into the saddle. Jack wasn't sure if he'd ever see them again.

Before they could leave, Lizzie flew up to be at eye level with Alice. "I don't want you to go!" she shouted.

"I don't want to go either," Alice said. "But I have to do this. It's my duty, as the Light Spirit."

"When will I see you again?"

Alice thought for a moment, wondering what she could tell her sister that might prove to be true.

"Every time you look up at the stars that fill the night sky. I'll be there, somewhere, looking at the same stars, forever and always," she said.

Nickoli reached up to grab Lizzie's wrist and pull her back to the ground. Lizzie slowly complied but never took her gaze from Alice.

Suddenly, the quart yard doors flew open, and Fire Kingdom soldiers poured into the clearing, including a girl wearing a Force Captain's uniform.

"Fly! Fly! Fly!" Nickoli shouted to Reezu. On command, the bird flapped his wings and began soaring up into the sky.

As Fire Kingdom soldiers began encircling them, Rosenia said one last thing to the departing kids. "Goodbye, my loves. Goodbye. Go, and restore balance to the world."

Jack, Fawn, and Alice looked down as more Fire Kingdom soldiers shuffled into the quart yard and began taking Nickoli, Rosenia, and the others away.

"No!" Jack shouted, half trying to leap out of the saddle. They were already high up in the air. Fawn and Alice had to hold him back.

After a few moments, they had flown away from the palace and over the remains of Elkmire. The city was nothing more than rubble set ablaze. There was no telling that yesterday it had been a loving town filled with hope and good times.

Jack couldn't bear it. He looked down at his chest. Hot tears flowed down his rosy cheeks and he stifled a cry.

Alice and Fawn looked down at their home. That was it for the Earth Nation. That was it for the home they all grew up in and loved so much. Even Mayday, the little cub, whined as she sat in Fawn's lap. The wind that once carried the scent of rain, now carried ash as it blew through the kids' hair.

Alice looked down one last time. "The Earth Nation . . . has fallen."

CHAPTER THREE

Whispers of Memories

Alice, Jack, and Fawn sat on Reezu as they flew through the early morning sky. After leaving Elkmire, they flew for the rest of the day. They had awoken early today to get a head start, to try and put more distance between them and any pursuers they might have.

Alice sat upon the bird's head, holding the reins. Fawn sat lazily in the saddle next to Mayday. And Jack paced back and forth in the saddle, looking stressed.

"Would you stop pacing?" Fawn said to him. "If we hit a bump, you're going to go flying off! What's making you so stressed anyway?"

"What's making me so stressed?" Jack exclaimed back at her. "I don't know, maybe because our entire city was burned to the ground and now the Earth Nation has fallen, or maybe because we're all alone on some quest to save the world, or I know! Maybe because I left my entire family to be captured by the Fire Kingdom!"

After his outburst, there was dead silence. Alice and Fawn had never seen Jack worked up like this before. He had always been the cool-headed and quiet one of the group.

"Jeez," Fawn signed. "Sorry I asked."

Jack flared up at this remark. "I guess you wouldn't understand, Fawn," he said. "Because you don't have a family to risk losing."

Fawn looked up at Jack. Her expression displayed all the hurt his comment had caused her. One look at Fawn's face made Jack realize he messed up. He softened his expression and plopped down next to her.

"I'm sorry," he said to her. "I shouldn't have said that."

"You guys," Alice called from where she sat on Reezu's head. "I know things are rough right now, but we can't afford to be fighting. We all lost something today."

"I know," Jack began. "You're right. It's just, I can't *believe* we left them all there. My mom. My sisters."

"They're strong. They'll be okay," Fawn said. "And Nickoli, and Lizzie too. They are counting on us to make this mission a success and hopefully go back for them one day."

"If they don't escape on their own first," Alice added.

"But we didn't have to leave them," Jack argued. "They could've come with us."

"It's better that they stayed," Alice said. "This way, they can take the Earth Nation back from the Fire Kingdom. Our parents and sisters all trusted us to be strong enough to leave on our own, to take care of ourselves, and this mess. Now we have to trust them to do the same."

"I guess you're right." Jack relaxed a little. "I wonder what they're doing right now."

In the dungeon underneath the Earth Nation palace, the only sound was the steady drip of water coming down from somewhere on the ceiling. There was no light, and the labyrinth of twists and turns and different floors made it difficult to navigate. The cells were made from metal. The floor, walls, and ceiling were made from a strange metallic material as an additional measure to confine earth magic users.

Commander Nickoli, Queen Rosenia, Lizzie, and the four princesses sat quietly in their cells. They were each put in their own, except for the three kids. Lizzie, Talula, and Bella Didi shared a single cell.

Suddenly, a small orange light appeared down at the end of the hall and gradually made its way toward them.

Force Captain Wildfire approached, exerting a small flame from the palm of her hand. Two Fire Kingdom soldiers came with her, each of them carrying several plates of food.

The soldiers dropped the plates at each of the occupied cells. This would be their new breakfast, lunch, and dinner: a dirty plate filled with green mush.

"Breakfast," Wildfire said sharply. "Courtesy of the Firelord. Enjoy . . . or don't. I don't really care." She snickered at the prisoners, but they didn't even bother to acknowledge her presence.

"So what?" Wildfire complained. "No, thank you?"

Silence.

"You know, I didn't *have* to come all the way down here. I am *not* a servant."

The prisoners continued to sit quietly in their cells. Not so much as even looking at Wildfire.

"Look at you, guys," she continued. "Prisoners in your own castle. How pathetic."

Before Wildfire could say anything else, another Fire Kingdom soldier rushed down the hall. "Force Captain!" he called. "A letter has arrived for you!"

"News from Firelord Ash?" Wildfire said eagerly. "How delightful."

She turned and started walking away with the other soldiers. And without looking back, she said, "I'd eat that glop if I were you. It's getting cold." And then the light diminished once more.

Once left alone, Nickoli sat up. "Now that that brat is gone, we can talk freely," he said to the others. "So, what's our escape plan?"

Aurora looked at him like he was crazy. "Our what?"

"Our escape plan!" Nickoli shouted. "How are we going to get out of here so we can go and help the rest of our children?"

Rosenia was directly across from Nickoli. She looked up at him with defeat in her eyes.

"Escape?" she asked. "There is no escaping this fortress. I should know. My husband built this labyrinth of tunnels designed to keep prisoners locked up. The plan is to merely survive. Hope that Alice can come back for us one day and we can forget this ever happened."

"How can you give up so easily!" Nickoli was extremely upset at this. "Your son is out there getting ready to do god knows what. My daughter is out there being hunted, and you expect us to just sit here, and what? *Hope* that everything turns out okay?"

Rosenia slumped down into the corner of her cell. She had nothing left to say.

"Alice is the Light Spirit," Aurora said. "This is her job. We have to trust that she can take care of things herself."

"She is thirteen years old, Aurora!" Nickoli argued. "She's a little girl, okay? She shouldn't be out there alone!"

Nickoli could hardly believe the things he was hearing. How could all of them be okay with this? There was no way he would sit in a cell and rot while Alice was out there fighting.

"She's not alone," Aurora responded. "Jack and Fawn are with her."

"Well, thank goodness for that. What would we ever do without them?" Nickoli almost regretted the words as soon as he said them, but it didn't matter. He had other things to worry about right now.

"You are underestimating them," Aurora began. "Sure, they might be kids, but they're not stupid. The two of them have been training for this, haven't they? For the past five years, they've trained and been sent out on classified expeditions searching for the scroll. Fawn has the most incredible combat skills I've ever seen. And Jack knows how to handle himself in a situation."

Aurora suddenly got very offended thinking about what Nickoli had said. Even if he was upset, she wasn't about to let him insult her brother like that.

"Oh, and for the record," she continued. "You are correct because if there's anyone you should worry about not being skilled enough, it *is* Alice. For *already* being a teenager, she has nothing to her name. By the time I was thirteen, I had already witnessed several major battles of war and had mastered the art of earth magic, just a reminder."

Afterward, the hall stayed dead quiet. Aurora had told Nickoli off. There was nothing left for him to say. He slowly slid his back down the wall and sat there, hopeless.

Waiting on the front steps of the interior of the palace was an anomaly. Anomalies were creatures originating from Dragonia. They looked similar to elves but had ears like a dragon, and long, curled tails. Anomalies had the ability of teleportation and were sometimes used to transport mail.

Wildfire walked over to the anomaly and retrieved a letter from her. The letter was concealed in a white envelope that had a red seal with a phoenix on it. *The phoenix insignia,* this letter came straight from the Firelord himself. Wildfire took the letter and stalked upstairs to a balcony on the second floor of the palace.

Now that she was alone, Wildfire quickly tore open the envelope and scanned the writing. As she read, she gradually got more and more infuriated.

She finished the letter and crumbled it in her hand as she gripped the railing of the balcony tightly. A strand of her hair came undone to dangle in front of her face. This was *not* okay.

After a few moments, Wildfire walked back downstairs to the entryway of the palace. The anomaly was still there and had been joined by Master Yagatsu who was standing in the open doorway of the palace.

"Well?" he asked, expectantly.

Wildfire waited a moment to respond. She was desperately trying to grab control of herself.

"It seems . . . the Firelord is . . . displeased with my attempt to capture the Light Spirit," she said, feeling her voice crack. "He is also unimpressed with my accomplishments." Hearing the words aloud made Wildfire's blood boil.

"So, what do we do now?" Yagatsu asked.

Wildfire took a deep breath, trying to collect herself. "We stabilize Elkmire with the might of the Fire Kingdom, just as the Firelord wants us to. And as soon as that's complete, we find the Light Spirit and we *end* her." Wildfire knew it would be risky to disobey the Firelord, but the end result would prove to be fruitful if everything went according to plan.

"Didn't you just say the Firelord specifically asked you *not* to pursue the spirit?" Yagatsu said, energy rising.

"He probably just wants us to focus on Elkmire for now," Wildfire said. "But he won't be complaining when I bring him the Light Spirit. Just think of how incredible that would be? If I, Wildfire Amulet, bring him the one being in this world who has the power to destroy everything? We could do so much! Who's to say there's not a way to take that power from her? And even if there isn't, we would still be getting her out of the way. Firelord Ash would *love* me, and then . . . and then maybe he wouldn't think I'm so useless."

"I think you are getting ahead of yourself, Wildfire." Yagatsu began. "If you want the young Firelord to *like* you more, then you should just do as he says. If you go along with this foolish plan of yours, and Firelord Ash finds out, there's no telling what kind of punishments will be enforced upon you."

Wildfire knew that this old man didn't know what he was talking about. Who cares if he was once Admiral of the Warrior Regiment? His old ways were dated, and he clearly didn't grasp the value of the Light Spirit. Besides, *his* time was over. *She* was the Force Captain now.

Just before Wildfire could tell Yagatsu off, and put him in his place, a dozen or so Fire Kingdom military vehicles pulled up to the front of the palace. The vehicles all bore flags with the yellow sun symbol on them.

Each section of the Warrior Regiment was commanded by a different Force Captain, each with its own unique symbol. Wildfire's symbol was a red and black flame, so who's was this?

Wildfire stormed through the open palace doors, onto the steps outside, with Yagatsu tailing her.

"Who is that?"

Alice laid on Reezu's head. She was tired, but the gentle spring breeze helped keep her awake as they flew over the endless Earth Nation forest. She heard Jack and Fawn laughing at something. Looking back, she saw them playing with Mayday.

Alice looked at the two of them as they played with the little cub. It was moments like these that she loved more than anything.

The sight stirred a memory from the back of Alice's mind. She remembered walking into a dimly lit room of the palace. She saw three little kids, about ages eight, nine, and twelve, sitting on the cushion of a window sill as they played a game. She had never seen these kids before, nor had any idea who they were or where she was.

The first child was a unicorn boy, with hair the color of snow and eyes a deep blue like the ocean. The second was a girl with long orange hair, ears and a tail like a wolf. The third was another boy. He looked just like the girl with orange hair and wolf features. The three little kids laughed as they played a game with cards.

As Alice remembered that particular moment in time, it just so happened, that a memory began to stir.

Five Years Ago, April 2040

An eight-year-old Alice stumbled through the Earth Nation forest. It was the middle of the night, and a terrible storm was casting thunder and lightning through the sky. Rain poured down hard and fast.

Alice had a bandage wrapped around her forehead, but it had gotten soaked, so she ripped it off. With the bandage off her head, a massive gouge was revealed right on her hairline. Blood seeped out of it and mixed with the rain on her face.

Alice could make out a light in the distance and some sort of structure. She gradually walked toward it. Before she had reached the light, exhaustion had taken its toll on the little girl, and Alice fell to the ground.

When she looked up, she saw a woman looking down at her. The woman wore a fancy dress and had a kind expression on her face.

Everything was hazy. Alice could sense the woman picking her up and carrying her to the nearby structure. Before going inside, Alice made eye contact with a little boy who was sitting on some steps. He had the biggest, bluest eyes Alice ever could have imagined. And then, it all went black.

When Alice awoke, she found herself laying in a large bed in a room so grand it had to be the epitome of luxury. She was no longer wearing the clothes she had been the night before. Instead, she had on a clean white skirt and a matching top. There was also a fresh bandage on her forehead. Besides her pounding headache, Alice felt much better.

She stood up and walked over to the door. She had no idea where she was, or what happened to her. Surely, there was someone who could fill her in.

She opened the door and peeked into the hallway. The hall was just as fancy as the bedroom, with silver and green decor throughout. *Silver and green,* Alice thought. *Colors of the Earth Nation.*

She heard voices down the hall and turned to see two people talking in a hushed manner. One of them was the woman who Alice remembered seeing last night. The other was a unicorn man, with long silver hair. This man shared a striking resemblance to the boy Alice had seen last night. Somehow, they had to be related.

"Where do you think she came from?" the woman asked.

"Likely someplace far away," the man said. "But she is most certainly *the one* so it wouldn't matter."

As Alice turned and began walking down the opposite end of the hall, the conversation faded away.

There was a set of double doors cracked open at this end of the hallway. A soft, yellow light poured in from them. Alice could hear the gentle laughter and giggles of young voices from beyond the doors

She gently pushed one of the doors open with a *creek.* Inside was a large circular room with a tree in the center. There were shelves with toys and books, large windows, and a staircase leading up to another door. The room seemed to be a playhouse of sorts.

Sitting on the cushions of the window were three young kids. The first, Alice immediately recognized as the unicorn boy from last night. Alice placed him to be about a year older than her. Next to him was a girl with long orange hair. She also had furry ears and a tail like a wolf. This girl had to be around the same age as Alice. The third child looked just like the girl. He was the oldest. Alice figured he must be twelve.

The three kids laughed and threw the cards they had been holding up in the air. Their game was over. After a moment, the kids noticed Alice standing in the doorway and their cheerful expressions quickly faded.

The wolf girl and boy stared at Alice strangely. The unicorn boy, however, gazed at Alice with his blue eyes filled with curiosity.

Suddenly, a hand grabbed Alice's shoulder. She turned to see the woman who had found her.

"Good. You're awake," the woman said. "Why don't we take off that bandage, and then you can come play with the other kids?" The woman held Alice's hand as she led her back to the fancy bedroom.

Once inside, Alice sat on the bed while the woman unwrapped the bandage from her forehead.

"Hmm," the woman said as she examined the gouge on Alice's hairline. "The bleeding has mostly stopped, but it will need more healing sessions over time. The cut is deep, how'd that happen?"

Alice scanned her mind for an answer to the simple question but found nothing. "I-I don't know."

"You don't know?" the woman said, unsurprisingly. "Well, I can tell you're a unicorn, although you don't look it anymore. So, it appears you've lost your horn. Can you remember anything that happened last night?"

"I was walking through the forest," Alice said. "It was raining, and then you found me."

"Alright, that's good. What about before that? Can you remember anything from before last night? Anything at all?"

Alice stared at the floor, searching her mind for any other memory.

"Do you know your name?" the woman asked.

"Alice."

Alice wasn't sure that that was in fact her name, but it had felt right, so she said it.

"Your full name?"

Alice thought for a moment. Full name? What was her full name?

"It's okay," the woman said. "Take your time."

Alice continued to scan her mind for answers but found none. She shook her head.

At that moment, a soft knock on the door sounded, and in came the man who Alice had seen in the hallway. "Sorry," he said. "I didn't mean to interrupt. I just wanted to come and meet you."

"You're not interrupting anything, *Aeolus,*" the woman responded. "In fact, we were just introducing ourselves. Weren't we, Alice?"

Aeolus extended a hand to Alice. She shook it gently. "Well then," the man said. "It's nice to meet you, Alice. Very nice. I'm King Aeolus, and it appears you've already met my wife, Queen Rosenia."

Alice's eyes grew wide. What in Infinity happened to her? Here she was, a unicorn with no horn, sitting in the Earth Nation palace, speaking to the king and queen?

Suddenly, laughing and shouting came from the hallway. Two girls appeared in the doorway. The first had long brown hair and was about twelve. The second had short brown hair and had to be ten. The two of them breathed heavily as if they had been running.

The girl with long hair looked down the hall and shouted, "We win again!"

After a moment, more kids appeared in the doorway. First was the boy with orange hair Alice had seen earlier. He ran in helping a toddler, with silver and brown hair, keep up. Next came the girl Alice had also seen earlier. She crawled on the floor, panting dramatically.

"I'm . . . so . . . tired . . . of . . . running!" The girl shouted between breaths. Lastly, another boy ran up, the one with silver hair and blue eyes. He bent over and breathed heavily. Almost immediately, he made eye contact with Alice, and could not look away. What was with this boy?

"Mom," the oldest girl started. "It stopped raining. Can we go outside now?"

Queen Rosenia turned to look out a window. "It's still pretty wet out there, *Aurora,*" she said. "I wouldn't want any of you to catch a cold, and *Jack* isn't as strong as the rest of you—"

The queen was cut off by the short-haired girl shouting, "Please, Mommy!"

Rosenia wavered for a moment as if making up her mind. "Oh alright," she said. "But only for a little while."

The kids cheered in response and ran down the hall. But the little unicorn boy stayed behind. Quietly, he peered at Alice from behind the door.

In the green valley behind the palace, the kids played. The girls stayed in the grass, doing cartwheels. The two boys and the girl with orange hair ran around the meadow in the distance. Alice sat underneath the single tree that filled the valley, alone.

Queen Rosenia and King Aeolus stood on the steps watching. "We'll need to keep it a secret," Aeolus began. "If word gets out to the dragons that the Light Spirit has returned, things could get very bad, very quickly. You said, Alice herself hasn't a clue what's happened. We should leave it that way. The less she knows, the better."

Before Rosenia could respond, a man with a sturdy build wearing a soldier's uniform approached. He carried a toddler in his arms.

"I got here as quick as I could," the man said as he sat down his toddler. The little girl immediately ran off to go play with the other kids. "Where is she?"

"Over there," Rosenia said. "Underneath the tree."

"That girl? She is much younger than I would have expected."

"Yes," Aeolus responded. "She'll need a watchful eye on her at all times. It'd be no problem for her to stay here at the palace, but things can get rather hectic around here with all of our own children. I don't know what to do with her."

"I can look after her," the man said without hesitation. "Things are quiet enough at my place with just me and *Lizzie*."

"I wouldn't want to put that kind of pressure on you, *Commander Nickoli*," Aeolus said hastily.

"It'd be no problem. As long as you're okay with it, sir."

"Alright then," Aeolus responded. "It's settled. Alice can stay with you for the time being, Commander."

Over underneath the tree, Alice sat idly, not knowing what to do. Suddenly, the girl with orange hair swung down from up in the tree. She startled Alice. She hadn't even noticed the girl approach. The girl swung back and forth upside down on the branch above Alice.

"Hi!" she said.

"Hi . . ." Alice responded.

The boy with orange hair, who looked just like this girl, also jumped down from somewhere in the tree. He laid down on the branch opposite from the girl and fiddled with a leaf, uninterested in the conversation.

And then, to Alice's surprise, the unicorn boy walked up from behind the tree. He jumped up and swung on the branch next to the girl.

"What's your name?" the girl asked.

"Um . . . Alice."

"Cool. Well, I'm Fawn. This is my friend Jack," she said motioning at the unicorn. "And that's my brother Kai." She pointed at the other boy.

"*Malahki,*" the boy corrected her.

"What were you doing out in that storm all alone?" Fawn asked, ignoring her brother.

"Ssshhh!" Jack interrupted. "We aren't supposed to ask questions, remember?"

"Right. Sorry," Fawn said. She flipped off the tree branch and landed smoothly beside Alice. "Want to come play dragon tail tag with us?"

"I . . . don't know how," Alice replied shyly. Jack jumped off the branch and extended a hand toward Alice.

"We'll teach you how to play," he said. "Come on, it'll be fun." Alice took Jack's hand and stood up. "Okay."

In the meantime, Malahki hopped off the branch and began jogging away.

"Kai!" Fawn shouted after him. "Where are you going!"

"*Malahki!*" he shouted back. "And I promised Aurora I'd play with *her.*"

Fawn signed and then ran off further into the valley with Alice and Jack at her side.

Back at the Earth Nation palace, Wildfire stormed through the crowd of the newly arrived Fire Kingdom warriors. Each warrior bore the symbol of the sun on their uniforms. They unloaded their vehicles and led their horses into stables as if they were already at home.

A young man with blonde hair that had a few orange strands and matching orange eyes hopped off one of the vehicles. His uniform was more detailed than the other soldiers, including a sash and a headband that was only ever worn by Force Captains.

"You there!" Wildfire shouted at him. "What are you doing here!"

The young man was not at all startled by Wildfire's harsh attitude. If anything, he seemed to have already been familiar with it.

"Relax," he said. "I'm just following orders."

"Orders? What orders?" Normally, Wildfire would receive news of newly arriving forces. Why is this the first she'd be hearing about it? She even received a letter from the Firelord this morning, and he hadn't mentioned anything.

"Firelord Ash specifically deployed my platoon from our station in Ekasas to Elkmire."

"And he didn't think to let me know?" Wildfire said, bringing all her anger out on this poor kid. "How hard is it to send an anomaly my way with some information! And besides, I don't need any help here, Force Captain. So, you're free to go."

"My platoon isn't going anywhere. Ekasas has been stabilized. If the Firelord wants me here, then I will stay here until further notice. You of all people should know that."

Wildfire couldn't believe what she was hearing. Just who did this guy think he was? This was *her* invasion, *her* plan from the start, *he* was an outsider.

Wait a minute, Wildfire thought. Something about this guy seemed strangely familiar. His blonde hair, the orange streaks through it, his height. He even talked like he had known her.

"Do I know you, or something?" she asked.

"You mean you don't remember me?"

Wildfire stared at him blankly. Sure, he was another Force Captain of the Warrior Regiment, but that didn't mean they would know each other.

The boy sighed as if a heavy weight had been suddenly set on his shoulders. "We were in training together for three years, remember? 107th cadet? We were promoted to Force Captain at the same time last summer."

Wildfire didn't generally remember people who she felt were meaningless, but after he mentioned it, she did remember this guy.

At the thought, an image popped up into Wildfire's mind. It was from last year, at the end of the summer when she had completed training and was immediately promoted to Force Captain. She kneeled before Firelord Ash alongside two others who had also been her in her cadet and were becoming Force Captains alongside her.

One of them was Eternus Endeavor, a boy several years older than her. He had come from an extremely wealthy and well-known family in the Fire Kingdom capital who her parents knew personally. He had the blonde hair with orange streaks that Wildfire was seeing at the moment.

The other cadet was a boy between her and Eternus' age, with orange hair, and ears and tail like a wolf, who Wildfire was not familiar with.

A small smile spread across Wildfire's face as she looked at the boy before her. "Oh right," she said. "Eternus was it? We're like old friends then, aren't we?"

"Sure."

"Well then, in that case, I have a favor to ask of you." Wildfire was getting excited. Having Eternus here to stabilize Elkmire was just what she needed.

"What is it?" he asked.

"Do you happen to know of the Light Spirit's return, Force Captain?"

Jack sat on the grassy ground of the clearing, fiddling with a stick. They had decided they'd flown enough today, and Reezu needed to rest.

It was late afternoon. The sky was an orange color. Fawn was curled up like a cat, sleeping next to Jack. She breathed softly. Alice was over by Reezu's head, tending to him.

For the moment, Jack was alone. Traveling had often led to his mind wandering, and it was moments like these when he thought of his past . . .

Seven Years Ago, January 2038

Jack stomped through the deep snow that covered the Earth Nation forest. This time of year, the trees were completely bare of any leaves.

Even though he was wearing large boots and a thick fur coat, Jack could still feel the iciness of the air, and he could see his breath in front of him.

Jack had only recently turned seven, so he struggled to carry the heavy bag filled with supplies on his back. Instead, he tugged it along the ground behind him.

He stopped walking to catch his breath. He was missing his two front teeth. In front of him, a small white cub that looked like a cross between a bear and a wolf, jumped around in the snow, alongside its owner. Jack looked up to meet his father's gaze.

King Aeolus was a unicorn. He had very long silver hair, striking blue eyes, and was remarkably tall, with a lean build. He smiled warmly at Jack before taking the supplies bag from him and carrying it the rest of the way.

Eventually, the pair, alongside the cub, made their way to a clearing. Aeolus pulled a small sword out of the supply bag and handed it to Jack.

"Jack, you're seven years old now," Aeolus began, with his husky voice. "Do you know what that means?"

Jack shook his head.

"It means you're not a little baby anymore. No more sitting in the nursery with Talula, eh?"

Aeolus repositioned the way Jack was holding the sword. "This is the proper way to hold a sword. You need to have a firm grip, but not too tight because you have to be able to swing the blade freely."

Aeolus held Jack's arm and guided him with several swings of the blade. After a few, he let go and let Jack try for himself.

Jack swung the sword as best as he could manage. One swing swooped too low and hit the ground. It flicked snow into Jack's face. The little boy's eyes grew wide. "Ah-choo!" he sneezed, before losing control of his footing and toppling over.

Aeolus gave a shy smile at Jack. He was trying not to laugh. He pulled a sword out from its sheath on his waist. This blade was very long. The metal it was made from was so shiny and reflective. Aeolus could see his eyes in it more clearly than in any mirror the palace had.

Jack looked at the sword in awe. He had always been very fond of the inscription on the blade. It read: *Never let fear decide your fate.*

Aeolus began swinging the sword with smooth, clean strikes at the air. He twirled around as if battling something as grand and magnificent as a dragon.

"The blade may be separate from your body," he said. "But don't think of it that way. Think of the sword as an extension of your own arm. Let it guide you."

Aeolus whipped around and threw the sword into the trunk of a tree across the clearing. It landed deep inside the tree, with nearly perfect accuracy.

He retrieved the sword and repositioned the way Jack was holding his, again.

"Now that you know how to hold the sword, let's practice a little. Try and touch me with your blade."

Jack made several attempts to touch his father's chest with the tip of the sword, but Aeolus was quick to dodge them. He gave Jack a free hit, which encouraged him to keep trying.

As the two of them danced around the clearing, the cub jumped up and down around them. Snow began falling softly from the sky like feathers in the wind. Jack sneezed again, and laughed, but never missed a beat as he and Aeolus swung their swords.

After a moment, the snow stopped falling and it melted from the ground. Green grass sprouted in its place. The trees were covered with thick leaves once more, and wildflowers grew along the trunks. Winter and spring had come and gone; summer was here.

Three years later, summer 2041

Jack swooped his sword underneath his father's attack, and just like that, he managed to draw the tip of his sword up to Aeolus' chest.

"I win again," he exclaimed proudly.

Aeolus laughed and ruffled Jack's hair as he ran his fingers through it.

"That's my boy!"

Jack was ten now. He had been training a lot with his father recently. It was something he loved doing because it was something he could share with his father, even if he wasn't good at physical activity.

A short while later, the pair, alongside a fully grown white dog, packed up their stuff and headed back through the forest.

Suddenly, they stopped as the sound of hooves thumping on the ground got louder as someone approached.

A soldier on horseback raced up to the king and prince with a grave expression on his face. Another horse, this one with an empty saddle, raced up beside him.

"My king!" the soldier shouted. "Forgive me for interrupting, but you're needed back at the palace immediately!"

"What's the matter?"

The soldier took an extra few breaths before responding as if pondering the severity of the situation. "They've breached Ekasas," he finally said.

A new sense of urgency sparked in King Aeolus. He immediately picked up Jack and put him on the second horse, before also jumping up and taking the reins. They took off quickly, with the dog running after them.

The next morning, Jack stood on the front steps outside the palace, with his mother and sisters. A large portion of the Earth

Nation army, all on either horseback or small vehicles, stood before them. Crowds of civilians gathered around near the palace, or outside their homes in the treetops to see them off. Everyone was saying goodbye to someone today. Rather it was a father, son, uncle, or husband; the men would leave to fight in Ekasas.

Queen Rosenia held a baby in her arms, and she hugged King Aeolus deeply. She breathed in his familiar scent. He smelled like roses.

Once she let go, tears were streaming down her cheeks. She placed her hand on the side of her husband's face, looking at him as if for the last time. And he kissed her, as if for the last time.

Aeolus kissed the baby's forehead and then stepped away from his wife to stand before Jack. Because Aeolus was standing on the ground, and Jack was standing on the steps, the two of them were at eye level with each other.

"Dad," Jack started. "I'm scared."

"Don't be scared, my son." Aeolus encouraged. "*Never* be afraid. You mustn't let fear decide your fate."

"Please don't go," Jack said so quietly it was nothing more than a faint whisper.

Aeolus sighed, and he hugged his son tightly. He looked up at the sun. "When the snow falls again, I will return home."

King Aeolus mounted his white horse, and marched off in the lead of the army, his dog included. Jack watched them go, and salty tears flowed steadily down his rosy cheeks.

Six months later

Jack stood on a balcony of the palace. It was December, his birthday was next week, and he was looking forward to his father's return.

He looked down at the city below. Snow covered the ground. And he looked up to the grey sky where snow trickled down softly like leaves from a tree.

Suddenly, Jack heard the sound of many hoof beats on the ground below him. He raced back inside, down a winding staircase, and outside to the front steps. His mother and sisters were behind him.

Jack looked at the returned army before him. It was much smaller than when they had left. There seemed to be more horses than there were men, and some of the soldiers looked severely wounded.

Jack trotted down to the last step. His eyes were wide and nervous, but he was excited to see his father again. He scanned the crowd of soldiers, but King Aeolus was nowhere to be seen.

A soldier wearing a Commander's uniform approached the steps. He walked, holding the reins of a white horse, the king's white horse.

The Commander took a knee before Jack and pulled a sword from his waist. With both hands, he presented the sword to Jack.

Jack slowly looked down at the sword. It was shiny and reflective. He could see his eyes in its silver sheen.

His stomach dropped, his mouth grew dry, and his vision clouded with tears as he read the inscription on the blade: NEVER LET FEAR DECIDE YOUR FATE.

Jack sat in the clearing, up against Reezu's side. The sun was setting, and he looked up at it. After a moment, he flicked away the stick he had been fiddling with, and with a heavy exhale, he moved on from the memories his thoughts had led him back to.

Wildfire marched swiftly through the Earth Nation palace with Master Yagatsu at her side. The palace was buzzing with life, Fire Kingdom soldiers filled every corridor and every hall.

"You can't really be going along with this, Wildfire!" Yagatsu shouted as they approached the exit.

"I've heard enough out of you, old man," she spat. "We're going after the Light Spirit, and nothing you say will stop me."

"Once the Firelord finds out that you outright disobeyed him, he is going to have your head!"

"Shut up already."

Wildfire flung open the doors and ran down the front steps outside the palace. Her entire platoon was packed and ready for departure on the vehicles out front. Wildfire hopped onto one of them and Yagatsu reluctantly joined her.

Force Captain Eternus waited nearby. He gave Wildfire a pained expression as if he too was dreading her decision.

"Don't give me that horrid face," Wildfire said to him.

"I just can't believe you're actually leaving to try and capture the Light Spirit, that's all!" he shouted sarcastically.

"Well, I am. Deal with it. And cover for me while I'm gone, got it?"

Wildfire knew she could trust Eternus. He seemed to always do what she told him. She remembered from the past, he used to boast about their "friendship" as if it meant something.

"No way," Eternus said. "I'm not getting roped up in this. I'm loyal to the Firelord, and only the Firelord. Not you, Force Captain."

"Ugh, you're really no help at all, you know that?"

Apparently, a year apart had changed Eternus some. However, that was nothing Wildfire couldn't handle.

"Look," she began in a nicer tone. "Eternus, just don't mention anything, alright?"

"What if someone comes looking for you?" Eternus complained. "I mean, what do you want me to tell people?"

"I'm sure you'll figure something out." Wildfire winked at him. And then waved her arm at the troops, signaling for them to move out.

As Wildfire's platoon departed, Eternus watched them go. He was hurt that Wildfire didn't listen to him. All he ever did was try and help her, but she never even noticed him. Eternus had been chasing that girl for years now. Maybe it was time to give up.

Fawn sat next to the fire with her knees drawn up to her chest. The warmth coming off the flames felt nice in the cool night air. Alice and Jack were asleep behind her, laying on Reezu's feathery legs. She had slept earlier, so she wasn't tired yet, and even so, Fawn had always been somewhat of a night owl.

She looked into the crackling of the fire, it was the same color as his hair, the person she had been missing for a while. Fawn remembered her childhood. She and her older brother Malahki used to run through the fancy streets of their hometown, the Piniel Dynasty.

Malahki had always smiled a crooked smile. His messy orange hair would bounce in the wind as he played with Fawn. She was very small then. He'd wink at her and tilt his head to the side with one of his ears bent, an image that stayed with Fawn constantly.

Malahki had been missing for nearly five years now. Fawn wasn't sure she'd ever see him again, the one person left of her family, the one person who cared for her back when no else did. She hoped he was doing okay wherever he might've been.

Almost as if on cue, Fawn felt the presence of someone sitting in front of her. She slowly lifted her head to see Malahki sitting across the fire from her. He looked the same as when she'd last seen him. His eyes met hers, and he tilted his head to the side, smiling his crooked smile.

And then, as quickly as he had appeared, he vanished. The apparition faded into the cool night air, leaving Fawn alone once more.

Fawn got up and laid down next to Alice and Jack. Perhaps she was more tired than she felt, considering she was seeing things now.

Next to her, Alice breathed softly in her sleep. Her dreams had always been extremely life-like, but tonight's dream was strangely more vivid than Alice could have ever imagined.

She stood in the middle of the forest. This forest was unlike the tropical rainforest of the Earth Nation. The trees were stocky oaks, and tall mushrooms were growing among them. It was more mystical and had a much warmer climate.

There was a pond in front of her. Colorful fish swam about in it, and lilypads dotted its surface. Strange creatures like jellyfish floated in the air. They glowed neon shades of white, pink, and lavender. It was pitch blackout. The only source of light was the moon peeking through the treetops and the glow from the floating creatures.

One of the jellyfish creatures came to rest on the tip of Alice's nose. The sensation made her tickle, and she sneezed it off. In response, a deep chuckle came from somewhere above her. Alice thought she was alone, and the sudden noise of someone startled her beyond control. She slipped and fell face-first into the pond.

"Oh dear," the voice laughed at her. The voice was unlike any voice Alice had ever heard. It was silky and rich but had a sharp undertone to it and a slight accent. Alice could not recognize the voice as someone she might've known, nor could she place the accent. But she could tell the speaker must have been a boy in his teenage years.

Alice spun around in circles looking up at the trees to find the speaker. In an instant, she spotted him. He crouched on the top of a mushroom just above her head. How had she failed to notice him earlier? A swirl of smoke and shadow clouded him from Alice's view and she could not make out his face.

He sat on the mushroom top, uncomfortably close for Alice's preference. "Who are you?" she asked him.

He held something like a pen attached to a string and inhaled from it. After a moment, he exhaled a huge cloud of puffy white smoke all over Alice. She coughed and covered her face with her hands. It had an overwhelming stench of vanilla to it.

The boy laughed more at Alice's reaction. She waved the smoke away, and once she did, the boy was gone.

Alice walked deeper into the forest, curious as to who this person was. She could hear him laughing up ahead and could see his shadow through the trees.

Alice followed the boy into a clearing. There was a small village filling the area. The entire village had been set on fire. Houses and shops collapsed and blackened in the fire.

Up ahead, the boy stood in front of one of the burning buildings. Alice ran through the decaying village to get there, but once she got to the spot where the boy had been a moment ago, he was gone.

Alice looked around, civilians were fleeing their homes. Women and children cowered away from the flames. Alice wanted to help them, but for some odd reason felt that she couldn't, as if it wasn't of her concern. Why did she feel that way? Why wasn't anyone helping these people? Was this the doing of that strange boy?

As if in response to her thoughts, Alice suddenly felt the presence of someone standing right behind her. The person was much too close for comfort, she could feel their hot breath on the back of her neck as they towered over her.

And then, to Alice's dread, a cloud of smoke and the scent of vanilla washed over her. He was right behind her, nowhere to run to now. The boy pressed his mouth close to Alice's ear and whispered, "Boo."

In an instant, Alice's eyelids shot open and she sat up. She looked around. Everything was okay now. She wasn't in the middle of the burning village anymore. Fawn and Jack slept right next to her.

Still, Alice felt on edge. Whoever that boy was in her dream gave her a sinking, gut-wrenching feeling. She rubbed her eyes, desperate to get the images out of her mind.

And then, with no warning at all, the scent of vanilla washed over her.

CHAPTER FOUR

Taesithia

Alice hastily packed her things away. She hadn't slept well last night after her dream, and she wanted to get a head start on traveling. Hopefully, she'd feel better once they were back in the air.

As she rolled up her blanket, Alice couldn't help but feel anxious about the dream she had. She remembered the fire, the smoke from what she thought was a hookah, the strange boy, and the way he laughed at her. And especially, the way he whispered in her ear . . .

And then a hand grabbed her shoulder. Alice was convinced the boy was real and had snuck up on her, but when she turned around, it was only Jack.

His eyes were wide with concern. "Hey, are you okay?" he asked.

Alice was in fact *not* okay. She was very shaken up, but she didn't want to worry Jack any more than he already was. He didn't deserve that. "Ye-yeah, I just had a nightmare, that's all. I'm fine."

"Well, then we should get going." Jack motioned to his left over the cliffside where smoke was trickling out of the trees from somewhere in the far distance.

Fawn who was playing catch with Mayday noticed the smoke as well. "Hey, someone's making a campfire!" she laughed.

"That's no campfire, Fawn," Jack said as he mounted Reezu. "It's the Fire Kingdom. And by the looks of it, they're getting close."

The three of them hurried up to collect their things. Alice took the reins and shouted, "Reezu, Fly! Fly! Fly!" In an instant, the bird took flight, flapping in the opposite direction of the smoke. The three kids turned around to stare back at their pursuers.

Wildfire stood on the front of one of the Fire Kingdom vehicles in her platoon. Several other vehicles rolled in behind her, and dozens of soldiers came in on horseback. They had traveled Southwest all night without stopping.

Wildfire held a telescope up to her eye. With it, she could see a huge bird flying away in the distance. It was them. She knew it. That was the same bird she had seen on the day of the invasion.

"Target acquired," she stated sharply.

Master Yagatsu came to stand beside her. Wildfire handed him the telescope and he had a look for himself. "Where do you think they're headed?"

"There's only one place out in this mountainous region of the Earth Nation," Wildfire said as she looked up in the general direction of where the bird had flown off. "They're going to Taesithia."

The three kids sat in the saddle as they flew through the morning sky. Jack and Alice were looking at a map, intently, and Fawn shoveled through their supplies. She opened a bag and dumped it upside down. It was empty.

"I hope there's a village nearby on the map of yours," Fawn started. "Because we're out of water, and the food's running low too."

"What?" Jack exclaimed as he set the map down. "My mom packed us enough food to last a week!"

"I have a bottomless stomach," Fawn replied.

"Yeah, no kidding," Jack said, picking up the map again. "Well, it looks like there is a small town on the top of this mountain we're coming up to. We can stop there."

"Ugh, can't we stop somewhere else?" Fawn complained. "I hate mountain food."

"Mountain food?" Alice asked.

"Yeah, like what can you grow on a mountain? Bean stocks? That town can't be the only place on the map."

"It's the only place close," Jack said. "We won't even have to make a detour to get there. It's straight ahead, just a few miles down. And don't worry, I'm sure they have something to eat besides bean stocks. What we should be more focused on is the Fire Kingdom. They've taken over the whole nation, this town included, so it'll probably be covered with enemies."

At this, Fawn extracted her long black claws. "Don't stress," she said, showing them off. "I have my own insurance."

Jack lifted his shirt to show his father's long silver sword strapped underneath. "As do I."

Alice looked at them from one to the other. Both of them had undergone training for this sort of thing. What had she done?

"I'll just stand back and let you guys do the heavy lifting," she said.

"You know, you're gonna have to learn how to defend yourself, Alice," Jack said to her. "Fawn and I can't always be there to protect you."

"*You're* the Light Spirit, for crying out loud!" Fawn exclaimed. "*You* should be protecting *us*."

"And how am I supposed to do that?" Alice argued. "I don't know any magic except for unicorn types: healing and light, which is not exactly something to use in battle."

"Ugh, I wish *I* had some type of magic!" Fawn complained. "I'd be a much better Light Spirit than you, Alice."

Alice rolled her eyes. Since Fawn was a wolfwalker, a type of skinwalker, she had no magic.

"Alice will need some teachers," Jack began. "People who have already mastered their type of magic, they can teach her what she needs to know."

"Okay, well where am I supposed to find these teachers?" Alice asked.

"I wouldn't know, but this town could be a good place to start looking."

"What's the town's name?"

"Taesithia."

Queen Rosenia was sleeping on the floor of her cell when she suddenly sat up, her eyes wide, and she was breathing heavily. She looked around from right to left, as if trying to get her bearings.

"Mom?" Aurora called from the opposite side of the cell block. "What's wrong?"

Rosenia looked around a bit more before answering. She was a frantic mess. Her face displayed all sorts of distress.

"I . . . saw something."

From where Nickoli sat in his cell, directly across from Rosenia, he looked at her intently. And then, he began smearing the green mushy food on the bolts and screws of his cell door.

The kids landed Reezu halfway up the mountain. They wanted to walk up to the town since it would draw less attention than if they flew in on a giant bird. They were in luck too because there was a wide grassy path that wined through the forest, up to the mountain's top, where Taesithia was located.

The forest was not at all like the rainforest of Elkmire. The trees here were much shorter and darker. The ground was smooth with grass and had little undergrowth. Little red birds flew around the treetops.

They had left Mayday with Reezu a little way down the path since they didn't expect to be staying very long.

The kids approached a huge arch over the path that was made out of the treetops. As they walked under it, a little white butterfly flittered past each one of their faces, as if welcoming them.

Past the arch, there was a small white sign with writing on it. Jack read it aloud. "Welcome to Taesithia."

Just under that, new writing had been imprinted on the sign in red ink. "Property of the Fire Kingdom," Jack read.

The kids looked at each other, a bit shaken, but then they continued up the path, swiftly.

Eventually, they made their way up to a wooden boardwalk that led up to the town situated on the mountainside. They ran up it and into the town.

As they went, a figure hid in the bushes behind them, watching them go. Little white butterflies fluttered all around the figure as it tucked away back into the bushes.

All the structures in the town were made from dark wood and there were small flowers that grew in between the cobblestone paths.

Jack, Alice, and Fawn stood there for a moment, in awe at the gorgeous town. But their excitement only lasted a moment because then they saw it . . .

A massive aqua-colored dragon sat on the peak of the mountain, peering down at the town with its golden eyes.

"Uh, guys?" Fawn said, nervously. "Are you seeing what I'm seeing?"

"A dragon," Jack replied.

"Wh-what's it doing here? Should we leave?" Alice asked, half turning around back the other way.

"No," Jack began. "Look at the way it's sitting, it's just watching, not attacking. I'm sure it's probably just under some sort of order to supervise the town. As long as we don't draw attention to ourselves, we should be fine."

"I've never seen a dragon in real life before," Alice said.

"Me neither," Fawn pitched in. "And it's a lot bigger than I would have imagined."

"What about you, Jack?" Alice asked. "Have you seen one of those things before?"

"Once," he replied. "It was when my dad took me and my older sisters out on an expedition, but I didn't get a close look."

Jack thought back to that memory . . .

It was winter. Jack had to be ten. He walked through the snowy Elkmire forest along a cliffside with King Aelous, Aurora, and Gaia who had to be eleven and thirteen years old.

Suddenly, an ear-splitting screech sounded from somewhere afar.

"Get down! Get down!" Aeolus shouted to the kids. He tackled them to the ground behind a line of bushes. They laid down flat on their stomachs, peering through the leaves, down at the cliffside.

Not long after that, two royal blue dragons flew by down below them. They were too far away to possibly notice Jack and his family, but still, dragons had strong senses, especially when in their dragon form.

Alice, Jack, and Fawn stepped away from a seller's stand. Each of them carried a knapsack filled with fresh fruit. The trees of Taesithia had been rich with all sorts of fruits, and the kids had plenty of money sent with them.

Alice looked at the view before her, the thousands of trees that made up the ground far below. "It's so beautiful here," she said.

"It is," Jack began. "But we should get going."

"But why?" complained Fawn. "It's nice here. Can't we stay awhile?"

"Weren't you the one who didn't want to come here in the first place, Fawn?" Jack asked.

"That was before I knew the trees here could grow more than just bean stocks! We should stay for a little, you know, look around, have some fun."

"I don't think that's a good idea with that dragon up there," Jack said. "Besides, we got what we came here for, and this town is crawling with the Fire Kingdom. It's risky for us to stay in one place for too long."

"Ugh. Fine," Fawn huffed.

The three of them began walking back down the boardwalk in the direction of the path that led them up the mountain. Before they could get very far, a group of Fire Kingdom soldiers began rushing uphill toward the kids.

Alice, Jack, and Fawn immediately swooped around and walked swiftly uphill in the opposite direction.

"Is it just me, or do those soldiers look like they're coming right for us!" Alice said, nervously.

"There's no way they could know who we are," Fawn began as they rushed through crowds of civilians. "We only left Elkmire a couple of days ago."

"Word travels fast in the Fire Kingdom," Jack said. "I'm sure every soldier was told to be on the lookout for a girl with silver markings on her face."

"How did they find us?" Alice shouted.

"Considering we are a unicorn prince, a wolfwalker, and the Light Spirit, I'm sure we are the type of crowd that draws attention," Jack said through his teeth.

"Great," Fawn exhaled.

As the three of them approached the top of the hill, more Fire Kingdom soldiers came down from that direction. The kids looked from front to back, but there was nowhere to run to. They were *trapped*.

"What do we do, Jack?" Alice worried. "What do we do!"

Jack hastily looked around, but it was no use. Fire Kingdom soldiers were everywhere, all coming right for them.

In that instant, a young boy floated down from the top of a building next to them. It was unclear as to how the boy defied gravity by floating down since he had no visible wings.

"Follow me!" he said to the others as he noticed their predicament. "I can get you out of here!"

Alice and Fawn looked to Jack for approval. With no other way out, he decided to lay his trust in this stranger. He nodded at Fawn and Alice and the three of them ran after the boy.

The boy raced through the network of buildings until he led them to a two-story building that had a ladder leading up to the roof. The boy completely disregarded the ladder and jumped. He somehow jumped effortlessly all the way to the roof.

Alice, Jack, and Fawn had no time to question the boy's strange abilities with the Fire Kingdom right behind them. They hurried up as fast as they could. The boy waited for them at the top and seemed to be taking account of the fact that his accomplices could not fly like him.

Once the others joined him, the boy ran along the rooftop of the building and jumped onto adjoining ones with Jack, Alice, and Fawn close after him.

Alice looked down at the ground to see the Fire Kingdom soldiers still in pursuit. If she or any of the others made one wrong step, they could fall and instantly be captured.

Eventually, they made their way to the end of the town. There were no more buildings to jump onto, and the ground was much too far below to land safely.

"Grab on, quick!" the boy shouted to them.

Without missing a beat, Alice wrapped her arms around the boy's back, and Jack and Fawn each grabbed an arm. Alice had no idea what this kid was about to attempt, especially because he was much smaller than them, but they had no choice but to trust him.

With the others holding onto him, the boy jumped off the building. At first, Alice, Jack, and Fawn started screaming, believing that this stranger had brought them on a suicide mission, but then they realized that they weren't actually falling. Instead, they were floating down at a rate that was somewhat slower than falling, and just slow enough to where they could control their landing.

Once safely on the ground, the boy set down the others before racing into the forest. "C'mon, we're almost there!"

The four kids ran into the thickness of the trees. Once inside the forest, Alice looked back to see that the Fire Kingdom soldiers had caught up, but hadn't quite made it to the forest just yet, thanks to this new kid's evasive maneuvering.

They continued following the boy until they reached what looked like a dead-end, the side of the mountain. The mountain's side was smooth and there was no way someone could climb it.

But to Jack's surprise, the boy walked over to a small crook in the mountain's side, to vines that covered an area. He parted the vines to reveal a tunnel boring into the mountain.

"Ssh ssh, in here," he said quietly.

Alice, Jack, and Fawn rushed inside and the boy followed after them. The tunnel was short and gave way to a massive clearing inside the mountain. The mountain acted like a bowl, with walls completely covering this secret area in the center. In the center of the clearing was a huge stone tower.

No wonder the boy knew of this secret place. He could practically fly and could have seen it from above.

The four kids rushed into the clearing and then fell to the ground from exhaustion.

"Wow . . . you guys . . . are heavy," the little boy said between breaths.

"Sorry about that," Jack began. "Thanks for getting us out of there. My name's Jack, by the way."

Alice and Fawn introduced themselves after him.

"You never told us your name," Jack mentioned.

"Oh me?" the boy asked as if he was ecstatic they had asked him for his name. He had light purple, almost pink hair, dark purple eyes, and freckles on his nose and cheeks, with pale skin. He was much smaller than the others. Alice figured he must be about ten years old.

"My name's Wesley. Wesley Anderson."

Force Captain Eternus stood on the front steps of the Earth Nation palace, alone. He nervously rubbed his sweaty palms together and shrugged his shoulders around. He wasn't sure he should be doing this. He knew it was the right thing to do, but he wasn't sure he should be doing this.

Suddenly, an anomaly popped into existence right beside him, teleporting from someplace else. "He's ready for you now," she said to Eternus.

Eternus exhaled sharply. "Let's get this over with."

He linked an arm with the anomaly, and in a flash, they teleported away. A strange folding sensation washed over Eternus and nearly made him sick. But the feeling only lasted a moment because then, they were standing still once more, although their location had changed drastically.

They now stood in the center of a large room that seemed to be an office of sorts. Everything in the room was a deep red color, with gold and black accents. Pillars supported the high ceiling in the four corners of the room, bookshelves lined the walls, and it smelled like firewood. The office was extremely fancy and so clean that it had to be completely spotless.

They had teleported all the way to a castle deep in the heart of the Fire Kingdom. This was the Firelord's palace in the capital, Palace City.

At the back of the room, in front of a large window with an ocean view, was a desk. A person sat in the desk chair facing the window.

"Thank you, Sadie," the person in the chair said without turning around. "You can see yourself out."

Although the speakers' composure was calm, cool, and collected, there was an underlying sharpness to his voice that made it seem as though he could slay you with only a word.

The anomaly, Sadie, bowed and then exited the room, leaving Eternus alone with the speaker.

"Thank you for having me, Firelord," Eternus said shakily.

The person in the chair spun around to face Eternus. He wore a dazzling red suit with long red gloves running up his sleeves. He had red, middle-parted hair. His skin was so fair, so pale, and so porcelain that his complexion was comparable to that of a doll's.

The Firelord wore an orange stone on a necklace around his neck. The stone seemed to give off some sort of light which gave it the illusion that it was glowing.

Another striking thing Eternus noticed about the Firelord was the flames sprouting from underneath his arms. The fire was fueling right out his body on the underside of his arms, through his clothes, but strangely didn't spread. It stayed completely controlled like wings.

Firelord Ash Levitt was an Inferno. A creature nearly extinct. Infernos have always been said to be half-phoenix and half-person. Ash had seemed to be the last of his kind.

The Firelord appeared to be very young, possibly even a teenager, but it was hard to tell exactly how old he was. Eternus looked at him, but a shadow was covering the Firelord's eyes, so he didn't know if he was looking back at him.

"Don't *thank* me," Firelord Ash said with a hint of annoyance. "Now I am rather busy, so if you could hurry this up, I might be less inclined to hurt you."

Eternus shuddered and desperately choked back his fear. "Uh, um, of course, your highness," he began shakily. "I just thought someone ought to tell you that Force Captain Wildfire, stationed in Elkmire, has left her post and has taken her entire platoon with her. She is supposedly chasing the recently returned Light Spirit, sir."

Ash stood up sharply and walked around his desk. He swiped his finger at the tiniest piece of dust that was nothing more than a spec and looked at it as if absolutely disgusted by it.

"Wildfire is chasing the Light Spirit? Even though I specifically asked her *not* to?" he asked, sounding more curious than angry. He paused for a long moment. "Interesting."

"Do you want me to track her down, sir?" Eternus asked.

"No," the Firelord replied quickly. He paused again. ". . . let her go."

"But sir!" Eternus said, alarmed. "Wildfire and her platoon are needed in Elkmire, and shouldn't she be punished? These crimes are comparable to treason!"

"*Let* her go," Ash said more sharply. "The girl is lazy. I have no use for her."

He paused once more, this time longer than before, and his eyes seemed to sparkle as he thought of something. ". . . *almost* no use," he finally said.

He started walking around his desk again, looking intently at the papers sprawled out on it.

"Maybe," Ash began sarcastically. "Maybe tracking down the Light Spirit will lead Wildfire into a *trap*. If it did, I wouldn't be surprised in the slightest.

"Time is almost up," he continued. "And I know they won't release him. I know they won't keep their end of the bargain. *This* is just what I need. Give them a *reason* to."

Eternus had no idea what the Firelord was talking about. And what was he planning to do with Wildfire? Eternus certainly hoped no harm would come to her because he turned her in. "What are you suggesting, sir?" he asked cautiously.

"It's not of your concern," Ash said triumphantly.

Eternus thought about their other problem, the Light Spirit. How would they defeat her? What if the Dark Spirit had also returned and the two of them were teaming up? What would they do then?

"This Light Spirit," Eternus began. "Do you know what she's up to? Or where she might be headed?"

Ash turned around to look at a map pinned to the wall. It was a map of all of Infinity.

"No . . ." he began innocently. His eyes lingered on a southeastern portion of the map labeled: ETAELLACA EMPIRE.

"But I have a pretty good idea."

Alice, Jack, and Fawn walked through the secret clearing in the mountains toward the tower in the center, with Wesley. As they trekked through the grass and flowers, Alice couldn't help but notice the little white butterflies that consistently fluttered around Wesley. They seemed to like him and followed him around everywhere without fail.

"You guys are going to love the tower!" Wesley said to them. "It's actually a library filled with books from all over Infinity!"

"This tower," Alice began. "Is it where you live?"

"No, my home is back in the Sky Kingdom," Wesley responded. "I used to hang out here with my friends Fallon and Daisy. But the dragons . . . they hurt my friends. And then they created a blockade on the Sky Kingdom border and I couldn't get back home. That happened last summer, and I've been stuck here ever since."

"That must have been so horrible," Alice said sincerely. Wesley was far too young to have gone through something like that. "I'm sorry."

"Don't be," the little boy said. "They've hurt us all, haven't they?"

"Huh?"

"The dragons. They've hurt everybody one way or another."

Although she didn't say it aloud, Alice thought that was a very mature thing for Wesley to say. She pondered on the thought of his culture. She had heard many stories of the Sky Kingdom and how it was much different than the rest of the world. She wondered if everyone there was as profound as Wesley.

As the group continued toward the tower, Fawn slacked a little way behind the others. She kept her eyes on the grass until she felt someone bump into her from behind. She stopped walking to see who the culprit was.

Fawn was shocked to see Malahki run past her and toward the tower. He turned to look back at her, his orange hair bouncing in the wind. He smiled at her, the same crooked smile Fawn had grown up with and loved so much.

She watched him go until his body faded into nothingness once more.

"Fawn?" Jack called from up ahead. "You coming?"

Fawn hadn't realized she had fallen so far behind. The others were all staring back at her.

"Oh, uh, yeah." She hurried to catch up with them.

Wesley flung open the double doors on the bottom floor of the tower. "Behold!" he exclaimed. "The secret library tower of Taesithia!"

Inside were hundreds of shelves lining the walls all the way up to the ceiling. There were ladders and walkways leading up to different portions the higher up you went. The entire tower had to be ten stories tall.

Alice looked up at all the shelves. For an instant, she could have *sworn* she saw the boy with the hookah from her dream, casually sitting on top of one of the shelves. But when she looked again, he wasn't there.

Suddenly, a small white creature flew down from somewhere higher up in the tower. It squeaked as it came to land on Wesley's shoulder.

"Hey there. Boo!" Wesley said as he petted the furry creature. It looked like a mouse with its large white ears and curled tail, but it had wing-like folds attached to its arms and legs that acted like a glider allowing it to fly.

"What is that thing?" Fawn shouted, taking a step back.

"This is Boo, my pet Feraroo!" Wesley answered happily.

"He's adorable!" Alice said as she petted the tiny creature.

Jack bent down to be closer to Wesley's height in order to get a better look at the creature. "I've never heard of a Feraroo," he said.

"They're a native species of Sky Kingdom," Wesley remarked.

"On a side note," Jack said as he turned to look at the library. "This library is incredible."

"Yup! It's incredible, and more importantly, it's hidden so the Fire Kingdom can't find it. I'm sure there's plenty of stuff in here that'll help you with all your Light Spirit secrets!"

Alice, Jack, and Fawn snapped their heads to stare at Wesley. *What did he just say?*

"How . . . how did you know about that?" Fawn asked hesitantly.

"Oh, uh, maybe I should've said something sooner," Wesley began. "But I've been expecting you guys for a while now."

"You have?" Jack asked in shock.

"Yeah, back home, a few years ago, the Skylord came to visit me to talk about a vision he had. He said the vision showed him that I would one day meet the new Light Spirit and that I would help her somehow. He wanted to give me the message to make sure I followed through with it."

"But how did you know it would be us?" Alice asked.

"I saw you when you first came into town. And then I saw the silver markings on your face, they're unmistakable. Everyone in the Sky Kingdom knows that."

Fawn stepped closer to Alice. "Are you sure he's just not messing with us?" she asked her. "I mean c'mon this sounds crazy."

"Things are different in the Sky Kingdom," Wesley said. "Stuff like that happens all the time. Everyone there is spiritually inclined and in tune with the universe. Everyone back home studies the spirits a lot, so when they found out I would one day meet the returning Light Spirit, it became the talk of the town. I was basically a celebrity! Well, before I involuntarily moved here."

"Wow," Jack whispered. "The Sky Kingdom sounds—"

Alice cut him off before he could finish. "Amazing," she said.

The thought of the Sky Kingdom and all its excitement made her heart race. The culture, the way the people could travel the world freely through flight. *That* was the kind of peace and freedom Alice had been searching for her whole life.

"Wesley, one day, you have to take us there! Can you?"

"Sure, I'd really like that. And everyone would love to meet you! Although with the dragons guarding the border, it might be a little tricky. But one day, we'll go there, I promise."

Alice smiled at him. A promise was enough for her. "So, you said this library had books from all over the world, on any subject?"

"Pretty much."

"Do you have anything on the—"

"The Dark spirit?" Wesley already knew exactly what she was going to ask about. "I had a feeling you were going to ask about that."

Jack and Fawn turned to look over at Alice. The Dark Spirit? She had never mentioned anything on the subject before, why was she suddenly bringing it up now?

Wesley used sky magic to jump all the way up to one of the highest levels of the library. Alice climbed up a ladder after him.

"Everything on the Dark Spirit is kept over here," Wesley said as he walked over to a shelf. He began pulling books from the shelf and tossing them at Alice's feet.

"That one is on Dark Spirit Achilles. This one is on the Dark Spirit in general," he reached up and grabbed a black and gold book from the top of the shelf that was covered in a layer of dust.

Wesley blew off the dust. "And this is the one I'm guessing you want to take a look at," he said. "It's on Dark Spirit Zaszage, the most recent Dark Spirit known."

He handed it to Alice. She looked at the golden trimming on the title. It read *The Demon Prince.*

"The demon prince?" she asked. She knew from stories that the last Dark Spirit was a dragon, so what could this book be referring to?

"Yeah," Wesley responded. "Zaszage was the son of the Dragon King, making him the Dragon Prince, right? Well, this book is from my home in the Sky Kingdom. You see, Zaszage was a dragon so evil and so wicked, that my people conjured up a new name for him: *The Demon Prince.* Lots of other nations have nicknames for him too. I've heard Prince of the Night, Lord of the Dragons, Slayer of Light, and that's just to name a few."

"But Zaszage was the Dark Spirit," Alice began. "Doesn't that mean he should have protected the world and been somewhat of a hero? Not a villain."

"Villain?" Wesley remarked. "Of all the terms I've heard used to describe Zaszage, villain is the least concerning."

"Well, you know what I mean."

"I guess you're right. And it's true, once, a long time ago when the world was still called Wonderland, the spirits did protect the world. And some people still think they should. But Zaszage didn't care. He used his power to hurt people. For the short time he roamed Infinity, he terrified creatures of all nations, even other dragons."

This was all shocking news to Alice. She had only ever briefly heard of the previous Dark Spirit. She knew he wasn't ideal, but had no idea it was just *this* bad.

"What happened to him?" she asked, her curiosity suddenly sparking. "I know he disappeared, but why? And where did he go? Is he dead?"

"That's the thing," Wesley began. "No one knows what happened to him. After one of the first attacks at the beginning of the war, he vanished. But he is definitely *not* dead. If he was, then a new Dark Spirit would have been born in order to take his place."

"Maybe the cycle is broken again?"

"Not likely, the event after Lexa and Akaos was rare, and it was caused by lots of trauma. And another thing, remember how I told you the Skylord came to visit me a couple of years ago?"

Alice nodded.

"Well, he told me something that he made me swear to keep secret. I guess it'd be fine if I told you though because you're the Light Spirit and if anyone can know, it should be you. But please don't tell the others, okay?"

"I won't tell them," Alice was quick to say. She almost hated the fact that she was able to agree to keep something from her friends so quickly and even without any context as to why. Was this who she was before she met Fawn and Jack? The kind of person to easily lie and keep secrets from those she loved? It seemed the person she was before was slowly starting to reveal herself.

"He said he could *feel* Zaszage's presence," Wesley whispered in order to limit the echo effects of the tower. "He said that the Dark Spirit's soul is so dark that it radiates across Infinity. He also mentioned how it had to be Zaszage specifically because he was unique from previous Dark Spirits and that his aroma carried a unique sensation to it."

"How could he still be alive!" Alice said almost a little too loudly.

Wesley quickly brought his finger to his lips. He looked over his shoulder to where Fawn and Jack explored the level below them, undisturbed.

"It's been over three hundred years," Alice said more quietly this time.

"My guess is magic," Wesley whispered back. "But who knows."

"This presence," Alice began hesitantly. "What did the Skylord say it felt like exactly?"

Suddenly, the atmosphere in the room began to drop as Wesley described it. Alice's hands grew clammy and a lump formed in her throat.

"He said it was cold and dark," Wesley started. "When he closed his eyes and thought of Zaszage, he saw smoke and smelled something sweet. I think it was a scent, but I can't remember for sure. The Skylord talked about being tricked, wickedly tricked and deceived by this monster in disguise that was Zaszage. Only he said the feelings weren't his own. They would be experienced by someone else someday."

Alice missed the second half of what Wesley said. The mention of the smoke and sweet scent was troublesome enough for her to get carried away.

"This scent . . . what did it smell like?" she asked.

"I don't remember," Wesley said at first. "The Skylord said it was very sweet. Sweet to cover up the evil it was hiding. Maybe like candy, or strawberries, jasmine, or—"

"Vanilla?" Alice interrupted. As soon as Wesley began to mention the sweetness, she knew what it had to be. She felt her stomach drop as she remembered the scent of vanilla wafting off the boy from her dream, or rather, *nightmare.*

"Yeah! That's the one!" Wesley exclaimed as if Alice had done nothing more than won a guessing game. He truly was the epitome of innocence and lack of worries,

Alice shuddered. Was that the boy from her dream? The Dark Spirit, the Dragon Prince? She could no longer hide her feelings of terror and they began to show on her face, to Wesley's notice.

"Hey, don't be afraid," the little boy said to her. "Zaszage hasn't been seen for three hundred years. It isn't like he's going to pop up tomorrow."

He placed a comforting hand on Alice's shoulder before he jumped over the railing and floated down toward Fawn and Jack, leaving Alice alone.

She thought about her nightmare from last night. If it truly was Zaszage who she saw in her dream, Alice would go berserk with fear. She typically wasn't afraid of anything, but this dragon rubbed her the wrong way. She thought about how close he felt to her. How close he seemed. How close he *was*. He was just out of reach, behind her shoulder and in her ear. Alice could have extended a hand and touched him. That's how close he was.

"He won't pop up tomorrow . . ." Alice repeated what Wesley had said. And even though the little boy didn't know it, Alice knew that that could be entirely wrong,

"We don't know that."

Princess Gaia sat in the corner of her cell with her knees drawn up to her chest, shaken as she listened to the conversation going on around her.

"And you said someone was inside this box?" Nickoli asked Rosenia.

"Yes, and it wasn't really like a box. It was more like a room. A small and darkroom," the queen responded affirmatively.

"And who was the person in this room?"

"I don't know. I couldn't see his face. It was too dark. But I think . . . I think he didn't want me to."

"He didn't want you to see his face? Why not?" Nickoli questioned uneasily.

"I told you already," Rosenia began pacing around her cell. "Something about this person doesn't sit right with me. He's up to something. I know it."

The queen picked up her pace as she marched around the four corners of her cell, deep in thought. She thought about the events that have happened in recent days. What could have triggered this vision so suddenly . . . the thought came to her in an instant. "Alice!" she said.

Nickoli perked up at the mention of his daughter. "What? Rosenia, what is it?"

Rosenia completely ignored him as if Nickoli hadn't spoken at all. "We . . ." she began. "We need to get out of here *now!*"

"Mom, what are you talking about? What's happening?" Aurora asked.

"It's Alice," Rosenia said. "We have to warn her before it's too late! She'll open the box and let him out! I know she will!" Her frustration was growing as she continued to think about her vision. This was a fate not written in Alice's future. This . . . *was bad.*

"Mommy," Talula said as she came to stand at the front of her cell. "What's going on? Is someone trying to hurt Alice?"

"No, no, everything is fine, Talula," Aurora said to her little sister. "We're just taking a few precautions."

Rosenia whipped around to face Nickoli. "Nickoli," she said. "Get us out of here."

"I'm already a step ahead of you," he responded as if he had been waiting for this opportunity.

"Do you guys have any of that green mush leftover from lunchtime?"

"Um, yeah, I think so."

"Alright then. Everyone, here's the plan."

Alice sat down with her legs dangling off the edge of the floor of the library she was on. She held the Demon Prince book in her hands, hesitating to open it. From the way Wesley described the Skylord's vision, it seemed as if the Dark Spirit was calling out to her. Alice hoped it was for a positive reason, but after hearing more about Zaszage from Wesley, she knew that would not be the case.

Alice opened the book up and was shocked by what she found. The entire book had been hollowed out, every single page had been cut into to form a square and hollow center. Inside the center was another book, this one was slightly smaller than its shell.

Alice looked at the pages of the Demon Prince book. Was it not real? A cover-up to hide this other book inside? It couldn't be, Alice thought. Because on the edges of the pages, she could see small words and letters that had been cut when the book was hollowed out. *Someone* purposefully did this. And if so, where were the pages of the book?

Alice pulled out the second book from inside the hollowed center. The cover had exceptional artwork on it. It was a drawing of a girl with fire for wings, and a boy with blue hair holding hands, with their foreheads pressed together.

The title read: *The Tragedy of Lexa and Akaos, an Era Forgotten.*

Alice was stunned to see this book. It wasn't just a story about the life of the previous Light and Dark Spirit, it was a gateway into the world before. A time portal explaining what happened between them that made the world the way it is now. But most importantly, it was a token of Alice's past.

Whether she liked it or not, Lexa was a part of her. One of her own past lives, the person she was a thousand years ago. Everything had begun with Lexa, and it had ended with her too. The answers she had been looking for, the reasoning behind it all, could all be explained in this book.

But, was Alice even ready for such a thing? After all, reading this book, finding out about her past, and putting the pieces together would all be a form of acceptance. She would have to accept her destiny, fate, and role in this world. She would have to accept the fact that she is the Light Spirit, she was Lexa, she was a thousand different people in a thousand different lifetimes. She was destined to save the world and she didn't have a choice.

But more than anything, Alice would have to accept that she was not free.

Wildfire stood in the middle of town. She despised Taesithia. The way the birds chirped all day, even if it wasn't morning. The way flowers grew through the cobblestone paths. The way people greeted each other at their stupid little shops. She couldn't wait to get out of here.

Yagatsu and the cat Nova came to stand beside her. Everything was going smoothly. The number of Fire Kingdom soldiers in this town had more than doubled with Wildfire's platoon here. Now there had to be almost three hundred soldiers all scouring this tiny town for the Light Spirit. Sooner or later, they'd find her.

"She's here," Wildfire said to Yagatsu. "I can feel it."

Jack stood on the second floor of the tower. He stared at the bookshelf on the wall across from him. He had noticed that the outside of the tower was slightly wider than what the inside seemed to be. If his calculations were correct, there should be a hidden room somewhere on this side of the tower.

He stepped closer and took a better look at the structure of the shelf. It didn't take him long to notice the slight gap at the top between the wood of the shelf and the stone wall. He had found it. Behind this bookshelf was an adjoining room,

He looked over the railing to where Wesley was across from him talking with Fawn.

"Hey!" Jack called. Wesley looked over at him as Jack pointed to the shelf. "What's through here?"

Wesley slid open the bookshelf that acted as a secret door. The shelf was more than triple the size of him, quite the physical act for a small boy, indeed. Wesley was surprised it had been Jack who noticed the secret door and not Alice, the Light Spirit herself, but he expected nothing less from a group of highly capable individuals.

Once the bookshelf had completely slid open, it revealed a tunnel digging into the mountainside.

"Um," Fawn said suspiciously. "Why is there a secret tunnel in a *library?*"

"The secret tunnel's purpose is to hide something," Wesley responded. "Would you unicorns do the honors?" he asked as he stepped into the dark tunnel.

In response, Alice extended her hand and began emitting light from it. Jack's horn began to glow a similar light, and between them, they lit up the tunnel enough to enter.

Wesley's little pet, Boo, whined as they went into the dark tunnel. "It's okay, Boo," Wesley said as he picked up the creature with a finger. "You can stay out here where it's bright." He then set the tiny white creature on a shelf just outside the tunnel before leaving.

As the four of them advanced down the tunnel, Fawn looked back the way they came. "This place gives me the creeps."

"No need to worry," Wesley assured her. "I've been down here a lot and it's almost empty so don't be afraid. Besides, we're almost there."

The hall came to a dead end. In front of them was a large wooden door with no handle. In the spot the handle would normally be was instead a small, deep hole boring into the thick door.

"A secret door?" Fawn asked.

"What's behind it?" Jack added.

"I don't know," Wesley began. "I've tried breaking this door, using sky magic on it, and even setting off explosions, but nothing I try seems to even make a dent in it. It must be reinforced by magic."

Wesley hunched over to look into the hole in the door. He stuck his finger inside. "But see this little hole? I think it's for a key."

"Whatever is in there must be pretty important if all this stuff has been set in place to keep it protected," Alice remarked.

Jack took a closer look at the shape of the hole. The farther back it went, the narrower it got. And thus, the wider the entrance was. It was almost like the shape of a sword.

At that moment, a loud ringing noise sounded from somewhere outside. It was surprisingly loud for being so far away and it startled Jack, Fawn, and Alice beyond control.

Jack slipped and fell to the ground from where he was by the door. Alice jumped and bumped into Fawn, sending her falling on top of Jack. And Alice followed suit, the three of them stacked on top of each other.

Wesley attempted to hold back a smile. He bit his lip as he looked from Jack, to Fawn, and then to Alice. And after a moment, he could no longer hold it in, and he burst out laughing at them.

"Uh, um, what was that ringing from?" Jack asked, trying to change the subject.

"That's the curfew bell," Wesley said as he whipped away a tear from laughing so much.

Fawn pulled herself off of Jack. Her cheeks were a vibrant red color. "The what bell?"

"Curfew," Wesley responded. "The Fire Kingdom makes all the civilians of Taesithia be inside by six o'clock. It's also when the miners from the mountains return."

"Just how long has the Fire Kingdom been here?" Alice asked.

"Five long years. The Fire Kingdom makes the men mine the ores and coal from the mountains to fuel their vehicles. And that dragon appeared as additional security almost a year ago now."

Before they could say anything else, a loud thump sounded from somewhere outside, followed by a deafening shriek.

At that, Wesley's stomach dropped. "Oh no."

"What?" Alice asked.

"The dragon! That's the dragon that hurt my friends. It knows the tower is here, but it never stops by! We need to go now!"

The kids took off back down the tunnel until they made their way into the library, and they closed the secret door behind them. Once back in the library, Boo joined them once more.

Wesley immediately used sky magic to jump up and up and up all the way to a window on the top floor of the tower. Outside, he could see at least a hundred Fire Kingdom soldiers that had encircled the tower, and the aqua dragon stood beside them.

Wesley's fear began to show on his face as he made his way back down to the others. "Not good! Not good! Fire Kingdom soldiers are out there and so is the dragon!"

"How did they find us?" Alice shouted, energy rising.

"What are we going to do!" Fawn said.

"I'll call Reezu. He'll come to get us!" Alice responded. She put two fingers in her mouth and blew to create a silent whistling sound.

"I hope he can really hear that!" Fawn doubted.

"How are we going to get out of the tower to get to Reezu, with them out there?" Jack said.

"The windows!" Wesley shouted. He started leaping back up to the top floor. The others climbed the ladders after him.

Wildfire looked up at the massive tower before her. "Can you smell them now?" She asked the dragon who stood beside her.

"Yes," it replied in a female-sounding voice. The voice had a metallic quality to it as if there were a hundred of her all speaking at the same time.

"How many?"

The dragon sniffed the air for a second. "Four kids, and some type of animal."

Wildfire walked closer to the tower. "Come out, Light Spirit!" she demanded. "I know you're in there. We have the entire perimeter surrounded. Give up, and come out!"

The kids huddled together underneath a window at the top of the tower. Below them, they could hear the Fire Kingdom Force Captain who had chased them there, shouting outside. If what she said was true, and that the entire perimeter was surrounded, then they had nowhere to go, not with them out there.

Wildfire waited.

No response.

"Fine then, don't come out. I'll come and get you instead!" She turned to face the soldiers behind her. "Show no mercy."

All of the ones who were Fire Blood Elves got ready to use their magic. The others stepped back to give them room.

"Ready . . ." Wildfire began. "Fire!"

At her command, the Fire Blood Elves shot fire at the tower, creating one huge blast. The bottom portion of the tower had caught fire and was excreting a thick, black smoke.

Satisfied, Wildfire turned to face the aqua dragon. "Your turn," she said to the creature. Wildfire took a step back as the dragon inhaled. After a brief interval, the dragon exhaled a smokey blue fire all over the tower causing it to blacken and crumble on the outside.

The bottom few floors of the tower were now ablaze with fire, and smoke filled the upper portion, making it difficult for the kids to breathe. Piece by piece, sections of the flooring on different levels began crumbling away, and the fire gradually grew upward.

Boo began to fly around erratically in terror. Wesley looked like he was about to burst into tears. Jack was coughing and clearly having a harder time breathing than the rest of them. And Fawn was completely helpless. Looked like Alice would have to take one for the team on this one and pull them together. Or else . . . she didn't want to think about what else.

Alice peered down at the bottom floor that was far below to see if there was a possible way out, but through the crumbling entrance, she could make out Wildfire pushing her way through the flames. As a Fire Blood Elf, she had no problem manipulating the flames to her advantage and safety.

Alice stuck her fingers in her mouth and whistled again, calling out to Reezu. "You guys," she began, confidently. "Pull yourselves together! We're getting out of this tower and we're doing it as a team!"

She grabbed Wesley's arm. "Wesley, get up!" The little boy complied, although he still looked terrified. "We can't escape downstairs. We'll have to use the window, and we can't do that without sky magic. We need a lift. We need *you*."

Wesley looked at her like she was crazy. His pupils dilated as he peered at her through the smoke. "Y-y-you want me to j-j-jump?" he asked, shakily. "I can't! N-n-not with all of you, you're too heavy!"

"You did it earlier, didn't you?"

"That height is not even comparable to this one! We'll fall!"

"No, we won't!" Alice assured him. "Just close your eyes or something! We'll be okay!"

The tower then made a horrible creaking noise as it tilted to one side. It was *falling*. The area Wildfire was using to climb up gave way to her weight and she fell back down to the first floor. She didn't waste any more time. Now that the tower was falling, there was no need to risk her own life. She ran out the entrance while there was still time.

Up in the window sill, Wesley adjusted to grab a hold of the others as best as he could manage. He took a deep breath as he looked down at the far below ground. If he was alone, he could slow a fall from any height with no problem, but carrying three people who were all bigger than him was another story. If he had a glider, he could fly with it and carry people easier, but he didn't have one right now. He was wearing a glider *suit,* but that was much different compared to an actual wooden glider and it wouldn't help him. Right now, all he had was himself, his experience, and his will to survive. Heights had never scared Wesley before because of his abilities, but this was shaking him up.

On Wesley's shoulder, Boo cowered behind his ear and held onto a piece of his hair. The little creature could fly on his own, but even he was scared for the kids.

"T-t-three," Wesley stuttered. "T-two." The tower crackled. "One!"

Wesley leaped out of the tower with the others clinging on to him. At first, they were coming down at a rate somewhat slower than straight-up falling, but as they continued downward, they started falling faster and faster until it was a race between them and the ground. They all started screaming. Wesley desperately tried to lift up, but it was no use. In an instant, they would splat onto the ground.

Not more than a second before the kids would have hit the ground, something blue and feathery swooped in and caught them.

Alice opened her eyes to find herself safely seated in the saddle of a gigantic bird. Reezu had come to their rescue after all. All four kids were still holding onto each other and it wasn't until Mayday came up and started licking them that they let go. The little cub assured them that they were all okay and Fawn wasted no time scooping her up to cuddle.

Alice jumped over to Reezu's head and hugged him. "Reezu! Thanks for the rescue, buddy!" The bird nuzzled his head up against her and purred a soft, deep melody. Reezu began flapping his wings harder in order to gain altitude to fly over the mountains.

Back outside on the ground, Wildfire looked up at the targets as they flew away. She was so close! The Light Spirit was right there. How had she missed her!

"Shoot them down!" she shouted at the soldiers. The Fire Blood Elves began shooting fire blasts at the departing bird, but it was too late, their fire didn't reach anywhere near Reezu.

In an instant, Wildfire's supernova ran over to the burning tower and climbed up the outside of it. Once at the top, it exhaled a massive ghast of flames that blew right into Reezu's path.

After a moment, the tower began to succumb to the fire and collapsed onto itself, with Nova still standing at the top. "Nova!" Wildfire shouted as her cat came crashing down to the ground with the debris. The cat cried out as she hit the ground.

Alice and the kids watched as a huge cat ran up the tower to shoot fire blasts at them. They ducked behind the edge of the saddle as the fire soared just above their heads.

Just when they thought they were safe, the kids shot up out of the saddle. Reezu was *falling* out of the sky. He had been hit with one of the fire blasts on his leftwing, and it blackened as the fire distinguished on his feathers.

The kids dangled out of the saddle, screaming their heads off. As Reezu fell, they seemed to defy gravity and were practically floating up off the bird's back. Jack had caught hold of Reezu's rightwing and was desperately clinging to Fawn and Mayday with his free hand. Alice had caught hold of the reins and Wesley clung to her.

Alice tried making her way closer to Reezu's ear, with Wesley. "Up, Reezu!" she shouted in desperation. "Lift up!"

After a second more of free-falling out of the sky, Reezu began flapping his wings again, this time weaklier than before, now that he was injured. But nevertheless, they flew away from the scene, and the kids fell back into the saddle with a thud.

On the ground, Wildfire watched the giant bird fly off and out of sight. She screamed in frustration. This was her chance and she blew it! There was no way she'd ever get that close again!

"Damn it!" Wildfire kicked a boulder that was beside her as hard as she could. The action backfired and she fell flat on her back, yelping out in pain as she did so.

The aqua dragon that had been standing beside the soldiers morphed into its avatar. A dragon she was no more, and instead, was a young woman with long aqua hair and golden eyes, with pale skin. She walked over to where Wildfire laid on the ground, helpless.

"Shall I go after them?" she asked the Force Captain, with her voice no longer sounding so digital.

Wildfire stared up at the dragon with her eyes blazing. The last thing she needed was someone else getting in the way *or* getting credit for *her* mission, *especially* someone from another nation.

"No! I don't need your help! This matter concerns the Fire Kingdom, *not* Dragonia!"

Without another word, Wildfire crawled over to where Nova laid in the rubble of the tower. The giant cat breathed heavily and whined softly as she suffered the pain of her injuries.

"Nova . . ." Wildfire cried.

Alice, Jack, Fawn, Wesley, and their animal companions trekked through the night under the canopy of the Earth Nation forest. It was late and they were exhausted.

Reezu's injured wing was now wrapped in a bandage after Alice and Jack had worked on healing it. But still, it would be days before he could fly again.

Eventually, they came to a cliff. There was a wide river at the bottom of the cliff, and an old bridge stretched across the chasm to the other side that was held up by a network of vines.

"Should we stop here for the night?" asked Jack.

"Let's just get across this bridge," Alice mentioned. "I want to put a little more distance between us and Wildfire before resting."

"Alright," Jack agreed.

All the kids looked incredibly tired. Had they not been so exhausted, and had there been daylight shining, perhaps they would have noticed that the bridge was in no condition, whatsoever, for holding passengers.

They shuffled into a single file in order to fit on the bridge, with Wesley in the lead and Fawn pulling up the rear.

As soon as all of them made it onto the bridge, a loud snap sounded from beneath their feet.

At once, the bridge gave way to their weight, and the kids screamed as they fell toward the rushing waters of the river. Except, they didn't fall all the way down, they got stuck in the network of vines that had held up the bridge. Each of them was wedged between the vines, they swung back and forth in the chasm.

One of Alice's vines snapped and she yelled out as she fell a foot or so deeper into the chasm. Wesley gradually began slipping out of the loose hold the vines had on him because of his small size.

"I'm going to fall!" he shouted.

"I'm going to end up in the river!" Alice yelled.

"No, you're not!" Jack shouted from between them. He looked around at their hopeless situation. They were all stuck. No one was coming to rescue them this time, and the Fire Kingdom wasn't far behind.

"We'll get out of this . . . somehow."

Fawn was wrapped tightly in the vines and was almost completely upside down as she stared down at the dark water below. Blood began rushing to her head. Everything was hazy, her vision blurry, her mind fuzzy, her body dizzy. The sensation brought forth flashbacks from a much different moment in time.

She thought of her brother Malahki. She thought of his messy orange hair, his laugh, his smile, the way he always cocked his head. And then . . . it all went black.

CHAPTER FIVE

Malahki the Deceiver

Piniel Dynasty, Seven Years Ago, July 2038

Fawn sat atop the rocks near the pond as she tossed bread to the coy fish. She was six years old. Her long orange hair had been braided in order to keep out of her face in the summer heat, and she was missing half her teeth.

In the surrounding area, farmers tended to the fields of crops that were grown just outside of the city. In front of Fawn, just a little way down the path was the massive white wall that surrounded the Piniel Dynasty of the skinwalkers. This was her home nation where she was born and raised as well as the generations in her family before her.

Fawn tossed the last of her bread to the coy fish and she leaned far over the rocks to watch them peck at it. Suddenly, the rocks began to crumble. She would have fallen into the water, but a hand pulled her back just in time. Fawn turned around to see her older brother, Malahki.

"Woah there little coy fish," he teased.

"Hey! I'm not a fish!" Fawn always hated it when he called her that.

"You are to me," Malahki replied cheekily. He knew Fawn absolutely hated water, and that's where his little nickname for her came from.

Fawn huffed and blew a piece of her hair out of her face that had come out of the braids, while Malahki smiled his crooked smile at her. His head was tilted to the side with one of his wolf ears bent, like a curious puppy.

Malahki was eleven and a wolfwalker just like the rest of his family. He and Fawn's resemblance was breathtaking. They had identical orange hair, green eyes, and freckles. If it wasn't for the age gap, they could've been twins.

On his back, Malahki wore a carrier that had been filled with firewood he collected. Fawn also had a carrier, but hers was empty.

"Since you gave all our food to the fish," Malahki began. "We should stop and get some more. C'mon."

He helped Fawn climb down off the rocks and they took off toward the wall.

Once inside, they ran through the busy streets of the Piniel Dynasty. Everything was made from white marble and quartz, which displayed the wealth of the nation easily.

As they ran, Malahki looked back at Fawn and smiled at her. This was their game of life—running through the fancy streets of their hometown and getting into all sorts of trouble. They were just kids at the time, and so little too, that everything had always been carefree and playful. It had always been just the two of them playing their games, like two peas in a pod. *This* was their story and they made the rules.

The kids made their way to the market where the city was busiest. They approached a fruit stand that was crowded with customers. Malahki glanced over at Fawn as if to say, *are you thinking what I'm thinking?* And she nodded back at him, *let's do this.*

On command, Fawn ran up to the seller of the stand and began tugging on his shirt. "Help! Help! I can't find my mommy!" she shouted in desperation.

Fawn dragged the seller out into the crowd of the market, leaving the fruit stand unguarded. And thus, *the game had begun.*

Malahki immediately took this opening and jumped behind the front of the stand. He pocketed whatever he could find. Fruits, money, seeds—everything went into his shirt and pants.

As soon as he had grabbed the items of interest, Malahki slipped back into the crowd without anyone noticing. Being sly and going unnoticed were his specialty skills, and being a certified ruffian living on the streets had certainly helped him touch up on those skills. After all, if he didn't find a way to steal, he and his little sister would go hungry. It isn't like their parents were going to feed them.

Malahki brushed past the very seller he had just stolen from in order to meet up with Fawn. They then hurried through the crowded white streets and away from the scene.

As they walked away, Malahki started laughing. He and Fawn could get away with almost anything. And wasn't that the best part of the game? The thrill? The fact that you can break the law and still make a clean getaway is what made the game all the more worth it. And as long as he could continue upping that thrill, Malahki would keep on playing.

As he laughed away, Fawn watched him. He laughed with his crooked smile and his orange hair bounced with his upbeat movements. The sight made Fawn laugh too for Malahki had the most amazing smile.

Slowly, the sight began to fade away as it fell to the darkness. Gently, the laughter of the kids dissipated into silence. Gradually, the memory that had been brought back to life became a memory once more.

And for the time being, Fawn was left to ponder in the emptiness of her own mind as she hung trapped in the vines, unconscious.

Jack desperately tried to wiggle his way out of the vines that he was stuck in underneath the broken bridge, but it was no use. He was stuck too tightly in them to move, and even if he did somehow manage to break away, there was still the rushing water of the river dozens of feet below him that wouldn't exactly make a cushiony landing.

On the contrary, Wesley hopelessly tried to hold on to the vines around him as he gradually slipped out of their grasp. The little boy kept slipping between their hold as if he was made of butter. He kept on reaching up, sliding back down. Reaching up, and sliding back down. At one point, he got flipped over upside down and was just dangling on with a vine he caught hold of with his mouth. Now, he simply clung to a single vine with his hands and feet, like a monkey on a tree.

On the other hand, Alice tried to stay completely still. She was hanging the farthest into the chasm than anyone else, with nothing more than a single vine wrapped around her wrist, to hold her up. One wrong move and she'd slip from its grasp and down into the river.

"It's no use. We're stuck!" Wesley shouted to Jack.

"We'll be fine. I have an idea, but this is all going to depend on you, Wesley," he responded.

"Ah, huh?"

"I need you to zap these vines with some electricity. Then they should snap, and we'll be freed."

"Electricity?" Alice yelled up at them. Where was Wesley going to find an electric current all the way out here?

"Yeah, Wesley should be electric," Jack said.

This was news to Alice. She had originally believed that Wesley was a Sky Blood Elf with the magical abilities of the sky allowing him to fly and float through the air.

"I didn't know Sky Blood Elves had electric powers."

"Sky Blood Elf?" Wesley said in disbelief as he again slipped from the vines. "I'm not a Sky Blood Elf!"

"You're not? Then what are you!"

"I'm a Pisces!"

"Like the zodiac sign?" Alice had never heard of a Pisces before. Now wasn't exactly the time for chatter, but it was helping her to relieve stress from their current predicament and the fact that Wesley also seemed to take the dangerous situation lightly, comforted her.

"A Pisces is a native creature of the Sky Kingdom," Jack began. "They are very similar to Sky Blood Elves because they possess sky magic, but Pisces do not share the pointed ears that elves do, and they are also blessed with electricity powers."

Jack went to turn his head to the general direction of where he presumed Wesley to be, only to be frightened to near death when the boy was dangling upside down right in front of his face. The two of them were nose to upside-down nose. Jack had no idea how Wesley had managed to get so close without him hearing or feeling a thing.

"Ahhhh!" Jack screamed.

"Ahhhh!" Wesley screamed back right in Jack's face.

Jack exhaled tiresomely. The little kid was certainly one to keep a leash on. "Wesley, you scared me."

"Sorry," the little boy said as he flashed a cheeky smile. "I came over here to try and zap the vines like you said."

"Do you think you can do it?"

Wesley started poking Jack's face as if trying to see what he felt like. "I can try," he said in between pokes.

Jack gave him a blank stare. *Seriously.*

Wesley stopped poking Jack's face in order to crack his knuckles. He stayed in his upside-down position holding onto the vine with his feet in order to get his hands free. He closed his eyes and took a deep breath. At once, his body began to charge up with purple bolts of electricity that looked like mini-lightning strikes. The bolts flickered around his entire body creating a buzzing sound.

Wesley opened his eyes which had gone completely purple. They now glowed like a smokey fire with no whites and no pupils. The bolts of lightning grew stronger and stronger in mere seconds.

And then, Wesley extracted the electricity from his body as he caught hold of Jack's vines with both his hands. Immediately upon contact, the vines absorbed the electricity, buzzed, and then turned black with a sizzle before snapping.

But the electricity didn't stop there. It continued to travel across all the vines that stretched the length of the chasm, blackening and snapping many of them, until it finally discharged into nothing at the back of the chasm.

The snapping of the vines caused everyone to fall a foot or so closer to the river. The vines were now much looser on Jack, and he began trying to wiggle his way out of their hold on him.

"I . . . think . . . I can get out now," he said in between breaths. Beside him, Wesley exhaled and reverted back to his normal state. Although his eyes seemed a bit watery now and his cheeks were red.

Jack managed to slip through the rest of the vines holding him up. When he reached up to hold onto a vine to use to climb up, it snapped and he plummeted toward the rushing river.

"Jack!" Alice screamed as he fell right past her.

In an instant, Wesley let go of the vine he was holding onto with his feet and fell after Jack, head first. Wesley brought his wrist to his chest and then opened up his arms like wings. He now had fabric from his jumpsuit attached to his wrist and sides of his body that acted like a glider.

Wesley used sky magic to dive faster after Jack, and right before he would have hit the water, Wesley swooped under Jack and caught him under his arm. It took the tiny boy a second to adjust to the new weight, and he and Jack splashed into the water briefly before soaring back up.

Alice took a closer look at Wesley's outfit. He had worn a white and blue jumpsuit with tall boots. She had noticed the two buttons on his chest earlier but didn't think anything of it. She now realized that the buttons connected to clasps on Wesley's wrist in order to open up the glider wrapped around his sides, which let him glide through the sky like a flying squirrel.

Alice watched as Wesley flew with Jack to a portion of the bridge that was not broken. To see him fly like that, so effortlessly and freely, was incredible. Maybe being the Light Spirit wouldn't be so bad after all because it meant she'd be able to learn how to fly like that as well. Flying like a resident of Sky Kingdom had to be the newest star in Alice's galaxy of dreams. And it just so happened that this star was tangible.

"Okay!" Wesley said as he landed with Jack. "Okay, that worked! I can zap the rest of the vines and catch you guys one by one!"

"Yeah!" Alice cheered. "We're going to get out here safely!"

"It won't work," Jack said as he took deep breaths. He seemed shaken up from what just happened and even seemed to be having a hard time breathing.

He took another breath and spoke quietly. "The electric current travels across all of the vines at once. There's no way Wesley could catch you and Fawn at the same time. Not to mention Reezu."

Alice looked up and over to where Reezu sat perfectly still in the network of vines with his feet dangling through. Mayday sat in the saddle and Boo flew around nearby. Reezu was big. Much too big for anyone to even imagine trying to catch. Alice had no idea how they were going to get him out, considering the fact he could not fly.

"You'll have to find something sharp," Jack said to Wesley. "That way, you can cut the vines individually to catch Alice and Fawn. We'll have to think of another plan to rescue Reezu."

That was smart, Alice thought. Wesley could fly away from the cliff to find something to use to help. She would have never thought of cutting the vines one by one. Jack sure did have a good head on his shoulders.

"Alright!" Wesley said cheerfully. "I'll be back in a jiff!"

The little boy leaped off the bridge with his glider open and soared off into the night.

"We'll uh, we'll just wait here!" Jack shouted to him. Jack looked over to the back of the chasm near where they had first got on the bridge, to where Fawn was dangling unconscious in the network vines.

"Just hold on a little longer, Fawn."

Malahki and Fawn ran up the steps of their white quartz house. Each of them carried some of the fruits they had just stolen from the market a few minutes ago.

The outside of the house was just as fancy as the surrounding buildings, with clean windows and flowers lining the steps. However, the inside was bare of any furniture and somewhat dusty, almost as if it were abandoned.

Malahki dropped the firewood he had collected at the front door and started making his way into the living room with Fawn close behind him.

Malahki stopped just short of the living room to stay hidden behind a corner and Fawn bumped into him.

"Hey! Watch where you're—" Fawn began, but Malahki cut her off as he quickly brought his finger to his lips. It took Fawn a moment to notice the sound of two people arguing in the other room. It was their parents, quietly shouting back and forth at each other, not something that was uncommon in their household, but recently, Malahki had been more interested in what they had to say to each other.

"This can't be happening!" their mother gasped. "There's no way we could have been found out!"

"Face it, Accalia!" the father cursed back at her. "We've been compromised and you know what happens next."

Malahki turned around the corner and Fawn followed him into the room. "Mom? Dad? What's going on?" he asked.

The adults were startled to see their kids enter the room. Their mother, Accalia, stood by a window at the back of the room. She had long orange hair and pale skin. Their father, Takara, leaned against the opposite wall. He had mid-length blonde hair and tan skin. Both of them were wolfwalkers with black ears and tails, and both of them were remarkably tall.

"Kids! You shouldn't be here right now!" Takara yelled. He was never very happy to see them, but now he seemed more stressed than usual.

Accalia rushed over to her children and began pushing them up the stairs. "Hurry! Go pack your things. We're leaving!"

"What?" Malahki asked. "Mom what's wro—"

"Be quiet! Just go and do as you're told!"

Malahki grabbed Fawn's hand and hurried up the stairs with her. Fawn looked at Malahki. He seemed distressed and were his eyes a bit glossy?

At the top of the stairs was a small loft that was filled with a bunk bed and a small dresser. Malahki grabbed a bag from the floor and began filling it with clothes from the dresser, hastily.

"Kai, what's going on?" Fawn asked him.

"*Malahki,*" he corrected. "And we're leaving."

"Leaving where?"

"I'm not sure." Malahki handed Fawn an empty bag. "Take this. Put your stuff in it, okay?"

Malahki trotted back down the stairs while carrying his and Fawn's bag. Fawn tailed after him. Suddenly, she bumped into Malahki as he stopped dead in his tracks at the bottom of the stairs.

Fawn peaked around Malahki's frozen shoulders to see what was going on in the living room that had startled him. It took the little girl a second to understand what was going on, but then it came to her. The dozen or so people who filled the living room who were all wearing fancy uniforms were members of the military police. And at the room's center, laying on the ground and currently being handcuffed, were Fawn and Malahki's parents.

One of the soldiers turned around and his eyes grew wide when he saw two little kids standing at the base of the stairs. He grabbed the attention of his comrades and a few of them approached Fawn and Malahki.

"Hey there, kiddos," the first soldier said in a somewhat friendly tone. He squatted down to be closer to the kids' height. "I bet you're wondering what's going on and I'll tell you, but first you guys are going to have to come with us. Is that okay?"

At first, Malahki stared at him blankly, but then, in a flash, the boy whipped around, scooped up Fawn, and ran up the stairs as fast as his legs could carry him.

"Hey! Come back!" the soldier shouted up at them. Malahki could hear their heavy footsteps gaining behind him, but it only urged him on even faster.

Malahki ran into the loft, set down Fawn, and then slammed the door behind him, locking it. He ran over to the bunk bed and climbed to the top in order to fiddle with a hatch on the ceiling just above it.

"What's going on!" Fawn cried. "Why are the military police here? Are Mom and Dad in trouble?"

Malahki completely sidestepped the question. "Jump up here," he said as he reached a hand down to her.

Loud bangs sounded on the door. Any second, the police would break it down. Malahki took that as his cue to lift Fawn up through the hatch and onto the roof outside. He followed a second after and closed the latch behind him.

The city was quiet and dark. The streets were empty and yellow light illuminated from all of the houses' windows. Malahki climbed down from the roof and onto the road, helping Fawn as needed. He then grabbed her hand, and without another word, they began racing through the night, away from the scene.

Fawn and Malahki hid behind the rocks of the pond just outside of the wall. They peaked their heads above the rocks just enough to see the path leading from the wall.

It was almost completely pitch black out there, away from the city. The only light came from the moon, although being part wolf certainly helped the kids with their night vision.

Fawn quietly sat next to Malahki. They had been waiting there for a while now. She had no idea what was going on, and Malahki wouldn't tell her if he even knew what was going on himself. Fawn suspected he must have known something that she didn't because of the way his pupils were dilated and his hand shook as he held hers.

He had told her they would wait there, behind the rocks of the pond, until their mom and dad came. But they had clearly seen both of their parents get handcuffed by the military police. There was no way they'd make it out.

"They're not coming," Fawn said hopelessly.

Malahki looked at his little sister. He could make out her orange hair and green eyes perfectly in the darkness. However, she wasn't looking right at him. Instead, she was gazing off in the general direction of where he was.

He felt sad for her. She was so little. She knew nothing of the choppy waters they were in, or at least, what their parents were in. To Malahki, his sister was his only friend. And he was her only friend. They had no one to take care of them, so they took care of each other. Without her, Malahki would have nothing. He wished so badly that Fawn could have a better life, that she didn't have to be caught up in this mess. He wanted to give her the world and everything in it, but that's rather hard to do when you have nothing.

"Just hold on a little longer," he said to her.

Wesley glided back into the chasm where Alice, Fawn, and Reezu still dangled helplessly from the vines. Jack sat very still on the small expanse of the bridge that hadn't fallen through. As Wesley approached that small expanse, he held up a sharp stick for Jack to see.

"Will this do?" he asked.

"I don't know," Jack said. "Let's find out. Alice? Are you ready?"

"Yes! Get me out of here, please!" she shouted. All the blood had drained from her arm that was hanging from the vine, and it was going numb. Alice was afraid she wouldn't be able to tell if it was losing its grip on her. Any moment, she could fall.

"Wesley?" Jack asked as he looked up to the boy who was flying around in circles above his head.

"And Wesley is up to bat again!" he said as he flew around with the stick in his hand. "Will he score? Will he not? I don't know, folks. Looks like you'll have to—"

"Wesley!" Jack shouted trying to get the kid to focus. "This isn't a game! Alice needs your help right now."

"Right, right. Sorry." Wesley flew down to where Alice was and grabbed hold of the vine with his hands and feet a little way above her. The sudden movement caused the vine to swing back and forth.

Wesley let go of his hold on the vine with his hands and swung upside down so that he was holding on with nothing but his feet. Now his upside-down face was at eye level with Alice's.

"Hi," he said smoothly.

"Hi?" she answered back.

Wesley grabbed hold of part of the vine just above Alice's wrist and sliced it in half with a smooth stroke of the sharpened stick.

The movement caused the vine to swing violently, and with nothing holding onto her, Alice fell. But just in time, Wesley slid down to the end of the vine with his feet and grabbed Alice's hand.

For a moment, Wesley stayed in that position. He was upside down, holding onto Alice's hand with both of his hands. He pulled her up, and for a moment, their noses touched. At that, Wesley's eyes grew big and his cheeks turned a vibrant red.

He almost froze but then quickly let go of the vine and flew up to the bridge with Alice holding onto him. Once safely next to Jack, Wesley quickly let go of Alice and scooted to the other side of the bridge. Was it hot out there, or was it just him?

Alice turned to look at Wesley. "Nice catch."

"U-uh yeah, haha," he said, scratching his head. "Don't mention it."

Jack noticed something strange was going on between the two of them, or at least with Wesley. He gave the boy a side-eyed stare, questioning him, but Wesley completely avoided the eye contact and quickly looked away and began whistling, casually. Jack decided he'd have to remember to ask the kid about this later.

He looked across to where Fawn was at the other end of the bridge. She still hadn't woken up yet. "Alright, Fawn, you're up next."

Fawn and Malahki sat behind the rocks of the pond, with their heads resting on each other. Malahki sat up when he heard the sound of footsteps approaching. He peeked over the rocks to see his mom and dad racing down the path from the wall.

"Wake up! Wake up!" he said as he shook Fawn. He hadn't realized she'd fallen asleep.

"Mm, what is it?" she said as she rubbed her eyes.

"Mom and Dad are back!"

It took Fawn a moment to figure out where she was and what was going on, but then her memories came back to her. The military police had taken her parents away, but somehow, they must've managed to escape, and now, they were leaving their home. They had always moved around a lot, in fact, they never did stay in one house for very long, but they had never left the protective wall of the Piniel Dynasty before. Where would they go now?

Malahki hastily grabbed his and Fawn's bag and raced out onto the path to greet his parents, but they raced right past him. If it wasn't for Takara shouting, "Let's go!" to them, Malahki would have assumed he and his sister were invisible.

Malahki whipped his nose on his sleeve with a sign, and then grabbed his sister's hand, before racing into the night after their mom and dad.

Two Months Later

Malahki carried Fawn on his back as he trekked through the rainforest. His mom and dad were a few yards in front of him, and they didn't slow for him.

The air here was much cooler, and even though it was autumn now, he could tell that wherever they were had to be much further north than the Piniel Dynasty to have such a cooler climate compared to his southern home. He shivered as a breeze blew past him. He had given Fawn his only jacket.

For the past eight weeks, they had traveled non-stop. They'd hiked over mountains, sailed on ships, and ridden on horseback, whatever kind of transportation they could get their hands on. And after all those days of endless travel, they had made it here to this tropical northern place.

Malahki carried Fawn with much exhaustion in his stance. He hadn't eaten in a couple of days. Most of the food he managed to steal he'd given to Fawn. He'd rather go hungry than see his sister starve. His eyes were dull and his tan skin was paling.

Suddenly, Malahki tripped over the root of a tree and fell to the ground with Fawn. Takara and Accalia did not look back or even wait for their kids to catch up. And Malahki sat there on the ground, on all fours, completely defeated.

Fawn stood up and reached for his hand to try and help him up. She smiled a tight smile at him. He looked up at her and reached for her hand. For Fawn to still be able to smile in such a horrible situation was one of the things Malahki admired about her. To be so broken, but yet strong enough to keep on pushing, that's what Malahki wanted to be for her.

Fawn helped her brother up and the two of them began walking side by side. They only made it a little way further before the exhaustion set once more, and Malahki fell again. He had pushed his body beyond limits. There wasn't any more strength left in his legs.

Malahki used the trunk of a tree to help himself stand up, but he fell. He stood again and fell again. He sat there at the base of the tree and buried his face in his hands.

Fawn looked down at him and tried not to cry. She grabbed his arm and desperately tried to pull him to a standing position, but it was no use; Malahki had given up. What could Fawn do to help? She couldn't carry him, and their parents were getting further and further ahead.

Suddenly, to Fawn's surprise, her mother looked back. Accalia then grabbed Takara's arm and said something to him. After a moment, they began heading back toward the kids.

Fawn's eyes grew wide. Maybe her mom and dad actually did care after all! Either one of them could easily carry Malahki.

"I know you kids are tired," Takara began as he approached them. "We've traveled a lot in a relatively short period of time. So, the two of you can stay and rest here for a bit, okay?"

Immediately, Malahki desperately tried to get up. He was nervous now because he knew something like this was coming. He had to get up, he had to move, and he had to fight.

"No! We're fine!" Malahki shouted in desperation. He stood and tried throwing Fawn on his back again. "We can keep on going! Right, Fawn?"

Accalia picked up Fawn and sat her down at the base of the tree trunk. Takara shoved Malahki back down next to her.

"*Stay* here!" he said sternly. "Just do as you are told!"

Takara began walking off again. Accalia went with him a little way before looking back. "We're gonna go now . . . we'll be back later," she said softly. And then the two of them disappeared into the trees.

Malahki didn't watch them go. He kept his gaze on the ground. Fawn sat quietly next to him as they waited for their parents' return.

Fawn watched as the blue sky between the treetops faded to orange, and then purple, and then to black. Morning arrived a few hours later but there was never any disturbance in the trees that would announce Takara and Accalia's return.

By mid-day, Malahki had regained enough strength to stand. He grabbed Fawn's hand and began trekking through the woodlands with her.

"Where are we going?" Fawn asked. She didn't want her parents to come back and realize that their kids were gone. "Shouldn't we wait for Mom and Dad to get back?"

"They're not coming back, Fawn," Malahki said without even the slightest hint of emotion. "From now on, it's just you and me."

Fawn didn't say another word.

Malahki and Fawn continued through the forest. A week had passed since their mom and dad left them. They traveled north in search of a town or village, but the forest was much too thick for anyone to build in. It stretched out for miles and miles, filled with trees towering dozens of stories high in the air.

Malahki stopped walking as he heard a strange noise coming from somewhere on his right. He waited and listened. And then it sounded again. It almost sounded like something plopping into the water.

Malahki walked with Fawn over to where the noise came from. He peeked through the trees and was surprised to find a clearing beyond it. The two of them parted through the trees and into the grassy clearing.

The clearing consisted of a small pond in the center with water as clear as glass and a gazebo that stood near the pond. From where she stood at the tree line, Fawn could see colorful fish twirling around in the pond.

Suddenly, a piece of bread dropped into the pond, making a plopping noise. It wasn't until then did Fawn notice the little boy sitting at the base of the gazebo who had been tossing bread to the fish. Fawn looked at Malahki. He had already noticed the other boy, but the boy hadn't noticed them yet.

Fawn gazed at the boy. She was mesmerized by his fair skin, silver hair, and large blue eyes. He was a unicorn and somewhere in between her and Malahki's age. Fawn had never seen a unicorn before, and never could she have dreamed of meeting anyone who looked like this boy. His hair looked like snow, and his eyes looked like the ocean. He was very different from her.

Malahki looked up and over the treetops. In the distance, not far away at all, he could see a silver castle towering amongst the trees.

The boy tossed the last of his bread into the pond. He then looked over his shoulder to the left, as he gazed back at Fawn and Malahki with his ocean eyes.

Jack and Alice had tied vines around their waist into a makeshift harness as they hung just below the bridge, on opposite sides of Reezu. Jack was over by the bird's tail and Alice at his beak. Wesley flew around in circles below them, and Mayday paced around in Reezu's saddle.

They were about to enact the plan Jack had come up with in order to save Reezu. He had originally wanted to rescue Fawn first, but the vines that held her up were connected directly to Reezu. If they tried freeing her, Reezu would plummet into the river. Their only choice was to hurry and get the bird out first.

"Here, catch!" Jack shouted to Alice as he tossed her a sharpened stick. She caught it with both hands, and Jack looked down at Wesley as he flew around just above the water. "All set down there?"

"Ready when you are!" Wesley shouted back.

Jack met Alice's gaze from where she was across from him. "One," he started.

"Two," Alice said.

"Three!"

They instantly began cutting the vines wrapped around Reezu as quickly as they could. As the vines gradually began to snap, Reezu fell lower and lower into the chasm with each one.

With only a few vines left, they cut another . . . and another . . . and another . . . until snap! The last vine snapped and the bird began falling right for the water. Reezu stretched up his neck and let out a cry.

But at that instant, Wesley started flying in a perfect circle just below Reezu, with extreme speed. He was going too fast for Alice to follow him with her eyes.

As Wesley gained speed, he created a whirlwind of air around him. While in the air, he flipped onto his back, placed his hands around his mouth like a microphone, and blew straight up.

The air came out of Wesley's mouth at a rate not physically possible for a normal person. And the air, along with the whirlwind he had created, flew upward out of the chasm with a massive gust, taking Reezu up with it.

The insane amount of wind blew past Alice and Jack with crazy force, sending them swinging on their vines to opposite ends of the chasm. Alice hit the front of the cliff wall gracefully and was able to catch herself on it. At the opposite end, where they had first boarded the bridge, Jack hit the cliff wall with a thud.

In the meantime, the wind storm had died down. Now, Reezu had been lifted high enough into the air in order to spread his wings and glide to the other side of the cliff without having to use his injured wing too much. Boo flew ahead, just in front of the massive bird, as if guiding him to land.

Wesley soared up high into the sky, twirling around in circles underneath the stars. "Woohoo! We did it!" He then swirled back down into the cliff to help Alice onto the solid ground on the other side.

At the back of the chasm, Jack reached up to where Fawn dangled just above him. Most of the vines holding her up had been cut with Reezu's, but one still held her at the waist. She was no longer upside down, and by the color returning to her face, Jack could tell she was waking up.

He cut the last vine and wrapped his arm around her tightly, as he dangled with nothing more than a single vine and a cliff wall to hold onto.

Fawn slowly came to and opened her eyes. She looked at Jack beside her, but her vision was too blurry to make him out exactly. "Jack?" she asked wearily. "W-what's happening?"

Fawn rubbed her eyes, and after a second, her vision cleared enough for her to see what was going on. She looked down to see that she and Jack were hovering dozens of feet up in the air above a river, with no clear way of making it back to land.

"Ahhhhh! What the—"

"Ssshhhh!" Jack interrupted her outrageous shouting. "It's fine, just hold on tight." He readjusted his grip on her, and she wrapped her arms tightly around him.

"This is crazy!" Fawn cried. "This is crazy! This is crazy!"

She tucked her head into Jack's shoulder in fear of looking at the water below and began whining like an injured animal.

"I thought you weren't supposed to be afraid of heights!" Alice shouted from the other side of the cliff.

"That's cats, you idiot!" Fawn replied back. "Wolves don't always land on their feet!"

"Maybe not," Jack began. "But I hear they are good swimmers."

He winked at Fawn, and she rolled her eyes in return. "Very funny."

Jack fixated his gaze on something past Fawn. Wesley was flying toward them, however. Fawn had no idea that he was approaching. Jack thought back to what his mother had told him and Fawn a few days ago when they left Elkmire. She had said for them to take care of each other. What did she mean by that exactly? She had said for them to stay together, for the sake of someone else. Jack hadn't had enough time to decipher the message, but he was working on it.

"Do you trust me?" he asked Fawn who was still cowering at his side.

"What?"

"Do you trust me?" Jack repeated.

"No," Fawn replied bluntly.

"Okay, well you're gonna have to," Jack said with a nervous smile. "Get ready to let go in—"

"Let go!" Fawn interrupted. "Have you lost your mind?" Fawn couldn't believe what he was saying right now. If they let go of this vine they were currently dangling from, they'd plummet into the water of that river.

At this point, Jack has noticed that Wesley had flown directly past him and Fawn. Wesley swooped around and began making his way back toward the two, sucking up air into his lungs as he approached at a quickening pace. Fawn had still yet to notice that Wesley was nearby.

"Three," Jack began.

"What? No—"

"Two,"

"Ah! You can't be serious!"

"One!"

At that instant, Jack let go of the vine as a huge blast of wind carried him and Fawn across the chasm and sent them flying to the land on the other side.

Fawn ducked and rolled, landing smoothly beside Alice. Jack didn't quite make it all the way and was left hanging onto the cliffside. Alice and Fawn helped pull him the rest of the way up, as Wesley landed beside them.

"See . . . that wasn't . . . so bad," Jack said in between breaths.

"Tsk," Fawn said sarcastically. "You're an idiot, Jack Everhart."

"And you still trusted me, Fawn Dekrano."

"So now that you have the scroll, you're heading all the way to the Etaellaca Empire to find the missing princess?" Wesley asked. He walked beside the others underneath the tree canopy. It would be morning soon and they were trying to find a safe place to camp out for the night, and hopefully get some sleep.

"Yes," Alice said. "And since everyone we know is stuck in Elkmire, we're on our own."

"We could really use a hand like yours, Wesley," Jack said, turning around to look at him from where he walked up ahead. "I understand that Etaellaca is on the other side of the world, but if you could come with us even for a short distance, it would mean a lot."

"Of course, I'll come!" Wesley shouted.

"Wait, really?" Jack asked, surprised. He thought it would have taken more convincing than that.

"Well, I mean there's nowhere else for me to go," Wesley said. "I was actually hoping I could come with you guys, but I didn't want you to think I was barging in on your plans. And besides, I love Etaellaca."

"You've been there before!" This was shocking news to Jack. How would a kid like Wesley have ever made it to the other side of the world alone?

"Several times actually," Wesley said nonchalantly. "The whole place is a pristine empire where the weather is always warm! And it's the cultural capital of the world, which makes it great for meeting all sorts of people!"

Alice smiled at that. It was the littlest and simplest things that seemed to make Wesley so happy. "You really like meeting new people, don't you, Wesley?"

"Heck, yes I do!"

The three of them all laughed.

"Once we get to Etaellaca," Jack began. "There'll be plenty of people to teach Alice the other types of magic." He turned to look at her. "You'd become a master."

"And for sky magic," Wesley started. "We could learn together!"

"And Fawn," Jack said looking back at her. "I'm sure there'll be some Fire Kingdom heads for us to knock out on the way."

"I'd like that," she said smiling. "I'd really like that."

"Great!" Alice said, genuinely happy. "Then we're in this together!"

Fawn slowed down and let the others go on ahead. They kept talking about their future plans, so they didn't notice as her smile faded away and she walked with her head down.

Elkmire, Five Years Ago, June 2040

An eight-year-old Fawn ran around the Earth Nation palace, playing tag with Jack, Alice, Malahki, Aurora, and Gaia.

Abruptly, Jack stopped running from Fawn who was about to tag him. He bent over, with his hands resting on his knees, and was gasping for air. After a moment, he started coughing heavily.

Malahki rushed over to Jack and helped him stand. Everyone else stopped running as well. They knew that when this happened, the game was over.

From another room, King Aeolus and Queen Rosenia rushed in with worried expressions on their faces.

"Not feeling good again, Jack?" The king asked his son. Jack shook his head as he leaned on Malahki's shoulder.

"Another cold," Rosenia said, feeling his forehead. "Not being able to keep up with the other kids is one thing, but this cough is another. I'll go make you some warm tea."

Rosenia hurried away while Aeolus scooped up Jack in his arms and followed her out. "Back to the infirmary for you, little guy." He turned his head to the other kids still standing in the room. "Aurora, Gaia, I believe there are some chores waiting for you out in the stables. And why don't the rest of you kids head home for the evening?"

"Jack can't play anymore?" Fawn asked.

"Afraid not," Aeolus responded. "We wouldn't want him to get any worse, now would we? Don't fret though, Fawn. I'm sure he'll bounce back in no time, just like always."

Alice, Fawn, and Malahki had made their way back home through the empty nighttime streets of Elkmire. Alice was inside the treehouse home already asleep.

Just outside of the main structure of the house, alongside the bridges up in the trees, were large, hollow spheres that dangled down from branches. On the outside, the spheres were a rough texture similar to that of a coconut, but on the inside, they were smooth and good for keeping the cool night air out. This is typically where Fawn and Malahki slept, each in their own sphere.

The two of them breathed softly. The spheres swayed back and forth gently with the breeze. It was dark. All was quiet.

Suddenly, a soft orange glow moved past Malahki's sleeping face. The light had come from a torch outside. Someone must have been carrying as they passed, but who? It was late, and this was the very outskirts of Elkmire, one of the last structures before the endless forest, so who was out there?

The light left as quickly as it had come. But that soft glow that brushed over his face was enough to wake Malahki. Or had he never been asleep in the first place?

He waited for a second longer for the torch to get just a little further ahead before he got up and hopped onto the bridge. He quickly ran across the bridges with quiet and sly footsteps and followed the torch into the forest outside of Elkmire.

All the while, Fawn was left sleeping, undisturbed.

The next morning, Fawn woke up early. She stretched her arms and yawned before hopping out of the cocoon. "Time to get up, Malahki!" she said as she popped her head into his cocoon.

Fawn was surprised to find that Malahki was not there. Had he already woken up? It was pretty early, probably not later than six-thirty, and Malahki had a habit of sleeping late. In fact, Fawn had always been the one to wake him up.

She looked around the area but didn't see him anywhere.

In the weeks following Malahki's disappearance, everyone in Elkmire was alerted of the young boy's absence. Volunteers scoured the forest beyond the city to no end. King Aeolus, Queen Rosenia, the princesses and prince, along with royal palace guards, spared no expense in the search.

The royal family along with Alice, Fawn, and hundreds of civilians searched through the forest.

"Malahki?" someone shouted.

"Malahki! We're here for you, buddy!" another called. But there was never any response. There wasn't a single clue as to where he might've gone. No footprints, no leads. It was as if Malahki had vanished into thin air.

Aurora was particularly worried about him. He was one of her closest friends. It wasn't like him to just run away and not tell her where he was going.

"Dad," Aurora began as she stood next to Aeolus. "Where's Malahki?"

The king took a deep breath before responding. He whipped a bead of sweat off his forehead and said, "Hopefully somewhere safe."

Malahki was never seen again.

Fawn stared down at her feet as they continued walking through the forest. In her heart, she wanted to believe that she would find her brother one day, that she would see his crooked smile and hear his laugh again. But in her mind, she knew that the chances of ever finding him were slim. She didn't even have a picture of him. For the time being, Malahki existed now, only in her memory.

Without warning, Jack, who was walking in the lead, came to an abrupt stop. Alice bumped into him, creating a domino effect of Wesley bumping into her, and then Fawn into Wesley.

"Why'd we stop?" Fawn asked.

"Oh no," came Jack's reply through his tightly clenched jaw.

"What's wrong?" Alice asked as she walked around Jack to see what he was seeing.

The others followed suit to find that the Earth Nation forest came to an end. Stretched out in front of them was an endless array of sand. There were no structures, no more trees, only a gentle sparkle of sun-colored sand that stretched out for infinity.

Jack turned around to face his accomplices. This would be their greatest struggle yet. "We've reached the desert."

Firelord Ash stood on a secluded balcony of the Fire Kingdom royal palace that overlooked the ocean. He breathed in the tang of the saltiness coming off the water. The fire that sprouted from under his arms like wings was the only source of light.

It was very late. The sun would peek over the horizon any minute. Ash hadn't slept at all that night, nor the night before. In fact, he could stay awake for days. If anything, he preferred it. Sleep had always seemed like a waste of time anyhow.

Ash looked across the sea to where the moon was gradually dipping below the water. He breathed in deeply and gripped the balcony railing tighter.

"My plan has been set," he said with a raspiness to his youthful voice. "All the ducks are in line. Just give it time, my brother. I've upheld my promise to *you*, my brother, and I will see it through until we reach the end."

He took another deep breath and glared across the sea at the moon as if speaking to *it*. "Soon. It'll be soon."

Ash let go of the balcony railing and rubbed his palms together. He finally took his gaze from the moon and looked up to where a phoenix was perched on the roof.

"Ryse," he called to it. "Come."

The bird flew down to land on the Firelord's shoulder as he made his way back inside.

Ash walked quietly through the empty palace halls, with gentle, slow footsteps. He rounded a corner and walked past two anomalies who were stationed outside of his study. They bowed to him as he entered, but Ash made no acknowledgment to them.

The fireplace near the window had been lit, and a hot cup of tea sat at his desk. Ash closed the doors behind him and sat down.

He hardly had time to take a sip of his tea before a sudden thumping noise sounded right outside the study. He stood and walked over to the doors.

He waited and listened.

Nothing.

"Sadie? Is that you?" he called to one of the anomalies.

No reply.

He cracked the door open just enough to allow light from the hall into the study, but that was enough for him to see it. The two anomalies that had guarded the study moments ago were now lying on the ground unmoving.

Ash kicked open the door further to let himself out. Both anomalies were girls, young girls. Their skin had paled and their eyes were wide open, frozen in shock. Ash checked for a pulse, but both of them were dead.

Both girls had deep slashes that looked like claw marks across their necks. Blood pooled around their heads.

Ash didn't bother looking around to find the perpetrator because he already knew who had done it. His dear old friend did have quite the temper. Even if he could not be there physically, Ash's friend certainly had his ways of defying physics.

Ash slowly looked up. At the base of the wall, just above where the anomalies had fallen, blood was being smeared by an invisible hand to form letters.

Ash watched until the sentence had been completed. With the blood ink steadily dripping from the letters, the statement read: MAKE IT SOONER.

And just after that, another letter formed. The message had been signed. A signature Ash had seen many times, in fact. This person's signature had become a trademark once, ages ago.

It was signed with a single letter . . . Z

CHAPTER SIX

Welcome to the Desert

Wesley's chest moved up and down slowly as he breathed gently in his sleep. A leaf from the tree above him peeled off from its branch and floated down to land on the tip of his nose. The little boy sniffled and then sneezed loudly. Because of his sky magic, the simple sneeze let out a huge gust of wind and sent him flying high into the air. After a moment, he came back down, sliding along Reezu's tail as a runway.

"Good morning, fellow adventurers!" he called with a big smile on his round face. It was around ten in the morning, not particularly early, but they hadn't gone to sleep until almost sunrise and the others were still tired.

However, Jack and Alice wasted no time in sitting up and groggily getting a move on. Fawn, on the other hand, rolled over and threw her jacket over her head. "Ugh! Keep it down, would you?" she complained.

"Oh, sorry!" Wesley said. "You're still sleeping, hehe." Fawn glared at him from behind her jacket.

Alice stood up, brushed herself off, and began fixing her hair. "Is it just me," she began. "Or is it *really* hot out here?"

"Well, we are near the desert," Jack said as he stared out at the endless sea of sand that stood before them. "And we've traveled pretty far south from Elkmire. The further south we travel, and the closer we get to the Etaellaca Empire, the hotter it's going to get, especially compared to the northern weather we're used to."

"Great," Alice said sarcastically. "If it's already this warm in the spring, just imagine how hot it's going to be when we reach Etaellaca this summer. I hate the heat. This is gross."

"It's not gross," Wesley said as he watched little white butterflies flutter around him. "It's just the beauty of spring! You know, birds chirping, flowers blooming, *and* it gets so hot that you'll wish you were tucked away in the snowy catacombs of Ice Nation!"

"Snowy catacombs do sound nice right about now. Let's make that a destination in our future," Alice decided.

Wesley walked over closer to her. "You know what I see in our future?"

"What?"

"Desert. A whole lot of desert."

Jack and Alice laughed at Wesley's remark. He was certainly right though because the Les Landes desert was massive and there was no safe way of getting around it. Even Fawn chuckled beneath her jacket.

"So then," Wesley began as he marched over to Fawn. "Let's get to it!" He blew a massive gust of wind right onto Fawn, sending her flying high up into the sky.

"Ahhhhhh!" she yelped.

In the meantime, Wesley stood with his hands on his hips, looking satisfied. That is, until Fawn came crashing back down right on top of him, squishing him into the ground.

"Ah!" he squealed.

Fawn laughed as she laid comfortably on top of him. "Haha. Nice try, airhead."

Jack stood right on the line where the grass came to an end, and just barely out of reach of where the sand began. He looked out at the endless dunes with a determined expression on his face. This is where the real journey would begin.

Behind him, Alice, Wesley, and Fawn sat on the grass with a map and a compass laid out in front of them.

Jack turned around to face them. "Crossing the Les Landes desert is going to be the *second* most difficult phase of our journey. The first will be traveling through the Fire Kingdom, but we'll face that bridge once we get there."

He began pacing along the line where the Earth Nation ended and the desert started, careful to never touch the sand.

"The desert has a powerful distractor spell on it that prevents anyone who enters from ever coming out."

"Magic that distracts someone?" Alice asked.

"Mm. Basically, once you enter the desert, your mind will succumb to the effects of the spell. The way a distractor spell works is that it takes your mind off of your target, or your ideal location. With your sense of direction paralyzed, and your judgment clouded, you become convinced that the direction you intend to go in is wrong."

"So, the distractor spell distracts us from going in the right direction?" Fawn asked.

"That's right," Jack said. "And it'll do a lot more to us than just that. I've heard stories of groups of people who enter and never come back out. Friends who become enemies once their mind is no longer controllable in the desert will start tearing each other apart just to go in different directions."

"It's that powerful, huh," Wesley mentioned.

"In a sense," Jack began as he stared out at the desert once more. "The spell doesn't want us to reach our destination. So, if we're trying to travel south, our minds, once inside the desert, will become convinced that the south is not the right direction. Or at least, it's not the direction we should be going in."

"Well then," Fawn said. "If we want to go south, then once we are in the desert, we can tell ourselves we're actually going west, in order to counterattack the effects of the spell. And then we'll just continue going south instead."

Jack could tell that Fawn thought she was onto something, and it was clever of her to be able to think like that, but unfortunately, he already knew that her plan wouldn't work.

"It's not that simple," he said, turning around to face the others. "Once inside the desert, you won't be able to think like that. All reasoning goes out the door."

"Then how are we going to get through it?"

"A distractor spell is a form of mind control. Creatures of light all have a light inside of them that protects their minds on some level. Unicorns and angels specifically have much more of that light than any other creature. Thus, they are immune to most forms of mind control, like this distractor spell. Because of this, as unicorns, Alice and I would normally be immune to the effects of the desert."

"Normally?" Alice asked.

"Well, Alice, you will be immune regardless because you are the Light Spirit. Your magic and soul carry more light than anything else in all of the Infinity. Your mind is perfectly protected at all times."

"As for you?"

"As for me," Jack said, turning around to face the desert again. "I carry enough light to be immune to most forms of mind control. But as a unicorn, I'm not sure I hold enough light to protect myself from a distractor spell of this magnitude."

"What do you mean?"

"The Les Landes desert is massive. It's more than four times the size of the Earth Nation, which means the distractor spell on it has to be extremely powerful. A normal distractor spell placed on a singular object would work nothing on me or any other unicorn. However, something of this size is bound to be a thousand times as potent."

"So, you won't be immune to the effects?" Alice asked. She was very concerned about the fact that she might be the only one who would have control of her mind inside the desert.

"Not likely," Jack said. "But it depends on what part of the desert the distractor spell is placed on. It could be the land itself, the air, or even the entire hemisphere of this region on the planet. We won't know for sure until we're inside, but I'd say it's a pretty safe bet that I'll be affected on some level."

Alice looked down at the map. The Les Landes desert covered much of the northern hemisphere of the planet. It would take them weeks to walk through it, not to mention the extra time it would cost them if they were going to be struggling against each other the whole way. Hopefully, Reezu's wing would heal quickly so they could fly instead.

Jack started pacing along the desert line again. "Once inside, Fawn, Wesley, and myself won't know our right from our left. On top of that, we'll be desperately trying to fight against each other, in order to go in opposite directions. It's between Alice and the animals on getting us through here in one piece."

"Oh, I see," Fawn said. "The animals will also be immune."

"Yes. As animals, they have a natural sense of direction, and a spell can't take that away."

"Animals will be immune . . ." Wesley said, almost as if to himself. He looked across to where Fawn sat directly next to him. He looked her up and down, from her fluffy black ears to her tail and sharp claws.

Fawn glared back at him from the corner of her eye. She knew exactly what he was thinking. *This little brat,* she thought.

In a flash, Fawn whipped toward Wesley and bit at the air in front of his nose with a snap. Wesley yelped and was just barely able to dodge the attack. He got up and ran. Fawn immediately gave chase.

"I knew the desert was somewhat cursed," Alice said to Jack. "But I had no idea it was this bad. I had originally hoped we'd be able to fly over the desert or the ocean with no problem."

Behind her, Wesley and Fawn started tackling each other. Boo and Mayday tried tugging their friends away from each other, but it was no use.

"That's another thing," Jack said, completely ignoring the chaos going on a few feet away. "Even if Reezu wasn't injured and we could fly over, the spell might affect us anyway. And traveling over the ocean poses another threat. The Fire Kingdom islands. We'd be sailing right over them, and those islands are known to be extremely militarily active."

"So then, this is the only way," Alice said, standing up. "We'll just have to make it work."

Wesley suddenly appeared next to Alice again. He stood there huffing with his cheeks warm. Fawn followed suit on the other side of Alice. The two of them kept on making faces back and forth at each other while Alice was lost in thought between them.

"I hate to put this much pressure on you," Jack said, placing a hand on her shoulder. "But you're the only one who can get us through there."

Alice looked up into Jack's glistening blue eyes. Was he worried? He seemed a little upset. Perhaps he was just tired. They hadn't slept much since they had left Elkmire and he had to be stressed out from being in charge all the time. This was the least Alice could do for him and to lighten his load.

"Mm." She nodded with a smile on her face. "Leave it to me!"

Wildfire rested her head on Nova's soft red fur. They were waiting inside a small shop in Taesithia for the owner to return from the back room with the healing herbs. Nova had been diagnosed with two broken ribs, and some internal bleeding, none of which were fatal, but the giant cat would surely be off her feet for a few weeks.

Wildfire gently stroked Nova's red coat. "Nova . . ." she whispered. "You're gonna be okay, I promise. Be sure to heal up fast, alright?"

Wildfire pressed her ear next to Nova's chest and listened to the slow beating of her heart. Nova had been Wildfire's pet since she was a little girl. She had raised this cat. Nova seemed to be the only one who understood her. They trained in the cadet regiment together, they fought in the Earth Nation together, and they had chased the Light Spirit together. And through it all, Nova never complained. She had always stood beside Wildfire proudly. Hopefully, this wasn't the end of their journey together.

Once Wildfire heard the sound of the door to the backroom creaking open, she quickly stepped away from Nova and leaned against the wall with her arms crossed over her chest. Master Yagatsu entered with the shop owner who was a petite Earth Fairy most likely a little older than Wildfire, but a few inches shorter. The two of them exchanged words in a hushed conversation.

"So, the herbs from this bag," Yagatsu began as he held a tiny bag. "Need to be given twice a day, with six-hour intervals?"

"Yes," the Earth Fairy responded shyly. She talked with her head down and her eyes looked away. She was clearly very afraid of the fact that there were Fire Kingdom officials in her home. "And you can give her the poppy seeds whenever to help with the pain."

"Got it," Yagatsu said. "Thank you very much for your help." The Earth Fairy just nodded her head in reply. Yagatsu reached into his pocket and held out one hundred sparks worth of Fire Kingdom money to her.

The Earth Fairy's eyes grew wide. "Oh no, no, no. You don't have to pay me of course," she said, taking a step back. "The Fire Kingdom owns Taesithia. What's mine is now yours."

Yagatsu placed the money on the shelf beside the fairy. "Well, Fire Kingdom or not, I am still a paying customer. I don't have any Earth Nation money, but that right there is around one hundred sparks, which is what we'd normally pay for these kinds of services in the Fire Kingdom."

The fairy looked at the red and black rectangular chips that served as the Fire Kingdom currency known as sparks. Why was this guy giving *her* money? He was Fire Kingdom after all.

With nothing else to say, the fairy smiled shyly and said, "T-thank you."

"It was simply due," Yagatsu replied. "We should be on our way now." Master Yagatsu pushed the table Nova was laying on out through the doors with Wildfire. The table was on wheels so it wasn't too difficult to move.

Outside, Wildfire's platoon all awaited on the vehicles for departure. It was time to move out now. They would continue heading south until they found the Light Spirit, or at least, that's what Wildfire told them.

The soldiers worked together to get the giant cat onto the lead vehicle. Wildfire hopped up and took to the front. She stared out at the forest below. It was time to get back to business.

"We've wasted enough time as it is," she said sternly. "Let's get moving."

Along with the bright sun, the air was thick and hot where the kids stood just out of reach of the sandy desert. Jack helped Alice adjust the rope-made harness around her upper body.

Everyone had one on, and the rope connected all of them together in a single file line with Alice in the lead, Wesley, and Fawn in the middle, and Jack pulling up the rear. Alice would lead them, and hopefully, the rope would help the others keep moving in the right direction.

"Alright, everyone," Jack began. "We've been over this. We need to be on high alert in case of any danger. We don't know what's out there, maybe nothing, or maybe something horrible. There's no reason to have Alice carry us forward alone, so do your best to stay focused."

Everyone else nodded in response. But Alice only stared ahead at the sand that laid out in front of her. This would be one of their greatest challenges yet. In order to make it through the next couple of weeks, they would have to work as a team, but in the end, it would all depend on Alice.

Reezu came tromping up beside the kids. Mayday laid down in the saddle and Boo flew around near them. "We ready?" Jack called from the rear.

"Sure," Fawn replied.

"Remember, don't pay attention to where you are going. Just follow the leader. The more you focus on where you're trying to go, the more you'll find yourself inclined to wander the wrong way. Follow the rope. No matter what you might think, the rope is right. Alice, lead on."

Alice took the first step out onto the sand. The others followed. She had lots of expertise with being outdoors but had never been in the desert before, and she worried she might lead the others poorly. She held the map and the compass in her hands. Alice concentrated on going south. Her main goal was to avoid doubling back because of going in the wrong direction. Since the others would be struggling against the effects of the distractor spell, she hoped to lead them safely through the most direct route possible.

Once they were a good few yards into the desert, Alice looked back at the trees they had left. They weren't in the Earth Nation anymore. The journey had officially begun and from here on out, things would only get tougher.

Being inside the desert, Alice didn't feel even the slightest difference in her mental state. She was as aware and alert as ever.

"Is everyone doing okay?" she called back at the others.

"Y-yeah. I-I'm f-fine," came Wesley's shaky voice from behind Alice. She turned around to look at them. Wesley was rubbing his palms together and looking around abruptly. Fawn bit her lip and stood with her fist clenched. Jack only stared at the ground, blinking slowly.

Alice looked down at the compass to ensure they were going directly south. Because all the sand looked the same, it would be difficult to navigate which way was true south. The pointer on the compass was pointed south, but it was shaking left and right as if there were additional forces acting on it.

After a moment longer, it no longer pointed south at all. It seemed to spin randomly, pointing in all directions even though Alice hadn't changed position.

"Uh, guys?" she said, looking back. "My compass is going berserk! I'm not moving at all but it's spinning all around."

"C-continue," Jack said quietly. "I figured it would do something like that."

Alice plodded through the sand. Without having the compass to rely on, how would they know what direction they were going in? It'd be fine for now, but after a while, they'd surely end up straying away from true south.

Alice tugged insistently on the rope when the others started to meander in the wrong direction. As they made their way further into the sand, she lost sight of the trees behind them, the Earth Nation was out of sight. They'd officially left home.

Alice began leading them up one of the first hills of sand that lay in the path. It wasn't super tall, but the sand was difficult to climb up. As they reached the top of the slope, Alice realized it would probably be even harder on the way down. Nevertheless, she took the first step down.

After only a couple of steps, she grew weary of the way the sand tugged at the soles of her shoes. Each step took immense effort just to lift up and make progress.

Suddenly, a tug on the rope caused Alice to fall headfirst into the sand. "We best head back," Wesley said.

Alice stood up and brushed the sand from her hair. "No, we just need to advance carefully down the slope. It'll be fine. I can see that it's flat after this hill."

"You've lost the route," Fawn moaned. "We're going the wrong way."

The others all holding the rope began looking backward. Wesley and Fawn started pulling against her together, and Alice found herself stumbling back the other way.

"Don't trust yourselves!" she said.

"We've reached an impassable hill," Wesley argued.

"Stop!" Alice shouted as she struggled against them. "Your instincts are blind out here. I won't let us get hurt. It's not that tall of a hill."

"Close your eyes," Jack's steady voice came from the rear. "Close them tight and follow Alice's lead."

"That's right," Alice said, relieved. "I'll keep us from falling all the way down. Let me guide us."

Fawn and Wesley mumbled uncertainty, but they did close their eyes. Alice leaned into her steps down the hill more than before. The others kept trying to stray and, even with their eyes shut, continued to second-guess their heading.

Eventually, Alice led them all the way to the base of the hill. The sand was completely flat from here as far as she could see.

"Stay with me!" Alice commanded as the others started hauling her to the left.

"You're leading us into the middle of nowhere!" Fawn cried.

"She's right!" Wesley agreed.

The two of them pulled against her so hard that Alice fell again. They dragged her across the sand, in an eastward direction. Alice called out in desperation, "Stop! Guys, stop! You're going the wrong way!"

"Ignore your instincts," Jack called. His eyes were closed and he moved with rugged, slow steps. He almost seemed lethargic, but whatever force the desert was putting on Fawn and Wesley wasn't taking total effect on him. "Go where she pulls us," he said.

Reezu waddled over to the kids and grabbed on tightly to the rope between Fawn and Wesley with his beak. He dug his talons deep into the sand to stop them from going any further out of the way.

"Keep your eyes closed," Jack said with a sign.

"I can sense danger," Fawn insisted.

"Your senses are messed up," Alice said as she braced herself against Reezu's side in order to stand. "Don't think, just follow."

Alice began heading in the right direction again, trying to move fast to keep their momentum flowing south. Glancing back, she saw that even with their eyes closed, her companions struggled to move forward. They followed her on stiff, hesitant legs. But they followed.

After a few minutes of running through the thick sand in the heat, Alice slowed to catch her breath. They were making progress now. Glancing back behind Fawn, Alice could see that Jack was trembling. Fawn dropped to her knees, moaning and grimacing. Wesley hummed a simple tune in a strained voice. Jack took deep breaths, beads of perspiration on his brow.

"Forward," she encouraged as she leaned against her companions to grind further into the sand.

"N-no!" Fawn shouted. "We're going the wrong way!"

"We need to go back!" Wesley said as he fought to turn around. Between the two of them, they easily pulled Alice and Jack backward.

Alice was running out of energy, and they hadn't even been in the desert for very long yet. There was no way they were going to make it another two weeks in there.

The sound of Wesley and Fawn shouting and fighting gradually became muffled by the wind that had suddenly begun to stir around the kids. The wind blew harder and carried sand with it that struck Alice in the face. Where had this sudden wind come from? She peered over to her left, and Alice was nearly frozen in place by what she saw.

Coming from the east was a massive dust storm. It was heading right for them and there was no way around it.

Firelord Ash finished writing the last few lines of the letter. It was addressed to *Force Captain Wildfire Amulet,* and it was signed *Firelord Ash Levitt.* He stuck the paper in an envelope and sealed it with the phoenix insignia. He rang the little golden bell that sat at the corner of his desk, and not more than a second later, an anomaly with long black hair came in.

"How may I be of assistance, Firelord?" she asked.

"Here," he said, holding out two envelopes to her. "Take this to Force Captain Wildfire Amulet of the Warrior Regiment, stationed in Elkmire. But, don't be surprised if she's not there when you arrive. And the second letter is to be delivered to Force Captain Eternus Endeavor, also of the Warrior Regiment."

"Y-yes," she replied, taking the letters.

"Oh, and one more thing," Ash continued. "Tell the other anomalies and guards not to take any night shifts for a few days. I wouldn't want them to get hurt."

"Does this have to do with what happened to Sadie and Elona?"

"Yes," Ash said, nonchalantly. "My dear old friend is getting rather excited now that time is almost up. It was a full moon last night, so he was particularly more anxious and stronger than normal. But still, we'll be cautious for a couple of extra days just in case. My dear friend does have quite the temper."

The anomaly looked at Ash silently. Had he lost his mind? Who in Infinity was he talking about? She only smiled and nodded at Ash. Now she understood what being locked up in a castle with no friends or family for three hundred years did to people.

"I-I'll get right on this," she said pointing to the envelopes. With a sudden flash of light, she teleported away, leaving Ash alone in his study.

"Go, go, go!" Alice shouted as she desperately ran across the desert. The sand storm was closing in on them. There was no way they could outrun it. The sand was hard to move in, and on top of that, Fawn and Wesley were fighting every which way the rope pulled them. And Jack seemed to hardly want to move at all.

The wind grew stronger and the sand around Alice swirled up into the air as the storm hit them. Once the storm was on them, a sudden gust of wind hit Alice with such force that she was sent flying backward for a dozen or so yards.

The air had been knocked out of her lungs. She couldn't move. She laid in the sand helplessly. The sand storm was so thick and so loud that she couldn't hear or see anything. She knew that the rope had come undone. Were the others somewhere nearby? Were they okay?

Alice desperately tried to take in air, but she couldn't. She couldn't feel her body. Had she broken her back? Is this what it felt like to be paralyzed? Totally helpless and afraid?

Something hard and curved pushed Alice up into a seating position. It was Reezu. He had somehow found her in the swirling storm of sand and lifted his beak under her back to sit her up. Reezu rubbed his beak along Alice's spine, and suddenly, she could breathe again.

She gulped in the air, but it didn't help much, as most of the air was carrying sand. The sand got in her eyes and Alice couldn't open them enough to see, even so, there wasn't much to see in the storm anyway.

The tiny rocks hit Alice like a thousand knives stabbing her all over her body. It hurt to move. It hurt to breathe. But she had to get to the others. Alice used Reezu as a shield and walked through the storm, holding onto him.

"Jack!" she shouted. "Fawn! Wesley! Where are you?" She yelled as loudly as she could, but her voice was drowned out in the wind. She wandered around in circles to no avail.

It was no use. The others couldn't hear her and she couldn't see them. Alice cowered on the ground and covered her ears with her hands. She felt Reezu lay down beside her, and he wrapped his body around her to protect her from the storm.

After what felt like an eternity later, all was quiet. It took Alice a second to realize it, but the storm was gone. She sat up and looked around. The storm was completely out of sight. In fact, there was no sign of it at all. How long had she and Reezu sat there in the wind? Thirty minutes maybe? More?

The sand had dried Alice's face, and now there were white streaks on her cheeks from where her tears had rolled the dust away. She stood up and looked around. There was no one anywhere.

"Jack!" she called out. "Fawn! Wesley! Please, guys." Her rope was ripped at the harness. Were the others still attached to each other? Maybe Jack had enough awareness to lead the others out of the storm? Not likely, Alice thought. He had seemed lost in more ways than one. He hadn't gone nuts like Fawn and Wesley, but he surely wasn't feeling like himself out there.

Alice walked around swiftly. She looked in all directions. The sand was completely flat for miles and miles in every direction. Had the sand buried them?

"Hello! Is anyone out there! Can anyone hear me!"

Alice stood there, alone in the middle of nowhere and completely helpless. She had one job. All she had to do was keep the others safe while they were defenseless and she couldn't even do that! It was all her fault, and now they were gone.

"Can anyone hear me?" she tried once more. The guilt and fear were unbearable. They were her friends. She needed them more than anything. Alice dropped to her knees and cried out. She let everything out. She screamed and cried and laughed all at once. But it was pointless. No matter how loud she screamed, no one would hear her.

Wildfire sat at the lookout post high up on a stake of the vehicle she was in. She liked it up there because it gave her a little privacy away from the soldiers and crew. And right now, she needed her privacy. They were storming through the southern Earth Nation at full speed in order to catch up with the Light Spirit.

Wildfire held a letter in her hands. It was addressed to her and was sealed with the phoenix insignia. She was worried. Had Ash found out that she disobeyed him? No, he couldn't have, or else he would have sent the military police after her, not have sent a letter. She tore open the seal and read the letter.

Dear to whom it may concern, in this case, Force Captain Wildfire Amulet. I have interesting news for you, Force Captain. I've changed my mind. I'd like for you to go ahead and pursue the Light Spirit after all. I originally failed to consider the possibilities of having such a powerful being under my control. I want you to find her. Do whatever it takes, chase her to the end of Infinity if you must, but all in all, you must bring me the Light Spirit, Force Captain. It is a task I can only entrust to you, Wildfire. You are the only warrior capable of such a meaningful task.

I have some additional information that may be of use to you in your search. I know where she is headed. The Light Spirit is on her way to the Etaellaca Empire. Her business there is not completely uncertain to me either, but that shall stay secret for now as it involves a private matter concerning my dear friend and I. Do with this information what you will, but regardless, you must find that Light Spirit. I suggest you wait to capture her until you both arrive in Etaellaca. My reasoning is secure, but it also involves a rather personal matter that is not of your concern. You can say I have "connections" in Etaellaca that may be of some particular use to you in one way or another.

Reach Etaellaca, dear Wildfire. Reach Etaellaca and find me the Light Spirit there and you shall be rewarded in more ways than one. You forever have my thanks and

*my appreciation. This service along with your sacrifice will
honor me greatly. And we do appreciate it, dear Wildfire.*

Your Firelord, and Admirer
Ash

Wildfire reread the letter again. And then again. She had to be
sure of what it said exactly. Her eyes scanned over the part where Ash
called himself her admirer. What did he mean by that? Was it a hint
that he felt a certain way about her? Perhaps the same way she had felt
about him this whole time? Was she finally getting what she wanted?

Wildfire was starting to get excited. Now she knew exactly what
she needed to do. Capture the Light Spirit. It was as simple as that.

She went back and read the letter a fourth time. There were
several parts that she didn't quite understand. Firelord Ash made it
adamant in the note that she reach Etaellaca before capturing the
Light Spirit. Why was that? He mentioned that he had connections
there. What connections? Maybe it was people who could help her
bring the Light Spirit back home? No, it couldn't be because Ash said
it was a task he could *only* entrust to her.

Remembering that part of the letter distracted Wildfire from
the questions she was asking herself. Firelord Ash trusted her and
believed in her, after all. He *liked* her, didn't he? And besides, that's
all Wildfire needed to hear, all she wanted to hear. Anything else was
besides the point, so she forgot about it altogether.

Wildfire skipped down from the lookout post to where Master
Yagatsu stood near the wheel of the vehicle. She handed him the
letter, "Here," she said. "Read this, now."

Yagatsu took the letter from her and Wildfire stood next to him
with her arms crossed while he read it. After a minute or two, Yagatsu
looked up but he didn't say anything.

"Well?" Wildfire asked, expectantly.

Yagatsu stood silently for a moment longer. "That is the strangest
letter I have ever read, Wildfire," he finally said.

"What? Didn't you see the part where the Firelord said he could *only* entrust this to *me?* And how he called me his admirer."

"That's exactly what I find strange about it. But I'm still thinking."

Wildfire could not believe what this old man was saying. He thought it was strange that Firelord Ash had finally opened his eyes to Wildfire? She had been waiting for this to happen and it finally was.

"Strange, really?" she said angrily. "So what? You're saying he said all that just to patronize me?"

"No, I'm saying I'm thinking!" he shouted back. He opened the letter again and pointed to several parts of it. "Look. He mentions this so-called 'friend' of his several times, and at the end, he referred to himself as 'we'. Who is that friend? And what connections is he talking about? It's also very suspicious that he even knows these things about the Light Spirit. And the biggest factor of all: how is it that *two* days after we leave Elkmire and disregard his order, he somehow changes his mind? The Firelord is most certainly up to something. Wildfire, he intends to use you—"

Wildfire cut Yagatsu off by snatching the letter out of his hands. She had made a mistake by letting him read it.

"You don't know what you're talking about!" she spat, feeling her voice crack. "You just can't stand it that for once I was right about something! I always told you Ash would eventually come around to me, and now you just can't accept that your old-fashioned dictatorship methods couldn't predict the outcome!"

Yagatsu exhaled sharply. It was nearly impossible to reason with Wildfire when she got like this. It was also nearly impossible to *ever* reason with Wildfire. As her teacher and guardian, Yagatsu felt he shouldn't just completely abandon her on this and throw her to the wolves to let her do whatever she wanted, but how else would she learn her lesson?

That was it. He had decided. He would step back and let Wildfire take her reins and set them on fire, and when she fell into the pit, she would finally understand what it was to have control in her life.

"Well then," Yagatsu began. "If that's how you feel. Go and do what you want. But you're merely a chess piece on the Firelord's board, nothing more than a cornered rat in a science experiment. Don't forget that playing with fire often leads to you getting burned."

Wildfire whipped around and began climbing back up to the lookout post. The words Yagatsu had just spoken left a gut-wrenching and uneasy feeling in her stomach. She heard what Yagatsu had said, about the Firelord wanting to use her. She wasn't stupid. She knew it too. But what if he wasn't? There was no way she would let that opportunity pass her by and she wasn't about to let Yagatsu silence her.

"Not if I can help it."

Fawn stormed through the desert with quick, purposeful strides. The dust storm had broken her harness and detached her from the others. What a relief that was! She couldn't wait to get away from them. They didn't know what they were talking about or where they were going. And Fawn certainly didn't want to leave her safety in their hands while they were out in a foreign and dangerous place.

Something sparkly on the ground a few hundred yards in front of her caught Fawn's eye. She picked up her pace as she made her way toward it. After a few minutes, she could make out a pond alongside a couple of palm trees.

"Water!" Fawn shouted as she splashed into the pond. The temperature of the water was warm, which was not very refreshing. Nonetheless, Fawn wasted no time in scooping a handful of water up to her mouth to drink.

After her thirst had been quenched, she crawled out of the water and laid on the damp sand, staring up at the palm trees. Suddenly, the trees began changing colors. They turned from their natural green hue to pink and then purple and then red and so on. Fawn sat up, blinking and rubbing her eyes.

"W-woah . . . what's . . . goin' . . . on?" Fawn mumbled, feeling her headache. Come to mention it, she felt horrible. Was she sick? Was it something she ate?

Fawn tried standing up, but couldn't seem to keep control of her legs. She stumbled around the pond, looking up at the trees until she heard a strange buzzing sound.

Her vision was starting to look fuzzy and her head was pounding, not to mention her wobbly legs, but she managed to turn around to where the sound was coming from.

Before Fawn could even finish turning around, something hit her right in the head and knocked her to the ground.

"Ah!" she yelped, falling over. She rolled over onto her back to look up at the palm trees that were still changing colors. Swarming around in the air alongside the disco trees were hundreds of giant flying mantises.

"Ahhh!" Fawn screamed as she got up and tried to run away. The mantises immediately started attacking her, or at least, that's what Fawn thought.

She yelped out, jumped about, and kicked sand around as she fought off the imaginary predators.

Jack's entire mind was deep in a trance-like state as he shuffled through the endless array of sand. He couldn't think, he couldn't see well enough to know where he was going, he couldn't talk, and he couldn't stop his legs from slowly marching him off deeper into the Les Landes Desert.

There was something white and furry flying around his face, trying to get his attention, but Jack didn't even have enough awareness to notice. Blindly, his legs kept going.

After many minutes had passed, Jack realized he had stopped walking. He was standing completely still. How long had he been standing there? Five minutes already? More?

More importantly, Jack realized he had control of his mind again. He could think again. His eyes slowly began to focus. There was something white sitting on his face and peering into his eyes.

It took Jack a second, but he realized that a furry white creature was licking his face.

"Ah!" He shouted out, falling backward. What was that thing? The creature flew around and came to land on Jack's knee. It was Boo.

"Oh," Jack said in relief. "Hey there, Boo." What had happened to them? Where were they?

The last thing he could remember was the dust storm separating him from the rest of his friends. As soon as the storm had apprehended them, he looked across to Alice and he tried to get to her, but she was blown away. He had been totally useless. And now they were separated, he didn't know how to get back to her, where she was, or even if she and the others had made it out of the storm.

Jack was starting to get himself worked up, but then he realized something. He had no awareness of himself or his surroundings a few moments ago, and somehow, he had still made it out safely. Therefore, the others should have made it too. But even so, where were they? He had to get back to the others, but first, he had to find out where he even was.

Jack quickly looked around. He had to find out what direction he had traveled in before losing consciousness again. Wait a minute, he thought. What had made him regain his consciousness in the first place? Was it Boo licking his face?

Jack felt the ground around him. He wasn't on the desert sand anymore. He sat on a stone. He got up and looked at his surroundings. The entire area around him for about a dozen yards in each direction was made completely of stone. It wasn't packed sand like sandstone; it was an actual rock.

"Boo, take a look at this!" Jack said to his only companion. "This is all solid ground. It's stone." The tiny creature looked at Jack as if listening intently. "I think we've found the answer to our question then. The distractor spell seems to only affect me on the sand, which means the spell itself is placed on the sand of the Les Landes desert. Nothing else here should be enchanted."

That explained why Jack was no longer under the effects of the distractor spell because this stone he now stood on was not enchanted by it. But this information didn't help him all that much in his current predicament. He still had no idea how to get back to the others or where he had wandered off to. And not to mention, it wasn't totally safe out there, that dust storm or any other dangers could appear at any given time.

"Boo," Jack called to the tiny creature beside him. "Can you tell which way is south?"

If Boo could determine which direction was which, then Jack could use that information to find out which way he needed to go in order to meet back up with the others, or at least in the same general area they had last been in together.

Boo hopped up on a rock and lifted his nose up in the air. He wasn't sniffing the air. He seemed to be feeling it, in a sense. After a moment, he spun around and pointed his nose directly left to where Jack was standing.

"Is that south?" Jack asked. Boo bobbed his head up and down. This was good, now Jack knew exactly what he needed to do. If his left was south, then that meant he had been traveling west while unconscious. He just had to turn around and go east until he found something.

"Now that I've gotten my whereabouts," Jack began. "I know how to get back to where I was. There's still one problem, the distractor spell. It doesn't affect me the same as it does Fawn and Wesley, but I don't have control of my own mind. Once I step back on the sand, my thoughts and actions won't be my own. Boo, can you help me get back to Alice and the others?" The tiny creature cocked his head at Jack as if wondering what plan he had conjured up.

Over the next few minutes, Jack explained his plan to Boo. The Feraroo sat there patiently listening to him talk, but Jack had no idea how much the animal actually understood. Although Boo had understood his questions earlier, so that was reassuring.

Once they were both caught up, Jack began ripping a piece of fabric off the back of his shirt. He tied one end loosely around his neck and the other end he tied around Boo's mid-section, as he hovered eye level with Jack. This was his plan. Boo would guide Jack eastward through the desert.

Boo didn't have a strong sense of smell so he had no way of telling exactly where the others were, but he did know which way was east, and that was good enough for Jack.

"Alright, Boo," Jack said as he took the first step off the stone. "Let's go find Alice."

"Jack!" Alice called out. "Wesley! Fawn! Where are you?" she yelled their names as loud as she could but at this point, she was only talking to the sand.

Suddenly, something tugged at Alice's boot. She looked down to see Mayday biting on it.

"Hey! What do you think you're do—" One look at the cub's round, sad eyes was enough for Alice to understand. She crouched down to stroke Mayday's black fur.

"You want to find Fawn. Don't you?" The cub whined a sad tune in response. "You sure you can find your way back to me?"

Mayday wagged her tail and licked Alice's hand. "Alright then. Go find her, girl. Be careful."

The cub skipped away into the sand. Alice trusted Mayday to find Fawn. The wolf had a good sense of smell and a natural sense of direction so she wouldn't get lost. And besides, splitting up would help them find the others faster, wherever they were.

Alice walked through the sand as fast as she could, the more ground she could cover, the better.

There was a hill not too far away in front of her. Perhaps, if she climbed to the top, she could get a better view of her surroundings and possibly spot the others.

Once she made her way to the base of the hill, Alice said to Reezu, "Wait here, buddy. I don't want you to strain yourself with your wing." The giant bird complied and waited at the base while Alice ran up to the top.

Once atop the sandy platform, a gentle and warm breeze blew past Alice. Her cheeks were red from the heat, exhaustion, and from crying.

There was nothing out there for miles. In every direction, the only thing Alice could see was sand. She was all alone. She didn't know where her friends were or even if they were okay. How had she let this happen? This was all her fault! If only she had been stronger or smarter or a better Light Spirit then none of them would be in this mess right now!

The thought of something happening to her dear friends because of her mistakes was enough to make Alice regret everything. She wished she had never found the scroll that night. She wished she never accepted the task. And more than anything, she wished she had never left home. Her, Jack, and Fawn could be in Elkmire right now instead. They could be running through the streets, sharing rose moose pudding, and playing through the forest knowing that life was good.

Except they couldn't. Because they weren't in Elkmire right now, and they weren't together right now. And most of all, Elkmire didn't even exist anymore. Her home, family, and friends were *gone*.

"No," Alice cried silently. And then her rage built up even more. Alice wasn't only homesick, but she had given up, and she was about to let herself go completely.

"No!" she shouted as she fell to her knees. In that one moment and in that one word, she released all her pent-up tension and it seemed to shoot out of her with a physical force. The sand around Alice blew away instantly and the hill she had been standing on was no more. It had been completely leveled to flat ground. Had she done that?

A sudden spark of light lit up around Alice's eyes, and she noticed that the silver markings on her face were glowing a gentle hue.

Wesley glided through the hot and thick air of the desert. The air was so heavy and was moving so slowly that it made flying very difficult for him. It exhausted him just to keep moving forward. His cheeks were red and perspiration collected along his brow.

For fear of falling out of the sky, Wesley decided to land. He closed his glider suit by clipping the buttons back to his chest and wrapping the wing-like folds around his sides. He wiped the sweat from his forehead along his sleeve and then continued walking.

He didn't know which way he was going but he trusted himself to go a safer route than the others. He hardly knew those people, after all. He had known those strangers for twenty-four hours and they had already dragged him out into the middle of nowhere. Wesley had risked his own neck for them enough times already. From now on, he would travel alone.

Abruptly, the ground beneath his feet began to rumble. He looked around but didn't see anything that could cause the ground to shake like this. Was it an earthquake? After a moment longer, the ground began shaking even more. Wesley was flung around violently to no avail.

But then, as quickly as the shaking had begun, it stopped. The desert floor was quiet and sound once more. Wesley sat up. This place was weird. He wanted to go back to Taesithia. They didn't have earthquakes there.

Before he could take another step, the sand in front of Wesley exploded into the air as a giant snake-like creature emerged from under the ground.

"Ah!" he screamed as the creature towered over him. It looked like a dragon except it had no arms or legs. Instead, its body was like that of a snake's. It had yellowish golden scales covering its entire body and beady green eyes.

"A s-s-sand serpent!" Wesley exclaimed. The serpent opened its massive mouth to reveal its sharp teeth and long, slimy tongue. It then screeched out a horrible, ear-splitting roar.

It dove right at Wesley with its mouth open and the tiny boy rolled out of the way with not more than a second to spare. The creature dove headfirst into the sand only to come right back up to attack its prey further.

Wesley took to the air and tried to fly away, but he was too slow. The serpent bit onto his leg and flung him backward. Wesley caught himself in the air just as the serpent turned around to get him once more.

The creature grabbed his leg again and Wesley's lower half was stuck inside its mouth. Any second, it could bite down on him and crush his internal organs causing him to bleed out, killing him. It would be a painful and excruciating death, and that's exactly why Wesley refused to allow that to happen.

He gathered up as much air around his right arm as possible and using sky magic to strengthen the wind, he slammed his fist down right on the serpent's nose with extreme force. The creature yelped out and released its hold on Wesley, dropping him. Before he hit the ground, a scale from the serpent's chest sliced across Wesley's forehead with a clean streak. The stinging sensation burned and he felt blood pour down around his eyes.

His hand was bruised from the blow he dealt with the serpent's weak spot, but his hand would heal, a crushed body, on the other hand, would not. The serpent slowly turned around to attack Wesley again, but it was too slow. Wesley had already soared up high into the sky, taking the wind with him, and kicked a sharp array of wind right into the serpent. It cried out another deafening screech before diving back into the sand and disappearing from sight.

Wesley gently glided back to the ground and stood on his sore, wobbly legs. His entire face was red with his own blood from the slice across his forehead. He had exhausted his body beyond his own limits, and Wesley slowly lost consciousness as he felt himself flop to the ground.

Alice ran as fast as she could to the sight before her. She could see what looked like Mayday dragging Fawn along the ground toward her. The cub made slow progress. Fawn seemed to be struggling against her pull and she clawed at the ground.

"Fawn!" Alice shouted as she dropped to her knees to hug her friend. "Mayday, you did it!" she said, petting the baby wolf.

"Alice?" Fawn asked. "What are you doing here? We need to get away from the mantis! They're trying to eat me!"

Alice starred at Fawn. What was she talking about? What mantis? After a moment, Alice noticed that Fawn's pupils were dilated and her skin felt all clammy. She lifted a hand to feel Fawn's sweaty forehead, and sure enough, she had a fever.

"Mantis . . ." Fawn said, feeling dizzy. "Buzz-buzz. I need more water!"

"Fawn!" Alice said, trying to get a hold of her. "What are you saying?" If she wanted water, perhaps she was suffering from some sort of hallucinations caused by dehydration. Alice went and got a pouch of water from Reezu's saddle where the rest of the supplies were.

"Here," she said, holding out the pouch to Fawn. She snatched the water from Alice and began guzzling it down all at once. After she drank all the water, she sat there with her eyes wide, peering all around at the sand-filled desert.

"How'd we get out here in the middle of the ocean?"

Nickoli, Rosenia, and the girls all sat quietly in their cells as the Fire Kingdom guards came around the corner to bring them their mushy, green dinner. The guards came three times a day with regular intervals, Nickoli had noticed. Now would be the third time they came today, meaning it was dinnertime, around seven-thirty.

The guards dropped the plates at each of the cells and turned to leave without exchanging any words with the prisoners. Nickoli watched them walk away down the hall and disappear around the corner. After they had left, he waited an extra two minutes or so just to be certain they were gone.

"Okay, let's go," he said to the others. At his command, Rosenia, Aurora, Gaia, Talula, and Lizzie began scooping their mushy food off the trays and applying it over the screws and bolts of their cell doors. Even Bella Didi, the little toddler, helped out. They kept on at it until they had used up almost all of the food. Although, they did save a small portion of it to eat.

Nickoli plopped down with his back against the wall with a huff. This was his plan, and so far, everything was going smoothly. He and the others had to get out of there and fast. Rosenia had warned them that something dark was awaiting Alice in Etaellaca. They had to tell Alice before she made it there, or else, it would be too late.

"Alright, everyone," Nickoli began. "If everything continues to go as planned, we should be able to escape in five days' time."

Alice dragged Fawn through the desert as she continued to search for Jack and Wesley. She had tied a rope around Fawn's ankle and pulled her along. Fawn had mentioned something about drinking out of a pond near "disco trees" and Alice figured she had drunk some sketchy water that was causing her to behave like that.

Alice thought about sending Mayday to go look for the boys since the cub had succeeded in finding Fawn, but the sun was setting and she didn't want Mayday to be out alone in the dark. She was also afraid of Jack and Wesley being out there, but there wasn't anything she could do about that at the moment. Alice had decided she wouldn't rest until she found them.

As she continued, something white lying in the sand up ahead caught Alice's eye. The object was surrounded by sand that had been disrupted and seemed to be almost flung out of place as if something had bulldozed through it.

A ray of the fading sunlight angled itself perfectly on the object in the sand and Alice could make out a small boy lying face down on the ground.

"Wesley!" Alice shouted as she dropped the rope and ran toward him. Fawn started rolling around the ground without her holding the rope, but Alice didn't care. She ran toward Wesley as fast as she could. He wasn't moving and she found her heart beginning to quicken its pace as she feared the worst.

Alice dropped to her knees and scooped up the tiny boy in her arms. His entire face was stained with blood from an open slice across his forehead. He had bruises and scrapes all over his body. Was he dead? The entire area of sand had been disturbed. What happened? Whatever it was, it must've been some fight.

"Wesley!" Alice cried. "Wesley, wake up! Come on, you have to wake up!" She shouted loudly, but the boy didn't stir. Tears began rolling out of her eyes and sliding down her cheeks.

This couldn't be happening. It was Alice's fault that they had gotten separated. Wesley was too little to handle himself out there. She'd never be able to live with herself knowing he was gone because of her. Alice hadn't known Wesley for very long, but he was a boy filled with life, innocence, and love. Alice refused to allow those aspects to die with him.

She pressed her ear to Wesley's chest and listened. More tears began flowing down Alice's face as she made out the slow and quiet beating of his heart. These were tears of joy, Wesley was alive. It seemed he had been flung around quite a bit and probably had internal injuries. Alice would have to work quickly if she hoped to save him.

She unzipped the front of Wesley's glider suit he wore and placed her hands on his stomach. She closed her eyes and breathed slow and deep breaths. After a moment, a bright and warm light began to emit out of her hands. Alice continued to heal him as she worked for her hands all around his stomach, sides, and chest. She imagined every bone, organ, and blood vessel that her hands were passing over and allowed her light to seep into those parts and heal what had been broken.

After several minutes had passed, Alice released her hands and the white light diminished. Wesley had been healed. He'd be okay now, although he probably wouldn't wake up for another few hours or so.

Alice wrapped a bandage around his forehead where the slice was and cleaned the blood from his face. She was exhausted now. It took a toll on her body and mind to work that amount of healing in a single sitting. Injuries like that would normally be healed over the course of several sessions, but Wesley couldn't afford to wait that long.

Alice sat with Wesley in her lap as Fawn stood up and started galloping in place. "Look at me!" she said laughing. "I'm riding a dragon!"

Fawn noticed Wesley laying on the ground and she stopped riding her dragon to look at him. She squinted her eyes at him as if wondering what he could be, and then it dawned on her.

"Ah! Forest Elf!" she shouted, jumping back.

Alice looked out at the setting sun. Because the desert was completely flat as far as she could see to the west, the sun was perfectly visible. It was massive, and Alice watched as it seemed to sink into the sand.

Just as she was about to look away, a small shadow appeared as it walked out of the sun from the west. Alice had to squint hard to see what it was. She gasped as she made out a figure of a person walking with his back to the sun. The figure walked toward them with slow, rugged steps.

Alice laid Wesley down on the sand and stood up. The breeze ruffled her hair as she watched the figure drew closer. It wasn't until the sun dipped below the sand, allowing all light to vanish from the sky, that Alice could make out Jack's face.

She ran to him. She ran to him with her arms stretched wide until she had reached him. Alice hugged Jack with all her strength, but he didn't hug her back. Instead, his arms laid limply at his sides.

"You're okay!" Alice said as she breathed in Jack's familiar scent. He smelled like roses. She pulled away to look into his eyes. His beautiful, blue eyes were completely dull. Bare of all life. Alice knew it was only because of the distractor spell but it hurt more than it should have to see him like that. She looked into his lifeless eyes a second longer, and for a moment, *she got the feeling that something terrible was going to happen in the near future.*

Alice quickly brushed off these feelings and tried to pretend that they had never happened. She was just happy that Jack had returned. They were all back together now.

Suddenly, a squeak sounded from Jack's shoulder. Alice turned to see Boo. She had almost forgotten about Wesley's little pet. There was a piece of fabric tied around Boo's mid-section and Alice followed it to see the other end wrapped loosely around Jack's neck. So, that's how he made it back. He must have gained enough consciousness at one point to tie the fabric and have Boo lead him back to the others. That was smart thinking. Alice would have never thought of something like that.

"Thank you, Boo," Alice said as she untied the little critter and stroked his tiny head. "You did good."

Alice grabbed Jack by the hand and led him back over to the others. She found that he did not struggle against being pulled in any particular direction. He wasn't fighting her, but he was totally lifeless, like a walking zombie with no inclination to go anywhere or do anything.

Alice tied the rope Fawn was connected to around Jack as well. She picked up Wesley and carried him on her back. It was time to get moving again. She was tired, and even though she had found the others, she felt lonely knowing that none of them were themselves right then. But yet, she remained determined. They were on a mission after all. No one said it was going to be easy.

"Come on, guys," Alice whispered. "We should get moving. We're the only ones who know about the task on the scroll. We have to get that information to the Etaellaca Empire."

"Alright, we'll stop here," Alice said. Fawn immediately plopped to the ground with a heavy sign. It was the middle of the night. Alice had carried Wesley the entire time they traveled and she also pulled Jack and Fawn along with the rope. She was beyond tired. Is this how the next couple of weeks would go for them? Alice forcing the others to tag along as she dragged them through the desert? After being in there like that for so long, she worried the others wouldn't even know who they were once the effects of the distract spell wore off.

Alice laid Wesley down in the sand, and she walked over to Jack and helped him to do the same. Reezu laid down beside them and Alice curled up next to his warm, feathery side. The temperature had dropped significantly. It was cold and dark. The only source of light were the stars and the moon. She looked up at the stars and thought of her sister, Lizzie. She hoped that wherever Lizzie was, she was somewhere where she could see the stars.

"We'll travel during the night when it's cool and rest during the day," Alice said almost as if to herself. It wasn't like the others were listening. "We'll start again in a few hours, just try and get some rest."

Alice shook Fawn from left to right, trying to wake her up. It was morning. They had accidentally slept the entire night. "Come on, it's time to get moving again."

"Mm, no," Fawn said with her head still in the sand. Alice decided to ignore Fawn's bad attitude for the moment. She had already awoken Jack and he stood idly nearby. She reached over to tap on Wesley's shoulder as he laid next to her, but before her hand even made contact, he spoke. "I'm awake," he said. "I couldn't sleep. Not after being knocked out for so long."

He sounded different, Alice thought. He had no pep in his voice and no spirit. "Are you feeling okay?" she asked him.

"Yeah. I'm much better. Thanks to you."

He was drained. Alice was too. This desert had taken a toll on them all. Hopefully, today would be a better day than yesterday. Alice stood up, and after ensuring that the rope was tied securely around each of them, she continued to march through the desert.

They hadn't walked for more than five minutes under the morning sun before the wind picked up and blew around the kids fiercely. Alice looked over to the east to find another dust storm headed right for them.

"No! No! No! Not again!" she cried out. She turned to the west and ran as fast as her legs would carry her. The others tagged along, but they didn't want to move and only slowed each other down.

"Run! Guys, we have to run, now!" Alice tried yelling. But her voice was drowned out by the storm that had closed in on them. She prepared herself to be blown away again and lose the others. She could only hope that this time, they'd find each other sooner and under better circumstances.

Except, she wasn't blown away. In fact, once the dust storm was on them, it slowly began to die down. Alice blocked her face with her arms from the sand. The wind lessened, and the dust settled.

Once the storm had completely cleared, Alice removed her arms from her face. Standing in front of her were three massive vehicles. At first, she feared the worst, that those were Fire Kingdom vehicles. But thankfully, they weren't. These vehicles were of a larger design than the ones from the Fire Kingdom Alice had seen previously and they weren't red either. These ones were the same sandy color as the desert.

Aboard the sand vehicles were cat people dressed in white garments. They had cloth covering their faces in order to guard them against the sand. Each one of them had either red, yellow, or orange cat ears sticking out of the tops of their heads, and a matching tail sprouting out of their lower back.

Alice didn't expect to find any friends in a place like this, so she remained on guard. These people had to be more enemies. She was in no position to put up a fight, and in cases like that, confidence was key.

"Who are you and what do you want?" Alice shouted to the onlookers, hoping to sound braver than she felt.

"We want to know who gave you permission to tread through these lands." One of the cat people responded with a heavy accent. He and a few others jumped off their vehicle and walked closer to Alice. Each one of them had eyes the color of fire. It was possible they could be Fire Kingdom.

The cat person who had spoken first walked even closer to Alice. She stood her ground. He looked different than the others. He was dressed in fancier clothing. He wore red face paint drawn into shapes underneath his eyes. His hair was snow white and his skin was fair. But his eyes and cat-like features were just as red as the others.

He spoke to Alice with a calm and smooth voice that carried an accent she was not familiar with.

"We are the guardians of the desert."

CHAPTER SEVEN

Trials

"What are you doing on our land with those animals of yours?" the cat-person asked. "From the looks of it, you're trespassing on sacred ground with several invasive species."

"We're only passing through," Alice said. The cat-people seemed to be quite practical. Hopefully, she'd be able to reason with them.

"We've come from the Earth Nation. Our bird was injured and we have no choice but to travel through the desert on foot. We're on our way to the Etaellaca Empire and we didn't know this land was sacred or that it belonged to anyone. I'm the Light Spirit, and I'm only telling you this because I'm hoping you'll let us off the hook. Unless you're Fire Kingdom, that is."

As soon as Alice mentioned she was the Light Spirit, the cat-people all stared at her with wide eyes. Some of them shuffled closer to each other and exchanged a few mumbles.

"You dare accuse our people of being part of that fiery filth nation while you ride in here from Fire Kingdom territory?" one of the females said angrily.

"Quiet, Antoina!" the leader said. "She hasn't accused our people of anything! If what she says is true, then we must give them hospitality."

"My apologies, Prince Urijah," the female said quietly.

"Prince?" Alice spoke up.

The leader gave a shy smile. At first, Alice had thought he was an adult, but now, she could see he was younger than that. In fact, he had to be around sixteen or seventeen, or so it seemed.

"Prince Urijah of Medina City, at your service, Light Spirit," he said, bowing.

"I've never heard of Medina City," Alice said.

"It's the only civilization out here in the Les Landes Desert. And truth be told, you haven't heard of it because it's not on any maps. Our city must remain a secret to most."

"Do you think you could take us there, Prince Urijah?" Alice asked eagerly, trying not to get ahead of herself. "We just need a day or two to rest and get back on our feet. The distractor spell has taken its toll on my friends."

"Certainly," Urijah responded without pause. "After all, you are the Light Spirit, a friend of the Flame Cats indeed. Although, before you can come to Medina, you'll want your friends to be relieved of that distractor spell. And that is why you must take the trials."

"What trials?" If it was some sort of test, Alice would gladly take it if it meant they'd be taken to the safety of Medina.

"The desert trials," Urijah said. "It will prove if you are really who you say you are and it will test your strength as well as make proof of your intentions. Should you pass the trials, the desert will lift the distractor spell on your friends and we'll take you to Medina."

"Okay," Alice responded. "I'll do it. Where do we go?"

"Come aboard," Urijah said as he jumped back onto the sand vehicle. "We'll take you to the sight of the trials. It's actually not too far from here."

After only a few minutes of being aboard the sand vehicle and plowing through the desert, Jack, Fawn, and Wesley began to return to their normal selves.

"Ugh, I think my head is finally starting to clear out of the poison water," Fawn said, stretching out.

"It's about time," Alice said. "If I heard you talk about riding on dragons or about the disco trees one more time, I'd have already left for Etaellaca on my own."

"Poison water?" Urijah asked.

"Yeah, I found some sketchy-looking water out in the middle of the desert and I drank it," Fawn said, nonchalantly.

"You must have a strong stomach. The water you're describing is dangerous enough to kill most people. The locals and I all know not to consume anything you find out here."

"I grew up in the forest of Earth Nation," Fawn replied. "I've tried just about every bush, plant, and flower there is, even the poisonous ones. Usually, I know just by the scent of something whether or not it's poison, but I'm not used to this desert."

"And yet you drank it anyway?" Urijah said, in disbelief.

Fawn nodded as if drinking potentially poisonous water was the only way to know for sure. Urijah looked at Fawn with an admirable expression in his gaze. Fawn didn't notice the way he looked at her, but Jack managed to catch the sight, although he didn't say anything.

"It feels so good to be back to normal again," Jack said.

"Oh, uh, right," Urijah stood up. "The distractor spell is placed on the sand of the desert. Once you're no longer touching the sand directly, the effects will be lifted."

"So, I noticed." Jack had been right, after all. "But I haven't figured out how you and the others are not affected. I'm guessing you're immune?"

"That's right," Urijah said. "My, Jack, was it? You're a sharp one, nothing seems to get past you. As cat people, we do have some interesting traits. Immunity to mind control is one of them."

"Why do you keep referring to yourselves as cat people and not catwalkers?" Fawn asked. "Aren't you skinwalkers like me?"

"A common misconception," Urijah said. "There actually is no such thing as a catwalker. The beings you're referring to, skinwalkers from the Piniel Dynasty, are considered to be half-person and half-animal, like yourself. They can be almost anything, a reptile, a mammal, a bird, and the list goes on. But there has never been a catwalker. There are lionwalkers and tigerwalkers, but not the domestic cat. And that's where us cat people come into play. We are our own unique species originating from one of the four elemental nations. The Water Cats from the Ice Nation. Tree Cats from the Earth Nation. Air Cats from the Sky Kingdom. We are exactly what a catwalker would be if such a thing existed but a little more advanced. We're not magical, at least not all of us, but we do have some properties and aspects that are considered to be a part of the magic world, such as immunity to mind control. Cat people are kind of in-between magic and non-magic user."

"Oh, I see," Alice said.

"You forgot the Fire Kingdom," Jack pointed out.

"What?" Urijah asked, seeming surprised Jack had mentioned it.

"You said there is one type of cat people for each of the elemental territories. Water. Earth. Sky. The fourth is fire. Why didn't you mention that? And earlier you referred to yourselves as being Flame Cats, which I'm assuming is the type of cat people originating from the Fire Kingdom. Care to explain yourself?"

Urijah was at a loss for words. He looked at Jack in awe with a glimmer of fear behind his red eyes. Some of the others aboard the vehicle began looking in their direction as if on edge.

"Yes, Jack," Urijah said, looking slightly deflated. "I was right to assume that nothing gets past you. You are correct. My kind and I are the Flame Cats originating from the Fire Kingdom. But please, allow me to explain."

Jack sat down beside Urijah. He crossed his arms and was slightly relaxed but would be sure not to let his guard down.

"The Flame Cats have not lived in or been a part of the Fire Kingdom for almost three hundred years. You see, those three centuries ago, just after the war began, there was a persecution against cat people. The persecution was worldwide, but it was most prominent and severe in the Fire Kingdom. People believed that cat people were sly and sneaky and were possible spies. It was true. There were many Flame Cats, as well as other types around the four nations working as spies. The governments of Infinity dealt with this accordingly and only punished those who were guilty. But the Fire Kingdom was already a disaster. It was like a purge. Civilians of the Fire Kingdom killed Flame Cats left and right, claiming that they were traitors of the nation. I remember it like it was only yesterday.

"Bodies of my kin littered the streets. It wasn't justice and it wasn't truthful. It was genocide. Once the persecution had neared its end, not many Flame Cats remained. Those who had survived were banned together, my family included. And we voluntarily left the Fire Kingdom and severed all ties with our homeland. We made the aching trek into the desert, as it was our only option of refuge. We learned how to survive and how to use the dangers of the desert to our advantage. We made a civilization, a new home: Medina. My father was appointed Sultan, and now we lead our people in a nation of our own.

"You see, Jack, I was hesitant to mention this because I was afraid you would not trust us if you knew we had Fire Kingdom in our blood. But please believe me when I say we are avid supporters of the Light Spirit. We don't believe in what the Fire Kingdom and the Dragons are a part of. I understand if you don't trust us. That is all I have to say."

"I trust you," Alice said.

"Me too," Wesley agreed. "It sounds to me like you guys are on our side! And besides, that was three hundred years ago when you were a part of the Fire Kingdom. You guys were brave to leave."

"Thank you, Light Spirit, and young sky child," Urijah said.

Jack looked into Urijah's red eyes. He believed the Prince of Medina was telling the truth, but still, some things he said sounded sketchy. "Just how old are you?" he asked.

"I was born on February 14th, 1732. I'm three hundred and thirteen years old."

"What!" Alice, Fawn, and Wesley shouted in unison.

"How is that even possible!" Alice asked.

"Cat people are immune to the effects of age," Urijah replied. "We cannot die of old age. We age at a normal rate until we are about eighteen, and after that, the aging process either slows down tremendously or completely stops. I'm not totally sure. There are disadvantages to being immortal though, like our health. A normal person can be severely injured or become very sick and still live. Things like a bruise or the common cold are nothing to you, but for a cat person, it is usually fatal. We'll die from almost anything if we're not careful."

"That's insane," Fawn remarked. "I know you said you guys are non-magical, but that sounds like magic to me."

"In truth, cat people are not normally born with magic. If they are, it is their elemental type. Flame Cats would have fire magic. Water Cats would have ice magic, and so on. But a cat person will only be born with that magic if they were born on the full moon. Otherwise, we are non-magical like a skinwalker."

"Why the full moon?" Alice asked.

"The moon is the source of all magic. And a full moon typically enhances magic for all creatures to a certain extent, some more than others. Although, none of the Flame Cats in Medina were born as fire magic users that I know of," Urijah finished.

The vehicle came to a slow and steady stop. Urijah got up and walked over to the front. "Oh, good," he called. "We've made it to the sight of the Trials. We're here."

Wildfire kept her feet firmly planted on the grass as she crouched down and scooped up a handful of sand from the desert that stretched out before her. The sand didn't feel any different than normal sand and it didn't look any different either, but still, something felt off.

"We'll continue through," she said to the soldiers and crew behind her. "As long as everyone stays aboard the vehicles or a horse, we'll be fine. And try to keep up because I'll gladly leave you slackers behind."

"I don't know about this, Wildfire," Yagatsu said. "This desert is a bad omen. We should stay in the Earth Nation and travel east to the coast and we can board a ship to Etaellaca from there."

"No," Wildfire demanded. "If the Light Spirit is traveling through the desert, so will I."

She turned around and mounted the vehicle in the lead of the troops. She waved her arm above her head, signaling to the others.

"Let's move!" she called.

And with that, Force Captain Wildfire's platoon of warriors charged into the Les Landes desert.

"Is this the sight of the trials?" Jack asked as he hopped off the sand vehicle and onto the stone below.

"It is," Prince Urijah responded.

Jack recognized the dozen or so yards of stone out in the middle of the desert instantly. "I've been here before."

"What? When?" Fawn asked.

"Yesterday. When we got separated, I wandered off without any sense as to where I was going until I stumbled upon this stone area. That's how I regained consciousness and had Boo lead me out. It's also how I figured out that the distractor spell only works on the sand."

"The entrance is over here," Urijah called as he walked over to a circular platform in the middle of the stone. The other Flame Cats all stayed near the vehicles.

"Stand on the platform."

Jack, Alice, Fawn, and Wesley did as he said. The four of them just barely fit on the platform with only an inch or two to spare.

"Once I lower the platform down into the ground," Urijah began. "You'll be in a hallway with doors on either side. Find the door with your name on it and enter. Once inside, your trial will begin. I shouldn't say anything about the trail itself, but you'll be given further instruction once inside. And remember, this isn't a game of wits. The desert simply wants a chance to decipher your intentions and will do so by seeing into your mind."

"The desert is going to read our minds?" Alice asked.

"No. It just wants to view certain aspects of your life. Based upon your previous experiences and decisions you've made in your life, it will deem you worthy or unworthy of treading on its sacred ground. You'll see once inside. Are you guys ready?"

The kids nodded. Urijah walked over to a rock. Hidden behind it was a small lever. He started cranking the lever, and as he did, the platform the kids were standing on gradually began sinking into the stone like an elevator.

Once they had been completely lowered into the hallway, the kids stepped off the platform. It was just as Urijah had described. A short and narrow hall with doors on either side.

Fawn and Wesley found the doors with their names on them quickly. They were right near the entrance. Jack's door was down at the end of the hall, and Alice's was just past his.

Fawn and Wesley didn't hesitate to go inside their doors. They disappeared inside and closed the door behind them. Jack paused outside his door. He stared up at his name engraved into the wood. How had that gotten there? Magic was his guess, but it was ever so slightly unnerving.

Alice waited in front of her door with Jack. She looked across to him. He seemed worried or scared. She opened her mouth to give him a few words of encouragement, but he opened his door and walked inside before she could get them out. His door closed behind him with a slam, leaving Alice alone in the hall. And without another moment, she too opened her door and walked inside.

On the other side of Wesley's door was a long hallway without an end in sight. The entire hall was made from mirrors. The walls, the floor, and the ceiling were all entirely reflective mirrors.

Wesley slowly walked down the hall. Everywhere he looked, he only saw reflections of himself peering back at him. What was he supposed to do? Nothing maybe? Just being inside this room alone probably allowed the desert to have access to his mind. If that was the case, then when would he know when to leave? Wesley ended up deciding it would be best just to continue along the hall for at least a little way before deciding on what to do next.

He hadn't made it more than ten steps down the hall of mirrors before the sound of children laughing came from somewhere near him. Wesley didn't see anyone ahead of him, and looking back, there was also no one behind him. But even so, the laughing continued.

"Play the song again!" the voice of a girl sounded.

"Alright, one more time then," a boy's voice responded.

Wesley would recognize those voices anywhere. He hadn't heard them in a long while, and he thought he'd never hear them again. Was he daydreaming? Or could it really be?

He slowly looked to his right. Inside the mirror wasn't his reflection staring back at him anymore but instead two little kids. The first was a girl with blonde hair and delicate, white fairy wings. The second was a boy with blue hair and pointed ears. Both kids were dressed in Sky Kingdom attire similar to Wesley.

Wesley felt his mouth drop. It was them. They were here. Fallon and Daisy. His best friends. But how? He had found their bodies, blackened and blue from the fire of a dragon. He had *buried* them. And since then, he had looked for them in everything. In a sea of people, his eyes had always searched for Fallon and Daisy, and here they were.

Wesley ran up to the glass and pressed his hands to it. They were so close, just behind the glass, but he couldn't reach them.

"Fallon! Daisy!" he shouted. "You're okay! You're here! You're a . . . alive."

Wesley broke into tears. He couldn't believe this was actually happening. His friends were alive and healthy. And they looked exactly the same as when he had last saw them.

Fallon held a ukulele in his hands. He and Daisy played with it. They made no acknowledgment to Wesley. In fact, it was as if they couldn't see him at all.

"Hey, guys?" Wesley cried as he crouched in front of the mirror. "Can you hear me?"

Fallon and Daisy continued playing with the ukulele. They plucked the strings and twisted the knobs but never did they look up to see Wesley.

"Fallon . . . Daisy, please, look at me. I'm here, we're all here again." More tears began flowing down Wesley's cheeks. He tapped on the mirror, and he cried out as he realized he was only peering into the reflection of memory. They couldn't hear him or see him because they weren't real, or at least not anymore.

"Please, look at me!" he shouted in vain. Fallon and Daisy remained oblivious inside the mirror. "Fallon! Daisy! I'm here! It's me, Wesley, your friend!"

Wesley started banging on the glass. "Come back to me!" He banged even harder, pounding his fist into the mirror. "I'm sorry! I'm s-so sorry! I'm so sorry that you died! I'm sorry that I couldn't save you!"

Wesley cried and cried. It was like dangling a carrot in front of his face. It was bittersweet to reunite him with his dear friends and have it only as a memory. They were so close but yet still so far, and it was as if Wesley was losing them all over again.

Fallon took the chip and began strumming a soft and familiar melody on the ukulele. Wesley had heard him play this song many times before. He closed his eyes and listened to the song. And as the hot tears continued to flow, he kept on listening as if he was really with Fallon and Daisy, as if they had never left him at all.

After a couple of minutes, the melody dissipated into silence. Wesley felt alone again. He opened his eyes. The mirror had several large cracks in it from when he had punched at the glass. Inside the mirror was not the image Wesley had seen a few moments ago. Fallon and Daisy no longer sat happily inside the mirror world playing the ukulele, but instead, they laid on the ground dead. Their skin was blackened and blued from the poison fire of a dragon.

Wesley screamed and cried at the same time. He kicked his legs at the mirror until his back was pushed up against the opposite side of the hall. But it wasn't enough. He could still see them.

Suddenly, Daisy sat up. There was blood pouring out of the corner of her mouth. "Why?" she whispered hoarsely as she stared right at Wesley. "Why didn't you save us?"

"I-I'm s-so sorry," Wesley whispered back.

Fallon turned his head to the side from where he laid and peered right at Wesley from inside the mirror.

"Why is it that you were the only survivor?" he asked calmly. "You didn't have to go to the market that day."

Wesley couldn't bear it any longer. If this was the trial, then he had failed. He curled up into a ball with his knees drawn to his chest and he tucked his chin between his legs. He brought his hands up to cover his ears and stayed that way until Fallon and Daisy's voices had been drowned out completely.

Fawn walked down the mirror hall quietly. She had walked down so far that she couldn't see the entrance anymore. She didn't know what to do or where to go, so she continued.

As she walked past one portion of the mirror, she saw someone inside looking out from the corner of her eye. She stopped walking and doubled back to have a second look. Inside the mirror was a younger version of herself, about three years old with her long hair braided into two braids.

Fawn stared at her timeless reflection with wide eyes. Her younger self smiled at her and waved. Hesitantly, Fawn waved back. The little girl turned and ran further down the mirror. Fawn lost sight of her younger self and quickly ran further down the hall after her.

Once Fawn had caught up, the reflection changed. Inside the mirror was herself once again, but this time about five years old. The five-year-old Fawn sat on the floor playing with blocks. And beside her was Malahki, about age nine.

After not more than a couple of seconds, the apparition of the two little kids vaporized into the air. Fawn understood it now. These were her memories. The desert was seeing into her mind and putting her memories on display.

She walked a little further and inside the mirror this time was her entire family. She was about six and huddled in the corner alone. Malahki was ten, and their mom and dad argued with him.

"You were *stealing* again?" Their mother yelled.

"I'm sorry! But I had to! Fawn and I had nothing!" Malahki shouted back. "You don't help us! You guys are not real parents! You only care about yourselves!"

"You little brat! You're going to get us all caught!" their father screamed. He hit Malahki with a heavy object and then the apparition faded away again.

Fawn signed and continued to the next part of the mirror. Here she saw Malahki carrying her on his back. They looked about the same age as in the last memory. Their mother and father appeared and shoved both of them to the ground.

"*Stay* here," Takara said to them as he walked away.

"We're gonna go now . . . we'll be back later," Accalia said.

Fawn walked to the next mirror. She saw herself at about eight years old swinging on a tree next to a girl with blonde hair. Malahki and Jack were beside her.

"My name is Fawn. What's your name?" she asked the girl.

"Alice," the blonde girl replied.

Fawn continued to the next mirror. Inside of this one, her eight-year-old self slept on the mirror world's ground beside Malahki. Suddenly, a torch appeared in the distance and the light illuminated Malahki's face. He awoke and ran after the torch, stepping over Fawn as he did so.

In the next mirror, Fawn saw herself and all her friends walking around the empty mirror world. They called out "Malahki!" and "Where are you!" but to no avail.

Fawn understood what was going on perfectly. The desert was processing her memories, trying to get a feel of her intentions. She had just watched her entire life play out in front of her like a movie. The apparition of her friends searching for Malahki faded away, and it was only then did Fawn realize that she had reached the end of the hall.

At the hall's end, to no surprise, was another mirror that faced her directly. Inside the mirror in replace of Fawn's own reflection was Malahki. He looked the same as when she had last seen him. He was twelve, with his messy hair and adorable freckles. He looked right at Fawn as if he was real and could actually see her.

He walked to the edge of the glass and placed his hand up against the mirror. Fawn walked to her end of the mirror and placed her hand up against his. The only thing that separated them was the glass of the mirror itself, but it was also the one thing that connected them.

Even though Malahki was born four years before her, Fawn had now out-aged him in his absence and was taller than her brother. He stared right into her eyes as if speaking to her with them.

"Malahki," Fawn began. "I love you."

To Fawn's utter surprise, Malahki answered. "Fawn," he began in his breathy voice. "I'm not even here."

Fawn's eyes turned glossy. "I know," she said. "That's the problem."

Malahki began falling backward into the blank, white world of the mirror as if slowly sinking deep beneath the waves of the ocean. He allowed himself to fall back. Fawn reached out for him but he didn't bother reaching back, as if he had accepted his fate. And Fawn had nothing to do but watch as he disappeared all over again.

When she turned around, Fawn was startled to see the writing on the mirrors underneath her feet. Written in red ink like blood were the words:

FIRST THE CAT. THEN THE DRAGON. THEN THE WOLF. HE IS MALAHKI. HE IS THE DECEIVER.

Jack sat up against one side of the hall with his knees drawn to his chest. In the mirror across from him, he watched a memory play out inside the white mirror world.

He was about nine years old, laying in the bed from what he assumed was the infirmary back home in the palace. A towel laid on his forehead and he coughed weakly. Somewhere in the distance, he could hear the sound of kids laughing and playing. Jack's younger self sighed as he wished he could be playing too.

Suddenly, a little girl popped up beside the bed. "Surprise!" she shouted.

"Ah!" Jack cried as he threw his head under the covers. But after a second, the girl pulled the covers back and crawled underneath them.

"Alice?" Jack said to the girl beside him. "What are you doing in here? You'll catch my cold!"

"But you're all alone when you get sick like this!" Little Alice responded cheerfully. "And I don't want you to be alone, not ever!"

Jack smiled at her. His eyes were somewhat red and so were his cheeks, but it made him feel a little better knowing that Alice had his back even if he was sick.

"Besides," Alice continued. "I can't catch your cold because your mom says it's not contagious!"

"It's not?" Jack asked.

"Oops, I don't think I was supposed to say that! Rosenia said to keep it to myself. I don't know why. But I'll tell you anyway! You're sick, Jack. That's just the way you are, but I'm sure you will get well soon!"

"Y-yeah," Jack said quietly. "Alice, can I tell you a secret?"

"Yes, Jack," came Alice's reply. Her voice didn't come from the memory inside the mirror. It came from down the hall. It didn't sound as high-pitched as in the memory either, in fact, it sounded like Alice herself from the present.

Jack quickly stood up. Out of the corner of his eye, he noticed the memory inside the mirror fade away. Down the hall, close to where he had entered was Alice, her actual real and thirteen-year-old self.

"Alice?" Jack called to her. "What are you doing in here? Is your trial over?"

Alice started walking toward him. "I came because there was something I needed to tell you. It's a secret . . . can you keep it?"

Jack was slightly confused. What was so important that Alice had to come and tell him now? The memory he had just watched made him slightly sympathetic and he decided to hear her out.

"Yeah, what is it?" he asked.

"I wanted to tell you that I—" Alice was interrupted by the arrow that zipped through the air from behind Jack's head that lodged itself in her abdomen.

Jack immediately froze up. He couldn't move, think, or talk. His eyes were wide. Where had that arrow come from? Alice slowly lowered her eyes to view the arrow in her stomach. She wrapped her hand around it and gradually pulled it out. Her blood dripped onto the mirror beneath her feet and more blood filled her mouth.

Alice dropped the arrow and fell to her knees. At once, Jack's senses came back to him. He rushed over to her as fast as he could, catching her in his arms. He placed his hands on the hole the arrow had punctured into her body and he tried to heal her, but it was no use.

"No, no, no, no!" he cried out.

Alice looked up at him, her eyes slowly closed and her heartbeat vanished.

"Alice!" Jack shouted as he shook her vigorously. "Alice! Alice, wake up! Stay with me!" his voice cracked. Was she really gone? Just like that?

"Alice . . ." he cried. "I never got to tell you. I never got to tell you that I—" Suddenly, Alice's body began fading away. It vaporized until Jack was holding nothing but the air in his lap.

It was *fake.* Alice wasn't ever in this room, to begin with. She was alive and well in her own hall of mirrors. It took Jack a few minutes to collect himself. It felt too real. For a moment there, he thought he had actually lost her.

Jack's brain began to spin. The desert was supposed to be searching his mind for memories, but what he just witnessed had never happened before . . . or maybe, not *yet.*

Alice walked with quiet footsteps down the hall of mirrors. She slid her fingertips across the glass on her left side as she peered into the endless number of reflections of herself. It was quiet, too quiet. There was nothing to see, nothing to hear, and nothing to do. So, she continued into the void to no avail.

She walked for another fifteen minutes or so, but there was nothing. Was it the same for the others? Was this the trial? Just walking down an endless hall of mirrors? Strangely, Alice felt like something was wrong. Perhaps the desert couldn't see into her memories like it was supposed to.

As she continued, she noticed something odd up ahead. The center of the hall was filled with mist. She couldn't see past it and the only way to go further down the hall would be to go through the mist.

Alice gently lifted her finger to touch the mist. She couldn't feel it, as if it wasn't there at all. She entered it completely with her hands stretched out in front of her so she could feel where she was going. The mist gradually got thicker and thicker. Before long, Alice could no longer see her hands in front of her face.

Eventually, the mist lightened up again and Alice broke away from it completely. On the other side, the hall continued as far as she could see, just the same as before.

Once on the other side of the mist, Alice could hear something. It sounded like a little girl was crying. She walked further down the hall trying to find the person.

"Hello?" Alice called out. "Is someone there?"

Instantly, the crying stopped and it was dead quiet once more. As Alice walked past one portion of the mirror on her left, she noticed a kid sitting inside the mirror. It was a little girl about seven years old with the longest blonde hair Alice had ever seen. The girl sat inside the mirror with her knees drawn to her chest and her head tucked away behind her long locks.

"Why were you crying?" Alice asked the little girl. Upon the question, the little girl snapped her head up to look at Alice. As soon as Alice saw the girl's face, she gasped and took several steps back.

The girl was *her*. A younger version of herself with the same blue eyes and silver markings on her face. Alice had no memory of her life before Queen Rosenia found her, so she had no telling of what she looked like before then or even what her early childhood was like. But even so, it was unmistakable.

The little girl was only slightly different compared to Alice now. She had extremely long blonde hair, especially compared to Alice's short hair tied into pigtails. The girl also had a unicorn's horn. It was small and peeked out of her head right on the hairline. Alice reached her hand up to touch her head right where that horn would be if she still had it today.

Large, clumpy tears poured out of the little girl's eyes and rolled down her chubby cheeks. She stood up and ran down the mirror.

"Wait! Come back!" Alice shouted as she ran down the hall after her younger self. When Alice made it over to a new panel of the mirror, her younger self stood completely still with her head down. Alice noticed that there were bandages wrapped around the girl's arms and legs. What could that be from?

All at once, the sound of clacking grew louder as someone wearing either boots or heels approached. The little girl shivered as a tall woman came to tower over her inside the mirror world. The woman was very tall with long black hair that flowed down past her waist. She bent over to cup little Alice's face in her hands.

"Tsk, tsk, tsk," the woman began. "Trying to run away again? I told you already. No matter which way you try to run, you'll get caught in the end." It was only after hearing the person's voice did Alice notice that the woman was in fact not a woman but a boy. He was a teenager whose long hair and feminine body style confused her.

The boy grabbed little Alice's arm and began tugging her away. "Come on now. We've got work to do if I want to finish those chains."

"N-no," the little girl resisted. "P-please don't, Isega," she cried.

Isega. Sega. Alice immediately recognized that name. That was the boy's name. But who was he? If this was a memory, then Alice had once known him. She was *afraid* of him.

"No?" Isega asked. "Well, you 'oughta make yourself good for something. Besides, I'm your big brother so you don't really have a choice." Isega tugged the girl away and the two of them vaporized into thin air.

Brother? Alice could hardly believe it. She had a brother? What was he doing to her? Why was she so afraid of him? What happened to her? Alice had so many questions, yet no one to answer them.

As Alice stared into the mirror, her own reflection began fading away as her younger self appeared inside of it again. The little girl laid on the clear floor of the mirror world, asleep.

All at once, a shadow appeared next to her as someone else came to tower over the sleeping child. He had his back to Alice, so she could not see his face and he wore a large cloak that covered his back. It wasn't Isega. Although this boy was around the same age as him, he looked much different than Sega from what Alice could tell. However strangely, something remained familiar about him.

The boy reached down to stroke the sleeping child's face. Alice could almost feel his soft fingertips on her face. Was this another memory?

"Sleep now, child," he said. Alice recognized the voice. She had heard it before and recently, too, but she couldn't quite place it.

"Dream," the boy said. "Sleep and dream of me." Alice walked closer to the mirror, trying to get a better look at him. His rich and silky voice along with his accent was so familiar.

Alice stopped dead in her tracks and she felt her throat drop into her stomach as the boy looked up and said, "That's close enough, Alice."

He could see her. A shiver ran down her spine. Something about this guy gave her the absolute creeps. "W-who are you?" she struggled to say.

"You'll know soon enough," he responded without turning around. "I hate to tell you to stay away because I am a person who is fond of touch, but with all this bright light around, you'd see my face if you were to get any closer. And I can't have that. Not yet."

"Are you a memory?" Alice asked.

The boy grabbed an object that was sitting near him. It was a hookah and he inhaled deeply from it. When he exhaled the cloud of smoke, a strong scent of vanilla filled the room. As the scent filled Alice's nose, her eyes grew wide and she immediately recognized the boy as the person from her dream a few nights ago. He scared her then and made an uneasy feeling in her stomach that she was also feeling at this moment.

"I am so much more than that," came the boy's cocky and taunting reply. Once the smoke from the hookah cleared, the boy was gone and so was the younger version of Alice.

"Alice!" came the sudden shouting of a different voice from somewhere beyond the hall. "Alice! Alice, wake up! Stay with me!"

It was Jack. She could hear his muffled voice coming from the other side of the mirror wall on the left. Why was he shouting for her? Was he okay?

"Jack?" she called to him. Alice looked around inside the mirrors one last time to be sure the boy and Isega along with her younger self had actually left. Only after confirming that she was alone did Alice take off back through the mist and down the hall to find Jack.

Alice busted through the door that led out of the hall of mirrors with such force that she fell through to the other side, landing on all fours. She had felt sure that the boy with the hookah who she had seen inside the mirror was following her, or at the very least, was watching. Every time she thought of him, she got an eerie and gut-wrenching feeling. Technically, she had no reason to be afraid of him. After all, she didn't know him and he hadn't caused her any harm. But the whole situation regarding this stranger was odd. The most concerning aspect about him was that Alice was certain he could be the mysterious and threatening Dark Spirit. However, that idea was little more than a theory. She didn't have any proof yet.

Down by the other doors, Alice could see Wesley huddled on the ground with Fawn and Jack near him. He was clearly very upset and it seemed as though Fawn and Jack were trying to comfort him.

As soon as Jack saw Alice, his eyes grew wide and he stood up. "Alice . . ." he said, jogging toward her. He met her on the ground and hugged her. "You're okay!" he exclaimed, sounding relieved.

"Yeah, of course, I am," Alice said. "What about you? Are you okay? I thought I heard you shouting earlier."

"I was. That mirror showed me some pretty messed up stuff, that's all." Jack had calmed down. From what he heard about Wesley's and Fawn's encounter with the mirrors, they also saw stuff that wasn't entirely accurate or truthful. It seemed the mirror was only playing with his emotions when it showed him the vision of Alice. Everything was going to be okay.

"What did you see inside the mirror?" Fawn asked as she walked toward them.

Alice froze for a second. What should she tell them? She didn't even know if what the mirror showed her was real or not. If it was, then somewhere out there, she had a brother named Isega and he had harmed her someway in the past. And there was also that boy from her dream, the one with the hookah. This was the second time Alice had seen him and the thought of bringing him up to the others felt entirely wrong. This was a matter she would keep to herself and no one else. Or at least until she found out who he was and what he wanted.

"Just some recent memories," Alice finally said. "Nothing special."

"Okay, same here," Fawn said. She had hoped the desert might've shown Alice some of her forgotten memories, which would help her find out what happened in her past. But since it didn't, they would just have to find out another way. "Wesley's was a little hard on him, that's all. But other than that, I think we are done here. Let's get going."

"Okay, yeah," Alice agreed as she got up and walked with Fawn and Wesley over to the platform that would bring them back up.

Jack walked right behind them. He noticed that Alice was twirling a strand of her hair and looking around quite a bit. He thought it was strange how she didn't see any memories from her early childhood that she had lost or forgotten. She was nervous and she was most definitely lying about what she saw in the mirrors. Jack had no way of telling exactly what she saw but he knew it was something unnerving. Alice had acted like this only one time previously. It was a couple of days ago, in the morning when she had mentioned having a nightmare.

That was it. Jack had connected it. Whatever Alice's nightmare had been about was what she saw in the mirror today. But what was it? Or, *who* was it?

"Congratulations," Prince Urijah exclaimed as he helped pull the kids off the platform and out onto the stone outside. "I can confirm that the desert has deemed all of you worthy of passing through. I can now take you to Medina to rest and gather whatever supplies you may need for the remainder of your journey. And as for the three of you, the effects of the distractor spell should have been lifted."

"Alright!" Wesley shouted as he ran over to the sand to test it out. The others followed after him at a slower pace.

"Urijah," Jack began.

"Yes, Jack?"

"The trial was supposed to be scanning our memories and I did see that happen, but I was also shown some things that weren't memories at all. Can you tell me what that was?"

Upon hearing Jack's question, Alice and Fawn began listening intently, as they too, were wondering the same thing.

"Look at it this way, Jack," Urijah said. "Time is not something that changes. You may perceive time to be always happening, coming and going, but it's not. Time is one single line that you travel along. In a sense, your memories from the past and events from the future are one and the same. Everything that has happened in your life and will happen in your life are coexisting right now. They always have been and always will be. The desert has the ability to perceive time differently than you and I, and sometimes, it gets confused on what part of the timeline we are currently standing on, and it may have trouble deciphering what part of your life you've already lived at this current moment in time."

Jack felt a lump grow in his throat. His hands became clammy and he rubbed them along his legs. "So . . . what you're saying," he began shakily. "Is that I didn't recognize what I saw in the hall of mirrors because it hasn't happened yet?"

"Precisely," Urijah responded. "But that doesn't mean it's for sure going to happen. You have the power to change the outcome based on the decisions you make. But regardless, whatever you saw in the mirrors has happened or will happen. Maybe not on this timeline with these particular versions of ourselves, but along another timeline, it may have already happened. Time is a difficult component of our understanding. In simple terms, the answer you're searching for is a yes, but please only accept that answer if it feels right with you, Jack."

Jack stopped walking. He couldn't believe what he was hearing. What Urijah was saying made perfect sense. The desert had shown him a memory of the future along a timeline where Alice *dies*. And if he didn't start making the proper changes, the same would happen in this timeline.

The image of Alice pulling the arrow out of her stomach filled Jack's mind again. He couldn't bear it any longer. It was *horrifying*. He turned to the side and threw up.

"Jack!" Alice shouted, rushing over to him. He waved her away and continued to throw up.

"What's wrong with him?" Urijah asked, coming to stand next to Fawn.

"I don't know," she said. "But he does have a habit of falling ill. Although normally, we'd be able to detect it a couple of days in advance. This is rather sudden."

Fawn thought about what Urijah had said about time. It made her think of the message that had been written in the mirror beneath her feet back in the hall. And only now did she realize it wasn't a message at all, but a *warning*.

Jack stood up and wiped his mouth along his sleeve. Alice opened her mouth to say something, but Jack interrupted her before she could speak. He didn't want her to ask.

"I'm fine," he said. "Let's just get to Medina." Without another word, the others complied. They hurried over to the vehicles where the rest of the Flame Cats waited with Wesley.

Alice walked a couple of paces behind them. She was thinking about the memories she had seen. She finally had an answer to what happened to her in her past. She had a brother. She had some type of family. It was a little overwhelming to imagine, considering she had never even thought about who her biological family was. She had always thought of Nickoli and Lizzie as being her family and thinking about her possible real relatives out there seemed like she'd be betraying the people who had actually raised and cared for her.

The only family she knew of, Isega, was scary. Is that the type of place she had come from? Alice hoped that over time, she would be able to find out the truth. She was on the track to finally put together the pieces of what happened to her before she turned eight years old. She had memories. She had a past.

The truly scary part was that the boy with the hookah, the one who had terrified Alice more than anyone else, was a part of that past. And learning more about her history would eventually lead her down a path that led right to him.

And there was nothing anyone could do to prepare her for that.

CHAPTER EIGHT

Medina

Alice watched as her younger self came running up to the glass of the mirror. She was back in the hall of mirrors from the trial, desperately searching for more answers regarding her past.

Her younger self was wearing fancy white clothes with gold trimming and her arms and legs were wrapped in bandages. She stood just behind the mirror, with her hands pressed up against the glass, looking right at Alice. Her cheeks were red and she breathed heavily.

"It's Sega," the little girl said to Alice. "He's coming." Alice could make out the sound of her creepy brother's boots clicking along the floor as he approached her younger self inside the mirror world.

Alice was scared for her younger self and there was nothing she could do to help. She walked to her side of the mirror and pressed her hands up against it so that their hands were almost touching.

Isega was right behind the little girl now. He held long, pearly-white chains in his left hand. The seven-year-old Alice's eyes grew wide as she sensed him behind her. She looked at Alice, pleading with her eyes. "Help me,"

"Turn around," Isega said to her. The little girl slowly complied. As soon as she turned around, Isega raised his arm. Alice gasped as she watched him swing a clean and fast strike at the little girl, violently slashing the chains with perfect control as if they were a part of his body. The younger Alice screamed and brought her hands to her face, but it was too late. In that one instant, Isega had done what he had wanted.

The little girl slowly turned back around to look at Alice on the other side of the mirror. Alice was horrified to see that her younger self had blood pouring down her entire face and there was now a gouge in her hairline where her horn was moments ago.

Alice awoke from her dream in a flash. She sat up and looked around, breathing heavily. She was sitting on a blanket on the top of one of the stationary sand vehicles. Her friends, as well as all the Flame Cats, slept nearby. It was the middle of the night. They were on their way to Medina and should arrive the next morning. They had left the sight of the trials four days ago and had traveled nonstop since then.

What she just witnessed back in her dream was horrifying. She had watched her own horn being cut off at the hands of her terrifying brother. Is that really how it went down? There was no way of telling, but it frightened Alice. She brought her hand up to her forehead where her horn used to be, wondering if that's how she had really lost it.

At once, Jack, who laid right next to Alice, sat up. "Hey, Alice, what's wrong? Are you okay? Why are you awake?" he asked, sounding more concerned than he should have been. Ever since they had left the sight of the trials, Jack had been extremely worked up. He had basically been attached to Alice at the hip. He wouldn't leave her alone for one second and he insisted on sleeping right next to her. On one of the nights, Wesley had laid down next to Alice and Jack made him move so he could be there. Alice had no idea what was going on with him.

"I'm fine," she said sternly. In fact, she was fed up with his strange behavior. "I'm always fine, Jack. I don't know what's been up with you lately."

"Me?" he asked. "What do you mean?"

"These last few days, you've been acting strange. I mean, you won't leave me alone unless I'm going to the bathroom! You're hardly eating, you're pale, and frankly, you don't look good, Jack. I'm worried about you."

Jack sighed heavily. "Yeah . . . I know, and I'm sorry. It's just that back at the trials . . . I saw something and I couldn't protect someone. I don't want anything like that to happen for real."

Alice smiled slightly. So that's what had been bothering him.

"Well, it's sweet of you to care so much," she began. "But I don't need you to look after me. I can take care of myself."

"I know you can," Jack said, feeling slightly ashamed for overreacting the way he had been.

"Then why are you acting so overprotective?"

"It's just . . . It's so hard to lose someone you care about."

"I don't want to lose anyone I care about either!" Alice said. "And at this rate, I will unless you start looking after yourself a bit more. Please, Jack? For me?"

Jack looked at Alice. Even though it was dark out, he could still see her blue eyes perfectly. So much had happened in so little time. Alice had a lot on her plate and a lot more would be added to it in the coming weeks and months, yet she was concerned about *him*.

"Yeah. Okay. For you," he said.

Although neither of them knew it, Fawn, who laid down nearby, wasn't asleep at all. She was awake and she'd just heard everything they had talked about. Fawn couldn't help but feel a little deflated.

Alice looked up at the gorgeous night sky. The moon was crescent-shaped that night and it seemed to smile at her. Not a happy smile. It was more like a smirk. A knowing and shark-like smirk that seemed familiar somehow.

Jack noticed her staring up at it. "It's a beautiful moon," he acknowledged.

Alice looked over at him for a moment, and then she looked up at the smirking moon again. Jack had no idea what was going through her mind right now, and she didn't want him to either. Something about the moon made her think of the familiar scent she had come to recognize easily.

"Yeah, it really is," she finally said. And as she looked up at that knowing smile the moon seemed to make, the scent of vanilla filled the air.

Wildfire stood near the steering wheel on her Fire Kingdom vehicle. The sun had risen not long ago and she wanted to get a move on as soon as possible. They hadn't been traveling through the desert at a fast enough pace for her liking due to the crew's inexperience in traveling on sand. Not only that, but the vehicles were also not equipped to deal with soft ground and they had gotten stuck several times.

Wildfire held a map up to her face. She was scanning it for a possible alternative route through the Les Landes Desert. During the past four days of traveling through the sandy wasteland, they hadn't come across the Light Spirit once. In fact, there was no trace of her at all.

"Ugh! Where is that stupid spirit already!" she complained. "It's been almost one week since we last encountered her!"

"I told you we shouldn't have come through the desert, Wildfire," Yagatsu said.

"Who do you think you're talking to like that!" she spat. "*I'm* the Force Captain. You don't get to tell me you told me so. And besides, there's no other way the spirit could have gone. I've checked the map and there's no secret route or shortcut to get you through the desert. Their pack animal was injured so they could not have flown over the ocean either."

"Then, in that case, be patient," Master Yagatsu suggested. "This desert is massive and as far as I can tell between our broken compasses, we've been traveling in a relatively straight line. We'll probably find her on the other side of the desert."

"This is ridiculous," Wildfire said. Upon closer inspection of the map, she noticed a strange mark on the southeastern part of the Les Landes Desert.

"Wait a minute." She held the map up to the sun. The light revealed a small star beneath the paper alongside the name: Medina.

"Medina? What's this secret star here?" she asked.

Yagatsu looked at the star and label that was hidden on the map. His eyes grew wide and he looked over at Wildfire. "It's nothing," he said.

"It's nothing? Really?" Wildfire said sarcastically. "What am I? Four years old? I know nothing means something."

"It's not important, Wildfire. We should just continue."

"You have five seconds to tell me what this Medina thing is before I kick you off this vehicle."

Yagatsu exhaled heavily. Even though Wildfire would never win against him one-on-one, he wasn't looking for a fight. He was a retired Admiral for crying out loud.

"Medina is the only civilization in the Les Landes Desert," he said.

"And you didn't think to tell me?" Wildfire complained. "That's important information, dingus. Why is there a secret on the map and why didn't you want to tell me? What? Are you a traitor or something?"

"No. It's like I said. Medina is the only civilization out here. I didn't want us to stop there because you have a habit of destroying things. It's a sacred place that shouldn't be touched and the people who live there are the last of their kind. That's why it's important for the place to stay secret."

"Well, thanks to you, it's not a secret anymore," Wildfire said happily. "Congratulations, we will now be going there."

"What! Wildfire, we can't—"

"We can. And we will. It's the only civilization out here and it's a secret to most people, huh? You couldn't name a better hiding spot for the Light Spirit."

Wildfire marched to the front of the vehicle. "Warriors! Let's move out! We're changing course! From here on out, we'll be heading southeast in the direction of a city!"

The soldiers who were all moving busily about the vehicles finished preparing the engines and slowly, they got on their way.

As the vehicles began trekking through the sand again, Wildfire thought about what Yagatsu had said to her.

"I have a habit of destroying things?" she quoted him. Wildfire smirked. "That could not be more true."

"There it is!" Wesley shouted happily as the city came into view. They awoke early this morning and hadn't traveled for more than an hour.

Upon hearing Wesley, Alice, Jack, and Fawn ran over to him near the front of the vehicle, not more than a few hundred yards ahead was a sand-colored wall, and beyond that, they could make out buildings that worked their way up near the tallest building in the center: the palace.

"Wow," Alice exclaimed.

"We're home, guys!" Prince Urijah said to the other Flame Cats from where he stood at the wheel. "We're home."

"How long have you guys been away?" Jack asked.

"Twenty-three days," Urijah said. "I leave every other month with my crew to collect water. Sometimes, it takes us longer than it should due to unforeseen predicaments out in the wilderness of the desert."

"Wait a minute," Fawn said, turning around. "I thought you said there was nothing safe to drink out here? Like the water I had that made me go all crazy."

"What I said was true. However, there is a certain oasis in the west that produces safe drinking water. It's the only reserve we know of."

"I wish I would have known that sooner," Fawn remarked. Urijah smiled at her.

As the gates to Medina opened up, the sand vehicles strolled through and hundreds of colorful flowers rained down on them. Alice looked up to see people standing on top of the wall dumping baskets of flowers that resembled all colors of the rainbow.

Alice, Jack, Fawn, and Wesley laughed as the flower petals rained down on them like snow. It was very loud as they slowly drove through the streets. People were crowded alongside the streets and on the flat roofs of their sandy homes welcoming them.

"Where do you get these flowers from?" Jack shouted to Urijah using his hands like megaphones.

"We have gardens at the palace. It's where we grow everything!" Urijah yelled back.

The civilians who stood near the sides of the road tossed flowers and bandanas at the vehicles. There were people dancing, holding hands, and tossing hats into the air. It was as if a massive celebration was going on. Everywhere Alice looked, people were celebrating and smiling. She also noticed that every single person was a Flame Cat. All of them had either red, orange, or yellow cat ears and tails.

There were colorful banners strung across the roadway and as they passed under it, someone tossed flower leis at the kids. They caught them and put them on. Everything was so bright and lively. People waved at the newcomers. Alice and Wesley waved back while smiling ear to ear. Jack and Fawn peered at the celebrating streets and crowds of people with wide, shy eyes.

As they made their way to the palace, loud booming noises sounded overhead. Alice looked up to see fireworks exploding in the sky. There were red, blue, yellow, pink, green, and purple fireworks shaped like stars erupting in the blue sky.

Once the vehicles pulled up to the palace, the loud noises of the celebration died down. Although it was still going on, just not this close to the palace.

"What's the party for?" Alice asked.

"It's a welcome-home type thing," Urijah said. "Every time we come back from the oasis, the people throw a huge celebration like this to welcome us home and to embrace good fortune. It's a tradition and it's said to bring good luck with the water crisis."

Alice nodded. It was hard for her to believe that these people were Fire Kingdom, technically speaking. Even if they were now part of their own district and didn't agree with Fire Kingdom customs, it was still where they came from. But they seemed so different. They were good, kind-hearted people. Alice felt bad that she had ever doubted them before.

The kids hopped off the sand vehicle with the other Flame Cats and headed up the sandstone palace steps. At the top, Alice could see a man and woman wearing crowns on their heads.

The Flame Cats that had taken the vehicles away to storage also took Reezu and Mayday with them. They said the animals would be most comfortable inside the garden where it was cooler. Boo stayed with Wesley.

The kids followed Prince Urijah up the sandstone steps to a platform that overlooked much of the city. Standing there waiting, was a man with long, braided white hair who wore a crown on his head. Beside him was a woman with similar white hair that flowed down past her waist who also wore a crown. Both of them had red eyes and red cat-like features. The woman seemed to be the same age as Urijah, around seventeen or so. The man possessed a strange ageless quality to his face. He did seem a couple of years older than the woman, but not much.

"Urijah," the man said as the two of them embraced. "Welcome home, my son."

"Thank you, Father," Urijah said before turning to hug the young woman as well.

"I'm pleased to see that you returned safely, as always. Son, you are a man of good fortune," the woman said to him.

"Only because *you* raised me, Mother," Urijah said.

Alice found it hard to believe that Urijah's parents seemed to be the same age or only slightly older than him. The three of them looked like teenagers, but in actuality, they had to be hundreds of years old.

Suddenly, a door nearby swung open and out came another Flame Cat. He had long white hair that had been put up into a ponytail and also wore a crown atop his head. This Flame Cat looked the youngest out of any of them. In fact, he appeared to not be a day over ten. He was around the same height and of the same stature as Wesley.

"Brother!" the little boy exclaimed as he ran over to Urijah and threw his arms around him in a hug. Urijah swung him around and they laughed happily.

"Alo!" Urijah cheered. "Little brother, how have you been? I hope you've been training in the techniques I showed you before I left."

"I promise I have! Every day, in fact, and I think I'm getting pretty good too!"

"Shall we have a look later this afternoon then?"

"Yes! Maybe we can even start with real shurikens!" Alo asked eagerly.

"I don't know if you're ready for that just yet, little man. But you'll get there in time, just as I did," Urijah encouraged.

Alo smiled. His gaze drifted over to Alice and her companions. He stared at them with wide, curious eyes.

"Brother," he began. "Who are these new friends?"

Urijah turned to look at them as if he had forgotten they were there. "Ah, my apologies!" he said hastily. "I nearly forgot to introduce our guests! Mother, Father, brother, this is Alice, Jack, Fawn, and Wesley. We found them in the desert trying to pass through. We did take them to the trials and it took its course and they have been cleared. I brought them here for rest and safekeeping until they're fit to travel again."

"I'm pleased. You did good, Urijah," the father said. He walked closer to the kids. "Well, young travelers, it's nice to meet you. My name is Mshai. I am the Sultan of Medina. This is my wife Rami. And our sons, Prince Alo and it seems you've already met Prince Urijah quite well then."

"It's nice to meet you as well, your majesties," Alice said with a courtesy. The others smiled and shook hands.

Suddenly, Rami's eyes grew wide as she took a second look at Alice. She walked closer to Alice and held her face in her hands, looking intently at the silver markings.

"My," she whispered in shock. "Child, are you the Sun Spirit?"

"Sun Spirit?" Alice asked, having never heard that term before.

"She means the Light Spirit," Urijah corrected. "It's just that here in Medina, we have our own legend that the Light and Dark Spirit were once the spirits of the sun and moon."

"Well in that case," Alice began. "Yes, I'm the Light Spirit."

"Good heavens, dear," Rami expressed.

"God made an angel," Mshai said with pure shock and honor in his tone.

Alice tightened her lips. She never knew what to do when there was this much attention on her. Although she had had a lot more attention on her now that it had been revealed that she was the Light

Spirit. Before, people didn't seem to care, and Alice was starting to realize that.

"That's so cool!" Prince Alo said cheerfully.

"It is!" Wesley agreed.

"So, where are you guys traveling to?" Mshai asked. "If that's not too personal. If it's classified, then no need to talk about it. I'm just curious."

"Well. right now. we are going to the Etaellace Empire as we have some business there," Jack said, stepping in place of Alice. He didn't want the others revealing too much about their mission, and he wanted to wrap up this conversation quickly.

"I have a question. If you don't mind," he said, changing the subject. Urijah nodded at him.

"This city is made from sand, so why is it that the distractor spell doesn't work here? Is it because all of us are simply immune due to being either Flame Cats, post-trial, or the Light Spirit? Or is it something else?"

"It seems I've forgotten to mention that Jack here is a sharp one," Urijah said, giving Jack a pat on the back. "To answer that question, it would be a mixture of your proposals. This city is no different than any other part of the desert. One would normally be prone to the effects of the distractor spell here as much as anywhere. We are all immune right now like you said. Although a normal person would be quite as lucky. We have a special object that resides here that protects one from the distractor spell. This object is our pride and soul and we must protect it at whatever cost. The object relieves a person of the distractor spell, should one make it to Medina without undergoing the trials, and it also protects the city from harm like storms, wild beasts, and other exotic events.

"Look up," Urijah said. "You can't see it, but there is an invisible barrier that acts like a dome, surrounding all of Medina. That's what the object creates, and that's what protects us all from harm."

Alice looked up at the blue sky. She couldn't see anything that seemed out of the ordinary or at all peculiar. She strained her eyes, but nothing was visible no matter how hard she tried.

"We are going through a bit of a rough patch, right now," Mshai added. "In recent years, the object, which happens to be a stone, its magical properties seem to be depleting. It's as if it's running out of energy. The guards who look after the stone have done everything they can to try and reverse this effect, but nothing they do seems to help. As a result of its energy depleting, the magical barrier is weakening. If we were attacked by anything, a storm, or even a sand serpent, then I'm certain the barrier would not hold."

"I'm curious," Rami said, stepping forward. "If this young girl is a reincarnation of the Sun Spirit, then some of its light is inside of her. I wonder how the stone will be affected by her light."

Mshai's eyes widened. "Yes, that would be most interesting. I had failed to consider that previously," he said. "Alice, would you mind taking a look at the stone then? If your touch can help bring it back to life, we'd be eternally grateful."

Alice wasn't getting at what they were saying. She didn't quite understand this whole Sun Spirit thing and she certainly didn't want these people getting their hopes up that her touch could save their precious stone. However, she did technically owe them since they had saved her and her friends, and it wouldn't hurt to try. She had already decided that if she could potentially help these people, then she would do exactly that.

"I can try," Alice agreed.

"Brilliant!" the Sultan exclaimed, cheerfully.

Prince Urijah led the way down a long and dark tunnel beneath the palace. They had passed many guards and sets of doors to get to where they were now. At the end of the hall was a large metal door with a keypad on it. Urijah punched in a code that was many digits long before a clicking sound unlocked the door and he was able to push it open.

On the other side, was a circular room that had no floor except for a narrow rim that stretched all the way around with a railing beside it. Looking down, the floor below was visible and at the center of it was a tall crystal pedestal with a relatively small orange stone that glowed a soft, dim light.

"There she is," Urijah said, glancing down at the stone. "The Sun Stone, Medina's pride and joy."

Jack, Fawn, and Wesley looked at the small stone. The light emitting off of it was not bright and a gentle humming noise came from it.

As soon as Alice's eyes met the stone, she felt a tingling sensation run down her back. The stone seemed to glow just a tiny bit brighter with her eyes attracted to it. Could the stone sense her light? It was almost as if it was calling to her, desperate for a touch of light.

"Come down this way, Alice," Urijah said as he made his way down a nearby staircase that led to the bottom floor. Alice took her gaze away from the stone and followed him down. The others stayed at the top.

"Isn't she a beaut?" the Prince asked as they approached the Sun Stone.

"It is a very beautiful stone," Alice responded. "How did you manage to score it?"

"It was a gift. So was the crystal podium it's sat atop. Without the crystal, the stone would not be able to hold a charge strong enough to produce the force field. Removing it from the crystal will instantly bring down our magical barrier.

"When I and the other Flame Cats made the aching trek from the Fire Kingdom to this region, we were fighting for survival. We were attacked by wild beasts, we starved, we had no water. I was sure we were not going to make it, but then a strange creature befriended us. He helped get us on our feet, taught us how to survive. He's the one who showed us the water reservoir out west, and he gifted us the Sun Stone to protect our civilization."

"Who was this person?" Alice asked.

"With us, he did not share his name. We simply called him our savior. But he appeared to us in the form of a young man with butterfly wings. After he taught us how to make it on our own, he disappeared. We never heard from him again."

"How strange."

"Alright then," Urijah said. "I want to see how the Sun Stone reacts to your touch, Alice. When you're ready, place your hand on the stone's surface."

Alice took a step forward and held her hand just above the surface of the stone. The light emitting off of it flickered and then glowed just a tad brighter. After a moment, she rested her hand on its surface.

Instantly, the stone grew warm against Alice's skin. She could feel her own energy rising as it glowed brighter and brighter.

"Incredible," Urijah whispered.

"Hey, it's working!" Wesley called from above.

The stone continued to glow brighter and thus, its temperature increased significantly. The Sun Stone now glowed bright enough to light up the entire room as well as the floor above.

"Ah, it's too hot!" Alice exclaimed as she flinched away from the stone. As soon as she let go, the Sun Stone stopped glowing as bright as it had while touching her. It was brighter than it was when they had initially entered the room, but only slightly.

Alice shook her hand out and whipped it on her clothes. The stone had left pink marks on her skin from the heat.

"Are you alright?" Urijah asked.

Alice turned to look at him. "I'm fine, it's just—"

"Your face," Urijah interrupted.

"What?"

"Your face, it's glowing."

Jack peered down at Alice. From where he was, he could see the silver markings on her face glowing a gentle, white hue. Alice brought her hand to her face. Nothing felt different, except she was more energized now.

"So it appears the stone only works to its full potential when in contact with you," Urijah said. "Otherwise, it returns to a state of low health. What about you? Did it affect you in any way, besides the heat?"

"Well actually, I feel like I have more energy," Alice responded. "Almost like it charged me up instead of the other way around."

"Yes, I expected something like that may happen. After all, you and this stone share the same properties of light, the sun. Well then, we best get going now. I have some new things I want to try based on this little experiment. Thank you for your help, dear Alice."

Alice smiled and nodded. Urijah turned and walked back up the stairs to the second floor where they had entered. Jack, Fawn, and Wesley followed him out of the room. Alice stayed behind.

She looked at the stone. If that Sun Stone could protect an entire city from harm, it could easily protect a group of four kids. It would be the key to getting them out of the desert and possibly even saving them from the Fire Kingdom. Alice had originally hoped to ask Urijah and his team to lead them the rest of the way out of the desert, but now that she realized it was apparently a big deal when he left and considering that he just got back, that was no longer an option.

The next phase of their journey was coming. They would have to travel directly through Fire Kingdom territory. This stone could produce an invisible barrier that would protect them from anything, and Alice could keep it fully charged with nothing but her touch.

Wait a minute, Alice thought. Just what was she getting at here? She shouldn't be thinking so selfishly right now, especially after these people just saved her and her friends. But still, it was a tempting thing to think about.

"Alice?" Jack's voice came from above. "Are you ready to leave? We need to go into town to get supplies."

"Oh, uh, yeah." Alice hurried up the stairs and practically flew past Jack and down the hall, away from the room with the stone.

Jack lingered in the doorway a second longer. He was wondering what was going through Alice's head while she was staring at that stone. He had been watching her for several minutes before he spoke up and said something. Just what was she thinking?

"And check out this meat I found!" Fawn exclaimed as she dumped her fifth bag of food on the sandstone ground out on the palace balcony. The kids had just got back from shopping in the town. Medina, strangely, did not have their own form of currency, nor did they use Fire Kingdom money. Instead, the people there traded goods. The kids had nothing on them to trade except for Earth Nation money, which the townspeople expected happily as a fair trade.

Fawn picked up one of her giant steaks and took a bite. "Ah, man," she said. "It's gotten cold."

"Boo-hoo," Wesley said sarcastically from where he sat on the wall of the balcony with his feet dangling off. "Check out what *I* got."

Wesley picked up a staff that sat beside him and he spun it around. Once spun around, the sides of the wooden staff opened up to reveal a blue glider. "I can use this to fly faster and carry more weight than with my suit. It also—"

"No one cares, airhead!" Fawn interrupted as she jumped up to stand on the wall beside him, looking out at the city.

"Take that back, Fawn!"

"I will not."

"I said take it back!"

As the two of them went at it while standing on a railing that had a drop of three or four stories, Alice pushed her way between them from where she stood on the balcony floor, in fear of one of them falling.

"Guys calm down, would you?" she began. "Wesley, that glider is very cool and I'm sure it will come in handy."

Wesley turned to look at Fawn and stuck his tongue out at her. "Ha ha!" He laughed. Fawn growled at him.

"And Fawn," Alice continued. "I'm sure that meat is . . . uh . . . tasty."

Fawn flashed a smile, her sharp corner teeth sparkling. "The meat's good and all," she said. "But it's nothing compared to *these* bad boys." She reached her hands behind her back and pulled out two unique handles from underneath her shirt. With a flick of her wrist, the handles popped open to reveal long and sharp switchblade swords. "With these, the Fire Kingdom won't stand a chance against me."

She started walking along the ledge while swinging the switchblade swords at an imaginary opponent.

"It's pretty interesting how the Flame Cat's system of trading works. Everyone is so nice and accepting too," Alice said cheerfully.

"Yeah sure, I guess," Fawn said half-heartedly.

"What do you mean by that?" Jack asked her.

"Well, it's just that I don't entirely trust these people. I mean independent or not, they are still Fire Kingdom. It's where they're from and it's in their blood. I don't want to stick around for too long, and I don't have any intention of ever giving these people the benefit of the doubt."

"That's pretty cruel of you, Fawn," Jack said. "These people have done nothing but help us."

"I know that!" she exclaimed. "But still, if I had the opportunity to put them in their place and show them just what their kind is to people like us, I wouldn't pass it up."

Alice's eyes sparkled at that. She didn't at all agree with what Fawn was saying about the Flame Cat's, but she had something in mind that needed Fawn's stubborn thinking involved.

"But I will say that I do like their swords . . . a lot," Fawn added holding the blades up again.

"How much did those cost you?" Jack asked.

"My entire share of our money, plus a squirrel."

Jack sighed heavily and shook his head in disappointment. Wesley started laughing at the sight, which drove Fawn nuts.

"Hey!" she shouted at him. "What are you laughing at, balloon boy?"

"Balloon boy?" he shouted back at her.

Before the two of them could go at it again, Alice reached up and wrapped her arms around Fawn's waist in order to pick her up off the wall and stand her back on the balcony floor.

"Alice!" Fawn whined. "What are you doing? He laughed at me!"

Jack walked over and started pulling Wesley off the wall as well. The little boy started kicking and wiggling out of his grasp. "Hey! What are you doing?" he said as Jack stood him back on the ground.

"We should go back inside," Jack said. "The sun will be setting in an hour or so and we need to leave in the morning."

"Right," Alice agreed.

Jack grabbed Wesley by the wrist and started tugging him back inside. "Come on, guys, let's go."

"Actually," Alice started. "I'm going to . . . help Fawn find some fresh warm meat before the markets close. You boys go ahead."

"What?" Jack asked as he stopped in his tracks. "Are you sure?"

"Of course, she's sure!" Fawn exclaimed, smiling ear to ear. "Meat! Meat! Meat!"

"We might as well stock up on some more before we leave," Alice said, thinking quickly. "It won't take long. We'll meet you back inside in a little while."

"Okay then . . ." Jack said as he went back inside with Wesley. The two of them turned a corner and began walking downstairs to the first floor of the palace.

Jack knew that Alice was lying again. Why would she want to go and get meat for Fawn? What was up with that? He knew her better than this, but Alice wasn't the brightest and she had always been very naive so of course she wouldn't be able to come up with a better lie. But why was she lying? What was she trying to cover up? Jack would have called her out on this white lie, but Wesley was right beside him. The ten-year-old was at an impressionable age and he didn't seem to have any parental figures in his life. Jack didn't want to teach him to not trust the Light Spirit, or even worse, to not trust their friends.

It hurt Jack's feelings to know that Alice was lying right to his face. They had grown up together and had always been so close. What was happening? Their friendship, along with Fawn and Wesley, needed to become stronger and more truthful than ever, not the other way around.

In the end, Jack decided he would talk to her about it that evening when she got back. But as he continued to walk down the stairs, he got the strangest and oddest feeling deep inside his chest. And at that moment, he knew that that conversation would never happen because they wouldn't get the chance to have it.

Rosenia, Nickoli, and their daughters sat very quietly inside their prison cells as guards approached from down the hall. They had to pretend like everything was fine. To the guards, tonight should seem like a normal night. Nothing will be left out of place nor should they suspect anything out of the ordinary. If all went as planned, the prisoners would escape and a couple of them would head off to find Alice and deliver a rather important message.

The guards stopped outside of each of the cells and placed the food trays in front, just as they did every night. Afterward, and without a single word, they turned and made their way back down the hall the same way as they had come.

Not more than a second after the guards disappeared around the corner did Nickoli stand up. "Coast is clear. Let's get going!" he said to the others hastily.

At his command, the others began loosening and unscrewing the bolts on their cell doors. Over the past week, each day, they had taken a share of their food and smeared it on all the screws. The acids in the food caused the screws to rust and weaken, allowing them to be taken out easily and without much force. This was only the first phase of Nickoli's escape plan. He wasn't super smart or very strategic, but he had his physical strength and he was quick on his feet in times of stress, and this is where he shined.

Nickoli popped his cell door off first and he quickly began helping Queen Rosenia from the outside. Once her door was off, they worked together to finish up on the cell containing Lizzie, Talula, and Bella Didi while Aurora popped her cell door off on her own with a strong kick.

Once the littlest girls were free, Nickoli started down the hall at a fast pace. "Phase one is complete. We're moving on to phase two, let's go!"

"Wait!" came Aurora's shout from behind. She was crouched outside of Gaia's cell trying to help her open it. "Gaia's door won't open!"

Nickoli doubled back to help them. They had to move fast. Time was of the essence and their targets were getting away. As he approached Gaia's cell door, he said, "Stand back," to the two girls. He also took a step back in order to ram his shoulder into the cell door with all his strength. The door broke off its hinges instantly and nearly collapsed onto Gaia who was frozen with fear. Out of breath, Nickoli turned to face her. "Let's go," he huffed.

The seven of them quickly raced down the hall following the exact path the Fire Kingdom soldiers had taken. Once they turned the corner, the very soldiers who had brought them food moments ago were now walking up a staircase at the end of the hall.

"Ssh ssh, come on," Nickoli said, giving them the go-ahead. The escapees advanced quickly down the dark hall and up the stairs on quiet feet after the soldiers. This was phase two of their plan. They would follow those soldiers out of the dungeon labyrinth. It was a risky plan. They had to be extremely quiet in order not to alert the soldiers to so much as turn around. They also had to stay a good distance behind them for the same reason. But if they stayed too far behind, they'd lose sight of the soldiers and their only hope of finding the way out.

The party followed the Fire Kingdom soldiers without incident for many minutes. They trailed a few yards behind them and lingered in the shadows of the hall to avoid the open areas. Lizzie and Talula kept up with the others surprisingly well. Nickoli had been worried that Bella Didi, still being a toddler, wouldn't understand that it was crucial for them to be quiet and that she might spoil their plan. But Gaia had kept hold of her little sister the entire time, careful to not let her make any noise, which the others were grateful for.

After nearly fifteen minutes of running down halls, upstairs, and down secret passages, the light from the first floor of the palace came into view. They were about to exit the dungeon and begin phase three of their plan, the final step to freedom.

Nickoli waited a solid five minutes after the Fire Kingdom soldiers disappeared behind the doors leading out of the dungeon before giving the go-ahead to the others. He had to be sure that no one was on the other side of those doors or else they'd be caught.

He approached the door alone and creaked it open ever so slightly. Soft, yellow light from inside the palace filled the dark dungeon hall. After peering inside the palace for a moment, Nickoli waved his hand for the others to come.

The seven of them stepped into the palace hall briefly in order to cross it to a storage room on the other side. Nickoli shut the door behind them with a heavy exhale of relief. The hard part was over. They had made it.

Rosenia grabbed a box from the top shelf inside the storage room and began rummaging through it, tossing items of clothing out as she did so. "There's another box on the bottom shelf," she said. "Get that one too."

Aurora grabbed the box which had similar articles of clothing inside as the first box. Every piece of clothing was a deep red color with gold and black accents. There were shirts, pants, skirts, headpieces, and jewelry too. And most importantly, everything was authentic Fire Kingdom clothing captured from real Fire Kingdom citizens.

Nickoli, Rosenia, Gaia, and Aurora completely drenched themselves in the Fire Kingdom clothing and disregarded their green and silver Earth Nation royal robes. Tonight, nobody should recognize them as former military and royalty of the Earth Nation. Instead, they would appear as honorable off-duty Fire Kingdom soldiers.

Once they had dressed, Nickoli began inspecting the others' new outfits carefully. He had to be sure that their disguises were convincing.

Nickoli took a red helmet off his head. "Gaia, you wear this," he said, passing the helmet to her. "You have blue eyes. A rarity for the Fire Kingdom, although not entirely unheard of. If someone sees, them it might raise some suspicion. The helmet should help hide that. The rest of us have brown eyes which is much more common for Fire Kingdom citizens."

Gaia compiled without a word. Now, they should all appear to be Fire Blood Elves instead of Earth Blood Elves. No one should be able to tell the difference. Phase three was nearly in action. There was just one more thing.

"Are you ready?" Nickoli asked, walking over to Talula, Lizzie, and Bella Didi.

"Ready," Lizzie said strongly. She turned, and with the help of Aurora, opened a small window at the back of the room.

It would be nearly impossible to hide Lizzie's green Earth Fairy wings, or Talula's unicorn horn, thus, they couldn't escape through the highly guarded palace. Not to mention they were far too young to pass as Fire Kingdom soldiers. The two of them would be a dead giveaway of their true identities. Instead, they would escape through the small window with Bella Didi and into the nearby forest until the others made it out. They were the only ones who could fit through the window and it was entirely up to them to escape safely on their own.

Nickoli crouched down to hug Lizzie. "I'll see you in the forest in ten minutes. If we don't make it by then, assume the worst and run far away without looking back. Find someone you can trust and deliver the message to Alice on your own with them. You can do it."

"Of course, I could do it," Lizzie said. "But I won't have to, because you're going to meet me in ten minutes. I just know it, Daddy."

Nickoli smiled and slowly let go of her. Once Rosenia, Aurora, and Gaia had said goodbye to Talula and Bella Didi, the three little girls slipped out of the window onto the grass below. Nickoli watched them run off through the night until they reached the forest. They had made it, and now it was his turn.

Rosenia closed the window and followed Nickoli to the door. He looked from her, to Aurora, and then to Gaia. All of them held determined expressions on their faces.

"Remember," he began. "If anyone says anything, just smile and nod."

"Right," Rosenia agreed.

"Alright then, let's roll," Nickoli opened the door and stepped out into the brightly lit hall without hesitation. Queen Rosenia, Aurora, and Gaia followed him a step or two behind. The interior of the palace had changed much since they'd last seen it. Portions of the floor and walls were blackened from the fire on the day of the invasion. There were storage boxes lining the halls, and many Fire Kingdom possessions were everywhere to be seen.

The foursome made their way onto one of the main hallways without incident. They hadn't seen any Fire Kingdom soldiers yet, but they could hear them everywhere. At times, Nickoli had to direct them down separate passageways that only they knew about in order to avoid being seen. The hall they were currently trekking through was filled with portraits of all the kings and queens that had reigned over the Earth Nation since its founding. Most of the paintings had been thrown off the walls or even had burn marks, resulting from the Fire Kingdom's hateful victory over the land of Earth.

At the hall's end, Rosenia suddenly stopped dead in her tracks. On the floor near her feet was a portrait of one king that she had some particular interest in. The sides of the painting were blackened and torn and there were a few rips in the center, but the King's face remained intact.

Rosenia's eyes grew tired as she witnessed the utmost disrespect that the Fire Kingdom had bestowed upon her husband's portrait. King Aelous' hair in the portrait wasn't as long as Rosenia had been used to because this had been painted in his younger days, likely when he was first crowned king. A tear streamed down her cheek as she remembered her beloved husband.

"Mom!" came Aurora's urgent whisper from up ahead. Rosenia snapped her head up to look at the others who were a few feet ahead of her. Past them, she could make out a Fire Kingdom soldier making his way toward them with a purposeful stride.

Rosenia quickly caught up to the others and the four of them resumed a fast pace down the hall. As the soldier gradually made his way toward them, Nickoli noticed he wore a fancier uniform than some of the other soldiers he had seen previously. This guy had to be ranked higher up in the regiment.

Just when Nickoli thought they'd be able to walk right past the soldier without interacting, the Fire Blood Elf came to a halt right in front of the escapees, blocking the path.

Rosenia, Aurora, and Nickoli all froze. A small mutter came from Gaia's lips almost like a cry for help. Luckily for her, the soldier didn't seem to hear it. For a moment, the group stared blankly at the Fire Kingdom official and he stared back at them without saying a word.

After what seemed like an eternity of silence, the soldier spoke. "Did the Force Captain send for you?" he asked briskly.

Upon instinct, Nickoli opened his mouth to respond, but then quickly shut it. Instead, he smiled tightly and nodded vigorously. The others joined him with more smiles and nods.

The soldier stared at them for a moment longer, as if seizing them up. "Well then," he began. "Get your uniforms on and meet him by the main entrance for the night patrol." The soldier saluted a Fire Kingdom-style salute that Nickoli was not familiar with, and then marched off.

The escapees stood in place for a few seconds longer until they could no longer hear the Fire Blood Elf's footsteps. Once the coast was clear, the group let out a relieved sigh.

"That was close," Aurora remarked.

"You made it!" Lizzie shouted from behind a bush as Nickoli, Rosenia, Aurora, and Gaia all poured into the forest.

"Ssh!" Nickoli said as he grabbed her hand so they could continue running. Talula and Bell Didi joined the group as well. "We're not out of the woods just yet," Nickoli acknowledged.

"But we made it out of the palace!" Lizzie mentioned. "What are we going to do now?"

"First, we'll gather supplies and determine some form of transportation. It's a long way to the Etaellaca Empire," Nickoli said. "And then we'll head off to find Alice and deliver the message . . . before it's too late."

Silence followed Nickoli's remark. They all knew the urgency and importance of this message, even the little ones. It was adamant that they reached Alice before she reached a certain someone. They were vying on luck and strategy while their opponent had the upper hand. It was a long shot, but Nickoli would take any chance he got in order to protect his daughter from her own reckless actions. In the end, he ran off into the night only hoping that he'd reach Alice before her pursuer.

Wildfire jumped down from her lookout post and landed lightly on the top of the vehicle near the steering wheel. The rest of the vehicles from her platoon pulled up beside her.

A smirk began to spread across her face as she thought of the grand scheme she was about to enact. This new plan would not only give her a change of pace from chasing her prey, but it would also lure that prey straight to her. It was a big risk, but who was she kidding? This whole thing had been risky since the very beginning. The Light Spirit had toyed enough with her and now Wildfire would be turning the tables on her and strike where it would hurt the most.

Wildfire peered over her shoulder to view the sun that was ever so slightly beginning to set over the endless array of sand. It was time. She turned back around to set her sights on the massive wall in front of her with closed gates. It was none other than the wall of Medina, and somewhere behind it had to be her target.

Wildfire's smirk that she wore on her face grew wider. She was thinking of the Light Spirit's lovely group of friends and how she was going to steal the life of one of them tonight. She couldn't wait to see the look of fear on the Light Spirit's face when it happened.

It was like Wildfire could see it already, and a dark chuckle suddenly escaped her lips.

CHAPTER NINE

Fallout

Jack stood in front of a window on the second floor of the palace of Medina. He gently stared out at the endless row of markets and shops that were beginning to close up for the day. The sun had just begun its descent and the sky was gradually fading into a deep warm hue.

Jack's eyes were wide with concern. He hoped Alice would be back soon so he could speak with her. It wasn't like her to lie to him like this, and what about Fawn? She had left with Alice willingly. Was she a part of this scheme too? He had no way of telling just yet, but he was determined to find out. And still, Jack had yet to shake a particular feeling of despair that made it seem as though this conversation that he desperately wanted to have would never happen. It made his insides churn and he nearly felt sick with apprehension.

Wesley, who sat at a table eating pie next to Jack, noticed his disheartened expression. "Want some pie?" he asked, holding a piece up on his fork for Jack to see. "It might cheer you up!"

"No thanks," Jack said as he took a seat at the table.

"I think I know what's bothering you," Wesley said quietly. The two of them sat there for several silent moments, looking out the window before Wesley finally spoke again. "You like her. Don't you?"

"Huh?" Jack asked, a little caught off guard.

"Alice. You must like her," Wesley said with the slightest hint of disappointment.

"And what might give that away?"

"The way you look at her, the way you're always concerned about her. I mean, I understand why. She's pretty, and fun to hang out with, *and* she's the Light Spirit."

"Actually," Jack began, flashing a smile. "I think you're the one with the crush, Wesley. Considering how you're talking about her."

"What?" Wesley exclaimed with red cheeks. "No! Of course not! Alice is great and everything, but girls are . . . gross!"

"Relax, I was only teasing." Jack relaxed slightly and even gave a small laugh. "Besides, Alice is too old for you anyhow."

Wesley averted his eyes from Jack and rested his head on his hand, looking disheartened. Jack opened his mouth to say something reassuring, but out of the corner of his eye, a flash of light outside the window caught his attention.

Down past the markets, Jack could make out the closed gates that gave access to Medina. The commotion had gathered around the gates with many Flame Cats rushing up to it. People began lifting wooden beams and putting them up against the gates as some sort of reinforcement. Several rumbling noises came from that direction followed by sudden surges of light all happening on the outside of the gates.

"What's going on out there?" Wesley asked as he too noticed the racket happening outside.

"I-I don't know," Jack replied at a loss for words.

Before they could say anything else, the loudest roaring sound of all and the brightest surge of light yet flashed near the wall. And not a second later did the gates come crumbling down.

Jack practically flew out of his seat and knocked his chair over. Wesley let out a sudden gasp and clawed at the window with his hands in disbelief.

The crashing of the gates created a massive disturbance on the sandy ground and the air near that area was filled with dust hiding the perpetrators from view. But after a few moments, the dust began to settle and Jack was horrified to see dozens of Fire Kingdom vehicles positioned in the gaping hole in the wall where the gates once stood just seconds ago. *They were being attacked.*

At that moment, Prince Urijah flung open a door into the room, out of breath and looking even paler than his already fair complexion.

"Urijah!" Jack shouted. "What's happening out there!"

It took Urijah a second or two to collect himself, but after a brief hesitation, he spoke.

"You said . . ." He paused to take another breath. "You said a Fire Kingdom Force Captain who was a young girl has been chasing you since you left home, correct?"

Jack nodded.

"Well," Urijah began. "She's out there right now, and she's brought her entire army with her."

"This can't be happening!" Jack cried. "That girl is relentless! She won't let up until she captures Alice!"

"You kids need to leave right away," Urijah said. "You must get away while you still can. Our healers inspected your bird. His injured wing is nearly healed and he should be able to fly you out of here without fail. Fly directly south until you reach Fire Kingdom territory. Don't stop flying unless you must. There are dangerous things out there in the desert. Wild beast, extreme weather, you name it, and you'll encounter it. We'll hold them off as long as we can. Please take the Light Spirit and escape!"

Jack and Wesley both stood completely still. The pressure was getting to them now.

"What are you still doing here!" Urijah asked in disbelief. "Leave! Now!"

Jack felt a lump grow in his throat. "We can't because . . . because I don't know where Alice is."

The look of shock on Urijah's face was something Jack could not describe in words. It was a mixture of fear, disappointment, sorrow, and aggression.

"What do you mean you don't know where the Light Spirit is!" he shouted. "She's your friend! She's important! *We* need her! *The world* needs her!"

"*I need her!*" Jack shouted back angrily. He had heard those things enough times already. Alice is the Light Spirit. Alice needs to save the world. All of Infinity needs Alice. Blah blah blah. What about him? What about *her?* Didn't anyone care what *they* wanted? Or what was best for them? Jack might've been thinking selfishly right then, but he didn't care. Light Spirit or not, Alice was his best friend. They had grown up together and he would do *anything* to protect her. And this moment was no exception.

"I . . . need her," Jack said again, more quietly this time.

"Then go save her!" Urijah shouted back.

At that instant, Jack immediately took off. He charged through the doors Urijah had entered and ran through the palace toward the nearest exit.

Wesley stood still in the room with Urijah. "Dude . . ." he whispered in shock, still thinking about the way Jack talked about Alice.

"Wesley!" came Jack's distant call from somewhere down the hall. "I'm assuming you're behind me!"

Wesley snatched his wooden glider staff and took off down the hall after Jack. He ran for a few steps, jumped, and then opened his glider suit so he could fly through the open hallway until he caught up with Jack.

It wasn't long before the two of them reached the exit and bulldozed through the front doors out into the middle of the city. Many buildings near the gates had already been set ablaze and Fire Kingdom soldiers poured into Medina from the outside.

Medina didn't have an official army. Instead, those who were able to fight would fight while the women and children rushed to whatever safety they could find.

Jack ran out into the midst of the onslaught. He looked from right to left, behind him, and back again, but he couldn't see Alice or Fawn anywhere. Time was running out. They had to find Alice before the Fire Kingdom did.

"Wesley," Jack began. "Fly around above and try to spot Alice and Fawn. If you find them before I do, lead them back to the safety of the palace. Whatever you do, *don't* land. Stay in the air as long as possible. Force Captain Wildfire might be after the Light Spirit, but that doesn't mean she won't come after us too."

"Got it!" Wesley tossed Jack his glider staff to carry and started running down an aisle between shops until he got enough momentum to open his glider suit again and fly high into the sky. Jack quickly lost sight of him.

The air was beginning to fill with smoke and the sky was quickly darkening to a deep red color. It wouldn't be long until nightfall. Jack took one last look around the area nearest to him before running off deeper into the city in search of Alice.

Wildfire stormed through the wide streets of Medina, easily blasting away anyone who came within reach of her. Fighting these Flame Cats would be mere child's play. And besides, she wasn't there to toy around with them. She had already set her sights on the main event: the Light Spirit. Wildfire might have to fight her in order to get to her friends. Whatever the case, she wouldn't be leaving here today without someone captive.

As Wildfire continued down the aisle of markets, a sharp and shiny object suddenly flew past just in front of her face. It barely missed her skin, but it did manage to slice a piece of her hair off. Turning toward the direction where the object had come from, Wildfire could see a small boy crouching along the side of the building. He hastily gathered more shurikens from his belt to throw at Wildfire.

Shurikens? Really? What would those do against a powerful fire magic user such as Wildfire? She stormed right for the boy as he launched shurikens at her.

"Ugh, you brat," Wildfire didn't want to waste any time playing around, but she might as well tidy up the area of pests such as this kid.

Wildfire was closing in on him and he desperately reached for another shuriken when suddenly, "Alo! No!" shouted a voice from the left.

Prince Urijah came running in order to protect his brother, but it was too late. Wildfire had already unleashed a massive blast of fire right at Prince Alo, striking him almost head-on.

The blast knocked Alo back several yards, sending him crashing into the wall of a building. Wildfire was satisfied. He wouldn't be getting up from that one any time soon. After all, a single bruise was sometimes enough to kill a cat person.

Wildfire whipped around and continued through the city while Prince Urijah ran to his helpless younger brother. She wondered where the Light Spirit might've been hiding. Perhaps, she should take to the high ground and get a better look from up there. Whatever the case, it was a small city. There were only so many places she could be.

"Come out, Light Spirit!" Wildfire shouted. "These little boys can't save you."

Jack whipped around a corner leading out of a row of markets and found himself back near the palace. Although he was on a different side of it than the main entrance. He had searched through the market area thoroughly, but there was no sign of Fawn nor Alice. He only hoped that Wesley would have better luck.

As if on cue, Jack spotted something strange coming out of one of the windows near the top of the palace. Upon closer inspection, he recognized Fawn hastily climbing down the outside of the palace wall with a bag over her shoulder. What in Infinity was she doing? Jack raced to the palace and by the time he got there, Fawn had descended from her climb down, unscathed.

"Fawn!" he yelled.

She turned around and seemed startled to see him there. "What!"

"Where have you been! And where's Alice? It doesn't seem like you care at all, but we're in a predicament and we have to get out of here *now!*"

"Ease up, would you?" Fawn complained. "Alice is fine. She's waiting for me up on the roof."

From the brown satchel that Fawn wore around her shoulder, Jack could see a slight glow coming out of it. Upon realization that Jack had noticed the glow, Fawn moved the bag to hide it behind her back.

"What's in that satchel?" Jack pressed.

"Uh, it's nothing important."

Jack exhaled heavily. He was fuming. Whatever game Alice and Fawn were playing, he had had enough of. He was going to put an end to this here and now. He grabbed Fawn by her shirt and dragged her over to an area that led up to the palace roof.

Wesley gilded near some taller buildings around one side of the palace. He hadn't seen Alice, Fawn, or Jack nor did he see any sign that they were nearby. In fact, he had begun to feel incredibly lonely.

With the heavy amount of smoke and fire in the air in addition to the heat, Wesley grew tired quite rapidly. He glided over to a nearby balcony and crouched on its railing in order to catch his breath. Looking down, he could see that most of the structures were on fire and several buildings near the front had completely collapsed.

It was getting late by the second. Just when Wesley jumped to start flying around again, a sudden blast of fire knocked him out of the sky. He fell a few feet but was able to catch himself on the railing. Looking up, Wesley was terrified to see a Fire Kingdom soldier jump down from the roof of the building to land on the balcony alongside him.

Except this wasn't any Fire Kingdom soldier. It was Force Captain Wildfire Amulet.

Alice slowly approached the edge of the palace rooftop. She looked out at the city below her and a strong case of deja vu washed over her. What she saw in Medina was the exact same thing she saw in Elkmire the day they had left. Buildings, homes, shops, and temples were crumbling down. Everything was on fire. People were screaming and running from the Fire Kingdom.

Alice felt her eyes swell up with tears. How could she let this happen? She knew exactly what it felt like to have her home destroyed by the Fire Kingdom, so why did she decide to turn around and have it done to these innocent people? *What was wrong with her?*

Fire and smoke began to cloud her view of the city. There was no going back now. She had done this. Tears streamed down her already damp cheeks. And for the first time, Alice felt the deep and sickening feeling of regret.

"Alice," came a familiar soft and husky voice from behind her. She turned around and instantly locked eyes with Jack. More tears poured out of her eyes when she looked into his stern and angry glare. He was upset with her, and he had every right to be. Fawn, on the other hand, displayed an unreadable and uncertain expression.

"Jack," Alice whispered hoarsely. "I'm sorry. I'm so sorry. It's my fault. It's all my fault."

"No, it's not," Jack said, to Alice's surprise. "You don't have to blame yourself for this. You're not the one who did this."

"I did," she cried. It was hard to hear him try and comfort her when he didn't even know the truth of the matter. "It's my fault. I did this. I hurt . . . *everybody*."

"What? What are you talking about?"

"The Sun Stone's barrier was already weak," she began. "But it still would've held the gates up, and the Fire Kingdom wouldn't have gotten in."

"Alice . . ." Jack said quietly, desperately hoping this wasn't going where he thought it was. "What are you saying?"

"The barrier fell. It fell because I took the Sun Stone! I took it so we could use it to protect ourselves! I made Fawn steal it! And then the barrier fell and the Fire Kingdom broke through! I knew this would happen but I still did it! Jack! Jack, why did I still do it? Please tell me why . . . why did I hurt all of those people?"

Jack's mouth dropped suddenly. He knew it was bad. But he didn't think it was this bad. He turned and snatched the satchel from Fawn's shoulder, aggressively. He opened the flap, and sure enough, inside was the Flame Cat's prized Sun Stone. It glowed a gentle hue.

Jack turned around and wiped his hands down his face. He suppressed the wicked and angry laugh that grew inside his throat. This was too much for him. They had been through so much already, but things had never been this bad. This time, it wasn't the Fire Kingdom's fault, and that's what angered him.

Jack turned back around to look at Alice. As soon as she caught a glimpse of his eyes, she collapsed to her knees. She had never seen Jack look this upset before, nor did she ever expect to. It pained her more than her own sins, to see him like that.

The fire that rained on the city below them was casting sun-colored rays of light into Jack's pupils as if demonstrating the rage of his own fire burning inside him.

Wesley hastily climbed back over the balcony railing after almost being completely flung off by Wildfire. She stocked toward him with long, powerful strides as he backed away.

"Where are your friends? Care to share, little boy?" she snickered. Wesley backed further away, toward the door leading into the building.

"Are we not talking today?" Wildfire teased. "Well, that's okay. If I can't find one of the others to take . . . then I'll just have you!"

She somersaulted into a fire blast aimed right for Wesley, but he was able to dodge it by using sky magic to jump to a height not physically possible for a normal person.

He went inside the building and slammed the door behind him. He had to think fast if he hoped to get out of this. Looking to his right, there was a window that was nothing more than a square hole in the sandstone wall, but it would work perfectly as an escape.

With a single fireless kick, Wildfire broke the door down and stormed into the room. Wesley immediately ran for the window. Outside of it, he could see the palace just a few buildings away. Standing on top of the palace roof, to his surprise and relief, he could see Jack, Fawn, and Alice. They huddled close together and almost seemed to be arguing. If Wesley could get to them, or even get their attention, he'd be saved.

Jack approached Alice with slow, gentle steps. She sat on her knees looking up at him with wide and teary eyes. He met her on the ground and wrapped his arms around her in a soft hug. Alice was instantly taken aback. She was expecting him to be furious with her, but instead, he hugged her.

The anger that filled Jack a few moments ago had vanished. He rested his head on Alice's shoulder and breathed in her sweet scent. She smelled like sugar.

"I'm sorry too," he whispered.

Alice sat there for a moment in a daze. Why was he saying this? What in Infinity did Jack have to apologize for? This was all her fault. He didn't have anything to do with this. This was all Alice's plan, to have Fawn steal the Sun Stone to use for themselves. Jack was the innocent one here. What could he be sorry for?

"I'm sorry that I got so angry with you," he said. It was at that moment that Alice realized what Jack meant. He wasn't apologizing because he did something wrong. He was apologizing because that's the kind of person he was. He was gentle, kind, and caring. It didn't matter what Alice did, as long as she understood that her actions were wrong. Jack would be there for her. He would help her clean up her mess and learn from her mistakes. What did Alice ever do to deserve someone like that in her life?

Alice returned the hug and wrapped her arms tightly around Jack, breathing in his rose-like scent. She was trying not to cry anymore, but she was hurting. It hurt that she had betrayed Jack the way she did. It hurt that she had done something so horrible. And more than anything, it almost hurt to love someone so much.

"Don't be," she said. "Don't be sorry, Jack. *I'm* sorry. I didn't mean to hurt you, or anyone. I just wanted us to be safe on the rest of our journey. I didn't mean to cause any harm."

"I know you didn't," he comforted. "And I should have been there for you more so you wouldn't feel so alone to make a decision on your own like that. From now on, we can't do things like this, okay? We have to talk to each other. No more secrets."

Jack pulled away from Alice but kept his hands on her shoulders firmly. He looked her in the eye in order to be sure that what he was about to say got through to her.

"You have to promise me that you won't do anything like this ever again," he pleaded.

"Yeah," Alice said, wiping a tear from her eye. "I promise." Jack leaned in and hugged her again, and she hugged him back. The two of them seemed to get lost in each other's sadness and regret. They stayed there like that for a long while.

Meanwhile, right behind them, Fawn looked on with wide and sad eyes. It shocked her to hear them speak to each other like that. As the wind filled with embers blew through her hair, Fawn felt a lump rise in her throat, and sorrow filled her heart.

In an instant, Wesley launched himself out of the window and brought his wrists to the clips on his chest to open his glider suit. Just when he thought he was home-free, a hand grabbed his ankle and yanked him back inside.

Wesley was flung to the opposite side of the room and he crashed through a table before landing in a corner. No amount of evasive maneuvering could save him now. He had been cornered. The fear inside his chest grew tremendously as he watched Wildfire approach him with a wicked grin across her face.

She gathered her strength to launch a blast of fire right at Wesley, and the little boy only put his hands in front of his face to try and protect himself. The last thing Wesley saw before the fire blast hit him was his friends standing on the palace rooftop just a little way away outside the window. They were so close, and yet they had no idea what was happening to him. Wesley tried to reach out for them in a last-ditch effort, but then it all went black.

Alice explained to Jack how she stole the Sun Sone and why she had Fawn execute the plan. Fawn was quick, agile, and she had experience in this sort of thing so if anyone would have success, it would be her. Alice also talked about how she knew Fawn would agree to do it because she was quite practical, easy to reason with, and she wasn't particularly fond of the Flame Cats. Alice could keep the Sun Stone charged by staying in contact with it as long as she could bear the heat radiating off of it. That way, a barrier would protect them from the Fire Kingdom and any other threats for the rest of their journey.

Jack understood that it was a solid plan, but it wasn't justifiable. "I can't forgive you for what you've allowed to happen," he began. "But I won't harp on it any longer. We need to get out of here."

"We can't leave without doing something!" Alice argued. "These people got their home destroyed trying to protect us. If we . . . if *I* had never come here in the first place, this would have never happened."

"Then let's leave!" Fawn shouted. "Wildfire will leave Medina to follow us!"

"Fawn is right," Jack said. "We're running out of time. Let's get out of here while we still can."

Fawn and Jack started walking away back toward the ladder that led down from the roof. Alice lingered behind a moment longer. She took one last look at the burning city.

"Wait a minute," she said in shock.

"What is it?" Jack asked.

"The Fire Kingdom. They're *retreating.*"

"What!" Jack and Fawn rushed back over to the ledge. Down below, Fire Kingdom soldiers ran back toward the fallen gates and boarded their vehicles in a hurry.

"I don't understand," Fawn whispered. "They didn't find the Light Spirit and the Flame Cats were no match for them in battle, so why are they leaving?"

"What if . . ." Jack began hesitantly. "What if they didn't come here for the Light Spirit."

"What else could they possibly want?" Alice asked. "That's what they've been after this whole time!"

"Hold on," Fawn said with a glimmer of fear behind her eyes. "*Where is Wesley?*"

"I was with him up until a little while ago," Jack mentioned. He still held onto Wesley's new glider staff. "I had us split up in hopes of finding you guys sooner. Although, I thought he would have spotted us by now."

"We need to find him right away!" Fawn expressed. "What if he's in trouble? Or what if he's hurt all alone out there? Jack, you should have never left him—"

Fawn's worrisome shouting became muffled as Alice stepped closer to the ledge. In the distance, near the fallen gates, she could make out Force Captain Wildfire striding toward the vehicles. At Wildfire's feet, she dragged the body of a small child by his collar.

"You guys," Alice said nearly too quietly to be heard over the others' shouting. "You need to come see this."

"One second!" Fawn yelled to Alice in between her argument with Jack.

"No, not one second! Now!" In response to Alice's sudden change in her tone of voice, Jack and Fawn hurried over to the ledge to stand beside her.

"Oh no," Jack cried silently at the view before him.

"It can't be," Fawn's voice cracked.

As Wildfire boarded her vehicle, she brought the unconscious boy along with her. But it wasn't just any young boy.

It was Wesley.

In an instant, Alice leaped off the palace rooftop and slid down the side of it until she hit the ground. Fawn and Jack reached after her, and almost went overboard as well, but they managed to catch their balance.

Once on the ground, Alice wasted no time in getting up and running toward the gates as fast as her legs could carry her. The air was hot and heavy. The wind was filled with smoke and carried embers with it. Alice quickly lost her breath, but she didn't slow until she stood upon the rubble of the gates.

Stretched out before her was the endless field of sand that made up the desert. She had gotten there pretty quickly, but she was still too late. All of the Fire Kingdom vehicles had already taken off.

The dust that the vehicles had stirred up in their hasty getaway was beginning to settle.

Jack was right. This time, the Fire Kingdom wasn't after her. They had changed up their strategy and went for a new target. It was the perfect plan really. This way, they'd be luring Alice in by keeping a hostage. The Fire Kingdom had taken the high ground in this fight and now they had the leverage that they needed to overpower their opponents.

Alice stood atop the fallen gates of Medina as she watched the Fire Kingdom vehicles get further and further away. She felt the hope of ever getting Wesley back shrink as the vehicles disappeared from sight completely. They had won. Was it really over already?

A sudden "Ka-kaa!" followed by a thump behind Alice startled her. She turned to see her ginormous bird Reezu with Fawn and Mayday in the saddle and Jack holding the reins. Reezu's wing was nearly fully healed and he was ready to get back in the air.

"Come on," Jack said as he reached down to help Alice onto Reezu. "We're not losing anyone out here."

As soon as Alice boarded the bird, Reezu took to the sky, flying fast in the direction Jack angled the reins. It was like the bird's wing had healed stronger than it was before, and he sliced through the air unchangeably.

As the Fire Kingdom vehicles came into view up ahead, Jack hopped down into the saddle beside Alice and Fawn.

"Alice, take the Sun Stone and keep it in your hands. We'll need its protective barrier around us if we hope to retrieve Wesley."

"Got it." Alice took the satchel from Fawn and reached in to keep her left hand firmly planted on the stone's surface. After a moment, the stone began to quickly heat up just as it did before, especially compared to its already warm temperature.

"I'm going to lower Reezu as close to the vehicles as I can get," Jack said. "With the invisible barrier around us, we should be able to get as close as we need to. Once I give the signal, the two of you will leap down onto the vehicle and do your best to rescue Wesley.

"Remember, the Sun Stone's barrier is going to stay around Alice, so as she moves, so does the barrier. Meaning that once the two of you leap off, Reezu and I will be unprotected. I'll fall back to stay out of the line of fire and try my best to swoop in as close as I can get once we're ready to take off. Because of this, once you're down there, you'll be relying on Wesley to fly you out. Can you do it?"

Fawn took in a deep breath. "Easy-peasy." She reached behind her back and pulled out her new switch-blade swords and flicked them open.

"Take this," Jack said as he tossed Alice Wesley's staff. "Wesley will be able to carry you guys in flight easier with this if need be. Also, try to keep in mind that we're not looking for a fight. Don't attack, just dodge and evade. Your main priority is to execute a rescue mission. We'll save fighting the Fire Kingdom for another day. Are we ready?"

"Ready," Alice affirmed.

Jack jumped back up to Reezu's head and took the reins once more. "Operation Take Wesley Back is officially in action. Good luck out there, guys. Let's go get him."

With Jack in control, Reezu began flying even faster than his already quick pace. The Fire Kingdom vehicles were only a stone's throw ahead of them. Reezu tucked his wings and dove down.

In response, the Fire Kingdom soldiers shot fireball after fireball at them, but each one was deflected away. A puzzled look crossed the soldiers' faces. They shot more fireballs and loaded cannons on the back of their vehicles. But every attack seemed to bounce off an invisible barrier and reflect back down on the Fire Kingdom themselves.

After realizing that their attacks were doing more harm to themselves than to their opponents, the soldiers stopped launching attacks altogether upon their Force Captain's command.

Jack eased Reezu into a dive that positioned them just above Force Captain Wildfire's vehicle. It was the perfect position for Fawn and Alice to jump down onto the moving vehicle.

Jack took one last look around to assume which escape route he would take once Alice left with the barrier. "Go! Now!" he shouted.

Alice and Fawn leaped over the side of the saddle and landed on the metal surface of the vehicle. Out of the corner of her eye, Alice saw Jack and Reezu take to the sky unscathed.

With her blades stretched out, Fawn immediately ran toward Wildfire who stood not more than ten feet in front of them.

"I'll distract her! You find Wesley!" she yelled as she passed Alice.

Alice took in her surroundings. There weren't that many soldiers on this particular vehicle. One held onto the steering wheel, and two propelled the engines at the back, positions they obviously could not leave. Near the front, just underneath the lookout post, was a small structure that led to the basement. That had to be where Wesley was.

Alice took off in that direction. She released her hold on the Sun Stone because now, the entire vehicle was within the barrier and it wouldn't do them any good. It also made her feel more secure to have her other hand handy.

She raced past Wildfire and Fawn who were locked in a battle of their own. Alice wanted to help Fawn, but she knew that her friend could handle herself. Alice also felt she might just get in the way and would ruin her one chance to find Wesley.

A moment before Alice reached the structure, a Fire Kingdom soldier jumped down from the lookout post to block the way. She hadn't even realized there was a soldier up there. The soldier was an older man who was a Fire Blood Elf with long black hair. He seemed familiar somehow and Alice realized she must have seen him with Wildfire previously.

The man instantly punched a flame aimed right for her. She dodged it by swooping her chest low underneath it in order to let the fire soar above her head. Alice ran around the side of him in an attempt to get away, but another blast of fire was shot for her. She quickly jumped above it. This guy was strong, and he probably had tons of experience in not only fire magic, but also in combat. There was no way Alice could beat him. But there was something about him that did pique her interest.

The soldier was old. Probably in his late fifties. After only a few seconds of dodging his attacks, she noticed that he wasn't nearly as quick on his feet as she was. Right now, being quick and agile was her only card to play.

Alice ran around the man in circles desperately trying to get him to trip over his feet so she would have a chance to get away. He could just barely keep track of Alice with his eyes and launched fire at her consistently.

She whipped around to turn the other way when suddenly an unexpected blast of fire came right for her. The soldier had noticed Alice was using a repetitive move to go around him, and he used that to predict which way she would turn next. Alice might've been quicker than him, but he had outsmarted her.

Thinking quickly, Alice spun Wesley's staff that she still had around in circles in front of her face like a baton. The air accumulated around the staff propelled the fire blast right back at the man, catching him off-guard. In the extra second he took to diminish the flames, Alice ran straight for the structure leading to the indoor section of the vehicle.

Right before she would have grabbed hold of the doorknob, a hand grabbed the strap of her satchel around her shoulder, yanking her to the ground. The soldier had recovered from her attempt to distract him after all.

The satchel carrying the Sun Stone fell from Alice's shoulder and the stone tumbled out of it, rolling right up to Wildfire, a few feet away. Alice jumped up and tried to retrieve the satchel and stone but it was too late. Wildfire had stopped toying with Fawn in order to pick the items up.

"Give that back!" Fawn shouted.

"Do you even know what this is!" Wildfire hissed angrily as she held the stone. "This is a Sun Stone, a relic originating from the Fire Kingdom! You've stolen from us! How *dare* you!"

"That must've been how they were dodging our attacks earlier," the male soldier began, walking toward Wildfire. "If that girl is the Light Spirit, her touch alone will activate it, even if the sun isn't out right now."

The sun? That was it! That's what charges the Sun Stone! It made total sense. Why hadn't the Flame Cats thought of that earlier? The reason why the barrier around Medina had weakened was that the Sun Stone hadn't been exposed to sunlight in so long. It needed to be recharged. The only thing that had kept it going was the crystal podium.

The male soldier and Wildfire were distracted by the stone. Now was Alice's chance. She could see Fawn a few feet away motioning for her to go.

Alice quietly and quickly opened the door to the indoor portion of the vehicle. Inside was a staircase leading down to the storage and resting cabins. Seated at the top of the staircase was a very nervous and distraught Wesley. His feet and hands were bound and a gag filled his mouth. He had a scrape across his forehead and a few minor injuries, but besides that, he seemed to be fine.

Wesley's eyes widened when he saw Alice. She pulled the gag out of his mouth. "Alice!" he cheered. "You came for me!"

"Of course, we did," she said as she began undoing his bounds. "We're a team, and teams stick together! We're not leaving anyone behind, not ever!"

Wesley smiled a soft smile. "How are we going to get out of here? Do you have a plan? The Fire Kingdom is out there. I can hear them still!"

"Jack is waiting for us with Reezu. That's our escape plan. But we still have to make it off this vehicle. Here." Alice finished untying Wesley and handed him the staff.

"My staff!"

"Now get ready to fly with that thing. Will go when I say."

Alice pressed her ear up against the door to hear what was going on outside. She could hear Fawn still fighting with Wildfire and the other soldier.

"Go find the Light Spirit already!" Wildfire yelled. "And watch out for that flying boy. He's a slippery one!"

Heavy footsteps that Alice assumed belonged to the man quickly made their way toward them.

"Wait . . ." Alice began.

The footsteps quickened their pace.

"Wait . . ."

They got louder.

"Get ready,"

He was right outside the door.

"Now!" Alice and Wesley flung the door open together and it slammed right into the man, knocking him over. They ran past him but out of nowhere, Wildfire appeared and snatched Wesley.

"You're not going anywhere!" she shouted in his ear.

From behind them, Fawn came running with her swords spinning actively. She sliced at the air in front of Wildfire in an attempt to give Wesley an opening, but there was no giving in. Wildfire clung to Wesley with one arm, and the satchel that held the Sun Stone in the other. In other words, she couldn't attack freely.

"Ugh! Here! Hold this, would you!" Wildfire grimaced as she put the satchel around Wesley. With her free arm, she blasted fire at Fawn, sending her backward. Right when she did, Wesley took that as his chance to kick the arm the Wildfire held him with.

"Ah! You brat!" she screamed as she let go.

Wesley spun open his staff to reveal the glider and he shot it forward and upward. The glider spun around in a loop-di-loop and as it came back toward him, he jumped up to grab onto it with his hands and feet. Once Wesley clung tightly to the glider, Alice jumped up and grabbed the back of it so that she was dangling from it. Wesley flew them back toward where Fawn had fallen.

"Don't let them get away!" Wildfire yelled at her companion.

"I've got this one!" he shouted as he captured Fawn.

Wesley swooped low right next to the man in order to give Fawn a chance at escape. He felt a hand brush past the satchel that he wore around his shoulder that wasn't his own.

A second later, Fawn jumped out of the man's hold on her and kicked him right in the side of his face before she jumped to grab on to Alice's leg as they flew above her.

Fireballs from every direction and from every car began shooting right at the kids. Wesley dodged them as best he could, but it was rather hard with the amount of weight he was carrying and considering the fact that Alice and Fawn were just hanging freely from the back of the glider.

He flew them straight up into the clouds above them where seemingly out of nowhere, Reezu appeared. Alice and Fawn screamed as the last few fireballs shot up at them before they fell into the saddle heavily. Reezu swooped around as soon as the kids were in and began flying back toward Medina at full speed.

"Shoot them down!" came Wildfire's distant shout. The vehicles came to a sudden halt and began to turn around in order to pursue the kids. But the vehicles were not designed to deal with sand, let alone turn around in it, and all of them got stuck in a sideways position.

As Reezu flew away without a scratch on him, Jack hopped down from the reins to sit in the saddle with the others. "We made it!" he cheered with a sigh of relief. "It looks like we still make a good team after all."

Jack, Alice, Fawn, and Wesley all hugged one another like a true family. The past hour had been one big emotional rollercoaster, but at that moment, it seemed as though things would turn out okay.

"We do make a good team, don't we?" Alice whispered with a tear in her eye.

Wildfire stood on the top of her vehicle angrily looking off in the direction the giant bird had flown off in. The soldiers all had shovels and sticks they were using to move the sand away from the tires where the vehicles had gotten stuck. It was a difficult job to manage since they couldn't stand on the sand. Instead, they had to reach from atop the vehicles.

A sarcastic chuckle escaped Wildfire's throat as a sudden realization dawned upon her. The chuckle grew into a laugh and the laugh grew into a cackle until the entire platoon was wondering what was going on with her.

"What could possibly be so funny?" Yagatsu asked.

"I put the Sun Stone in the satchel . . ." Wildfire said as if it were a joke. Master Yagatsu stared at her blankly, as if he didn't understand, which only angered Wildfire further.

"I put the satchel on *him!*" she pointed off in the direction Wesley and the kids had gone in.

She whipped her hand down her face and smacked her lips in astonishment. How could she have managed to pull off something as stupid as that? How had she been so careless?

"Maybe," Yagatsu said, reaching into his pocket. "But that boy isn't very observant."

He pulled out the Sun Stone that he had snatched and tossed it to Wildfire. It looked like they had lucked out after all.

"You sneaky old man," Wildfire smiled.

"Here's your satchel back," Wesley said as he passed it over to Alice.

"We're nearly back to Medina," Jack said as the city began to come into view in the twilight sky. "You should keep a hand on the stone, Alice, so we can have a protective barrier just in case anything happens."

"Okay, right." Alice reached her left hand inside the satchel. She felt around but didn't sense the stone anywhere. She opened the flap and peered inside. Alice's heart skipped a beat as she realized the stone was *missing*.

"Is everything okay?" Fawn asked as she noticed Alice gasp.

"The Sun Stone . . . it's not here." Alice admitted.

"What!" Jack and Fawn shouted in unison. Fawn snatched the satchel and looked inside, as did Jack.

"This cannot be happening!" Jack exclaimed. "After everything we went through to get it in our possession and to save Wesley, now it's *gone?* What are we going to tell the Flame Cats? What are we going to tell Prince Urijah?"

"Sun Stone?" Wesley asked. "What about the Sun Stone? What are you guys talking about?"

Jack realized that Wesley had no idea about what had led up to this moment. He wasn't there when Alice explained that she and Fawn stole the Sun Stone. On second thought, it was probably better this way. Jack didn't want Wesley to get roped up in this and he also didn't know how the little boy would react to hearing what Alice had done.

"You don't mean you . . ." Wesley began hesitantly.

"Nothing," Jack stated sharply. "It's nothing really."

Although Wesley was not convinced that it was indeed "nothing" that they were talking about, he was cut off from asking anything else by the deafening screech Reezu suddenly let out.

"Reezu!" Alice shouted. "What is it, boy?" She peered over the side of the saddle and what she saw shook her core. The others joined her to see the dozen or so Fire Kingdom vehicles positioned right in front of the fallen gates. Each vehicle bore a flag with the yellow sun symbol. Jack instantly knew that this was not Wildfire. And he was right, as there was a young man with blonde hair wearing a force captain's uniform who stood at the front of the army.

In fear of being shot down from the sky, Alice lowered Reezu to the ground a few yards in front of the new Fire Kingdom platoon.

Not more than a second later did the sound of engines coming from behind them grow loud.

The kids turned around. Coming to a halt just behind them was Force Captain Wildfire's platoon. They had somehow gotten unstuck and made their way back here.

Alice looked to her front, and then to her back. They were now facing a new enemy, another Fire Kingdom Force Captain and his entire platoon. The stakes had doubled and there was no getting away this time. The kids couldn't make it past the Fire Kingdom into Medina and they couldn't escape through the desert either. *They were trapped.*

Their only way out of this would be through a fight. Jack realized it instantly. In his mind, he always thought that in order to be victorious, you'd also have to make a sacrifice.

He came to the conclusion that in order for their team to pull out a victory, *he* would have to be the one to make the sacrifice.

CHAPTER TEN

The Boy of Life and Death

ildfire and the other Fire Kingdom Force Captain hopped off their vehicles and began walking toward one another. Because the ground near the gates on the outside of Medina was made from stone, they didn't have to worry about the distractor spell affecting them.

The two of them walked for a few paces and then stopped with Wildfire behind the kids and the other Force Captain in front of them. Was this part of Wildfire's plan all along? Alice thought. To have reinforcements trap them?

"What are you doing here, Eternus?" Wildfire asked, sounding more curious than angry.

"Following orders, just like always," the other Force Captain replied matter of factly. "About a week ago, I received a letter from the Firelord. He thought you could use some help out here."

So it wasn't part of Wildfire's plan after all. It had been purely by coincidence that this other Force Captain, Eternus, had ended up there. If it wasn't for him, Alice and the others would have escaped Wildfire and been on their way by now.

"I don't need you baby-sitting me," Wildfire began. "If you're here, then who's watching over Elkmire?"

"Force Captain Kelevi. I heard a word from him this morning that the prisoners escaped. The Firelord ordered more forces to Elkmire during my absence for this reason."

"Blatant christ!" Wildfire cursed. "I can't let you fools do anything without messing something up!"

"Look at it this way," Eternus suggested. "They don't matter anymore because now we have the Light Spirit."

"*I* have the Light Spirit," Wildfire corrected. She was well aware of the fact that if it wasn't for Eternus showing up here at the right time, she wouldn't have the Light Spirit at her fingertips. But she also didn't have any intention of sharing credit for this accomplishment.

While Wildfire and Eternus continued to talk, Jack took the moment to converse with his own team inside Reezu's saddle.

"Alright, here's the plan," he started. "I'm going to distract them and once you guys see an opening, get away as fast as you can. Keep flying and don't stop until you're somewhere safe. I'll try to get the Sun Stone back and return it to the crystal podium. The barrier will be restored, protecting me and the Flame Cats."

Jack knew that this plan would never work, at least not for him. But it was all he could come with at the moment. There was a small chance for Alice and the others to succeed in getting away, and that small chance was good enough for him, even if it meant his own demise.

"No, Jack," Alice said. "That plan is suicide. You said it yourself that we're not losing anyone out here. Don't you realize that includes you too!"

"Yeah, Jack," Fawn agreed. "We need you."

Jack shrugged and looked away. "No one needs me."

"*I* need you," Alice said sternly.

Jack looked back at her. His eyes were watery. He was afraid, and not for himself. He was afraid that the others might not make it out of this. He was afraid that Alice might not see the light of day after tonight. But hearing her say that *she* needed him gave him all the strength and bravery in the world.

He grabbed Alice's hand. It was warm.

"It'll be okay. I'm your prince. I'm the oldest and the leader of this group, rather you guys like it or not. It's my job to make the plans and it's your job to follow them. Out of all of us, Alice's life is the most important. I hate to say it, but it's the truth. There's only one Light Spirit. We need to follow the best course of action to keep her alive at all times. As your prince, I've decided that this plan is Light Spirit Alice's best chance for survival. Anyone who goes against this plan is a traitor of the Earth Nation royal court. I'm sorry to do this to you, but this is the way it has to be."

"Nothing I say will change your mind, will it?" Alice asked.

"Unfortunately, not." He smiled.

"Jack, I don't like this," Fawn cried out.

"Why do you have to be the one to go?" Wesley complained. "Let me go! I'm faster, I can outrun the Fire Kingdom any day!"

"Wesley," Jack began. "You were captured by the Fire Kingdom today. Did you forget about that? And you're still so young. I couldn't live with myself if I had you do this and something happened."

"And what if something happens to you?" Fawn asked. "What do you expect us to do then, huh?"

"You'd push forward," he said strongly. "You keep going no matter what. You make it to the Etaellaca Empire and you save the world."

"Not without you," Alice consoled.

"Hear me out," Jack said. "It's true I might not make it out of this. I might be captured or even killed. I'm not ignoring that, but that's the reality of our situation. No matter what, we will be together again. All of us. Rather I make it out of here with you guys on Reezu or if I die at the hands of the Fire Kingdom. We will be together again! Someday . . . somewhere."

"Somewhere above the clouds," Wesley said.

"What?" Fawn asked.

"It's what we say in the Sky Kingdom. If we can't be together here and now, then one day we'll be together again somewhere above the clouds."

"Yeah," Alice said. She held her hand out in front of her. "To meeting again somewhere above the clouds."

The others put their hands forth and said together, "Somewhere above the clouds."

Jack looked at each one of his friends. He admired their bright, sad eyes and their hair that blew in the ember-scented wind. His eyes teared up and his voice grew weak.

"Yeah. Okay."

Jack hopped off of Reezu and began walking toward Wildfire. He stopped just a few paces short of her.

"Alright, now that we're all here," he started. "Just who are you and what do you want?"

"You mean you haven't guessed?" Wildfire said sarcastically. "I'm a Fire Kingdom official with more honor in my little finger than there is in your entire body, boy. And I think you already know what I want, at least part of it. I'm taking the Light Spirit. She's the key to making my dreams a reality."

"There has to be another way," Jack pleaded. "Are you really willing to go that far for something you want? How selfish of you to build yourself up at the expense of others."

"You can call me whatever you like. You and your friends are no match for my army. Give up now and live. Or you can fight, and die trying."

"We don't have to fight!" Jack argued, trying to buy time. "There's been enough blood spill for one day, hasn't there? It's late. We're all tired and far from home. Let us rest and move this battle to another day."

"Another day?" Wildfire questioned. "If that's so, then you must want to prepare for our battle. Do you *really* want to fight me?"

"I don't. I don't want to have to fight anyone. But if I must in order to protect those that I love, then I will gladly draw my sword at anyone who seems to be a threat."

"And that's what makes you weak."

"No. It's what makes me stronger than you."

Wildfire grimaced at that. "Enough chatting. This chase ends here and now. Soldiers! Prepare to engage!"

"No!" Jack shouted. "Please, we don't have to fight! Why are you doing this! Why!"

Wildfire stared at Jack with a threatening glare. "I told you already . . . *there's something I want.*"

In that instant, Wildfire created a wall of fire and sent it right for Reezu where Alice and the others still remained. The wall of fire blew right past Jack's right side, and the heat from it was enough to make him tremble.

"Reezu! Fly!" he commanded from the ground. Reezu instantly took off. The firewall passed underneath his talons with an inch to spare.

As Reezu flew up and away from the scene, fireballs began shooting at him. Without the Sun Stone to protect them, Fawn had to keep a steady hold on the reins and have Reezu dodge the attacks. In the midst of all the chaos, Alice looked down and instantly locked eyes with Wildfire.

"Maybe you can avoid me," Wildfire shouted up at her. "But *he* can't." She set her sights on Jack who stood unarmed just a few feet away from her. Wildfire jumped and exerted flames from the bottom of her foot, launching her high into the sky. On her way down, she flipped and the tail of fire streamed right for Jack. He rolled out of the way and drew his sword. He quickly realized that a sword, being a close-distance weapon, would do him no good when his opponents could attack from a long distance.

Jack stood as Wildfire began stalking toward him. A moment before she reached him, she suddenly jumped to the left. Turning around, Jack could see Prince Urijah standing on the rubble of the fallen gates. He chucked another shuriken at Wildfire that missed her by a hair.

More of the Flame Cats began pouring out of the city and engaging into combat with all of the Fire Kingdom soldiers. It was a relief to have support, but Jack knew it wouldn't be long before the Fire Kingdom overpowered them. All they had to do was hold out long enough to give Alice and the others sufficient time to get away.

Wildfire ignored the Flame Cats and left them for the soldiers to deal with while she attacked Jack with flame after flame after flame. He did his best to dodge, but she was faster than them. One punch of fire blew past his arm and burned through his sleeve, leaving a mark. He used his sword as a shield, but it wasn't enough. Another powerful blow came from Wildfire and Jack was blasted to the ground.

Fawn had already flown Reezu away from the battle, but looking back, Alice could still see the fight. "No!" she shouted as she saw Jack fall to the ground. She climbed up Reezu's neck to where Fawn sat on his head holding the reins.

"Turn back!" she demanded.

"We can't!" Fawn yelled. "This was the plan, remember? Jack . . . he-he'll be okay."

Alice grabbed Fawn's wrist and dragged her back down into the saddle.

"Hey! What do you think you're doing!" Fawn complained.

"I'm saving a life, you idiot!" Alice jumped back up and took the reins. She turned Reezu around mid-flight and headed for the battlefield. Once they were back in range of the fire magic users, fire blasts shot up at them once more.

Alice couldn't dodge the attacks as well as Fawn could, so instead, she landed Reezu a short distance away from the fighting. Reezu let out an ear-splitting screech as Alice forced him down from the sky near crashing balls of fire.

Alice ignored the saddle and jumped right off of Reezu's head onto the far below ground. She could hear Fawn say, "Ugh! This again!" as she passed her.

Fawn drew her swords and Wesley opened his glider to take to the sky. Even though they were very well aware that this could cost all of them their lives, they hurried after Alice into the blood frenzy.

Fawn stood still as a dozen Fire Kingdom soldiers came running at her with either swords or hands of fire. She waited until they reached her, their loud battle cries made her ears ring. Once the soldiers were within reaching distance, Fawn twirled around with her swords outstretched. She spun so fast that the soldiers couldn't follow her with their eyes. She made sure to pass by each one of them.

Fawn stopped to catch her breath once she was sure she struck them all. She turned around to face them again. They all stood completely still with shocked expressions. Fawn stared back at them and whipped a drop of blood from her cheek.

"You missed," one of the soldiers said.

Not a second later, each of the soldiers Fawn had attacked fell to the ground. Some of their limbs detached from where Fawn's blades had sliced through. Others had their stomachs empty of its contents. All of them flopped to the stone ground and bled out.

Fawn stalked up to their bodies and glared down at them with a look of disgust. "I never miss."

Wesley zipped through the sky as he dodged the fireballs being shot at him from below. Not only did he have to remain aware of his surroundings in order to avoid being knocked out of the sky, but he also had to deflect blows from his airborne opponents.

Fire fairies flew after him left and right with either swords or bow and arrows as their offense. Wesley was grateful that fairies did not have fire magic abilities. Otherwise, he'd be in a lot more trouble.

He was faster than then and much better at dodging the fireballs which he used to his advantage.

Wesley had devised a strategy that seemed to work against the fairies. He would fly in any direction as fast as he could in order to gain speed, momentum, and air. Then he would whip back around at the opponents following his tail and kick a blast of wind at them, knocking them down from the sky.

He was careful not to hit them too hard in fear of injuring them. All he needed to do was get them down from the air to protect himself and to prevent them from hurting any of his friends.

Once a fairy would get knocked to the ground, Wesley noticed they would be weary taking to the sky again. As this pattern continued, fewer fairies remained in the air for him to tackle. He'd have to take his abilities to the ground soon in order to be of more help.

Alice ran through the war zone as fast as her legs would carry her. Many attackers came at her left and right, but she easily dodged them. Most of the soldiers were large, bulky men who were clumsy and not very quick on their feet, so it made things easier on her in terms of getting away.

As one particularly large soldier came for her, she jumped and kicked him in the head before running past him. A pair of smaller guys charged her with one coming from the left and one from the right. Alice stopped dead in her tracks and let them come right for her. A second before they would have stabbed their swords into her, she ducked. Instead, the soldiers stabbed each other, killing them both instantly.

Alice ran a few more paces and then the center of the battlefield came into view. It was smokey from the number of fire blasts being shot, but she could make out Wildfire and Jack battling each other.

Wildfire danced around Jack on fast and unpredictable feet. Jack stayed steady and strong on his legs, only slicing his sword at Wildfire when he saw a good opening. He could tell that his sword made her a bit uneasy. Perhaps, the Fire Blood Elf wasn't familiar with the techniques used by a swordsman.

Wildfire was slowly getting closer to Jack with each jump or flip she made. She was coming in for a direct attack. Jack used this opportunity to run right for his opponent while slashing with strong, quick strokes. Wildfire dodged the attack with a single, extraordinarily high jump. Before she landed, she extended her leg and kicked Jack's wrist with a force so great, he heard it snap. His father's sword was instantly knocked out of his hand. It tumbled through the air and hit the ground many feet away, leaving him unarmed.

Jack's gaze shifted from the awkward bent position of his wrist, to where his sword lay in the midst of the battle near the feet of many fighting soldiers. There was no way he'd be able to get to it. He hadn't the time to. He was injured, exhausted, and unarmed. There wasn't any grand scheme or complicated strategy left for him to execute, whatever came at him next would mean the end.

Wildfire took the opportunity to blast a fire kick at Jack. It hit him with an extreme force that sent him flying several yards away. He tumbled over himself a few times before hitting the ground hard. The fire had scorched his arms, leaving red marks that stung horribly.

From where she stood a few yards away, Alice trembled as she saw Jack get blasted away.

"Jack!" she shouted.

Alice made a beeline right for Jack. He was still a good distance away from her. She knew it would be nearly impossible for her to reach him before Wildfire did, but she had to try. Even if she somehow did make it in time, what could she even do to help? There was no way she could defeat Wildfire in a fight. If she had trained her whole life like a proper Light Spirit, she'd have a good chance. But instead, she'd spent the last five years playing and taking it easy. How shameful of her.

Instead of Wildfire making her way toward Jack, she turned around and walked a few paces away. She walked to where a fairy that had fallen from the sky lay unconscious. Beside the fairy was a bow and arrow. Wildfire picked it up and began stalking toward Jack.

Jack tried to get up, but he fell. He rose and fell again. He stayed on the ground on his hands and knees. Looking up, he could see Wildfire through the smoke several yards away. She held a bow and arrow in her hands. She positioned the arrow on the bow and raised it, aimed right for him.

"No!" Alice cried to herself as she ran to try and get to Jack. She had almost reached him. Maybe she could still save him.

From across the battlefield, Urijah heard Alice's shout as he sparred with a trio of Fire Kingdom soldiers. He defeated them and looked over his shoulder. He could see Alice running right for Jack who had an arrow pointed at him a few yards away. In an instant, he understood what she was planning.

"Alice! No!" he shouted. But he was too late. Alice had reached Jack just as Wildfire let the arrow fly.

Alice stood before Jack, and time seemed to slow down. She turned around and felt the wind blow through her hair. Suddenly, she could smell the fire and smoke that had been around her this whole time. It was overwhelming. Her eyes wheeled up from the heat and fumes. Unable to move, she watched as the arrow sliced through the air and rammed its way towards her.

Jack saw the arrow coming right for Alice. His mind thought back to what he saw in the hall of mirrors at the sight of the trials. He remembered the feeling of guilt when he saw the arrow strike Alice then. That vision was a warning. A vision from the future, now the present, that he could have avoided. He could hear Urijah's words echoing across his mind, *"You have the power to change the outcome based on the decisions you make."*

At once, Alice's senses came back to her and the world revolved back to its normal timing. She felt a pair of hands grab her shoulders from behind and shove her to the ground a few feet away. She hit her head on the stone ground hard and got the wind knocked out of her. Her hearing paused, and for the moment, there was no sound around her. The shouting of soldiers, explosion of fireballs, and clanking of weapons all stopped. She could still see those events happening in her peripheral vision, but no sound came from them. All was quiet.

She sat up. Standing before her, a few feet away, was Jack. He had his back to her. He stood completely still . . . as if frozen in time. He slowly turned around to face Alice. Standing behind him, Alice could make out Wildfire. The bow she grasped was still raised, but its string was empty of the arrow it held seconds ago.

Jack's wide, glossy eyes met Alice's. He gently looked down at his chest. Alice followed his gaze there. A sudden gasp escaped her lips and she felt her eyes well up as she peered at the arrow lodged firmly in the middle of Jack's chest. Blood poured down from it, turning his shirt red. He seemed to move in slow motion as he lifted his arm and wrapped his hand around the arrow to pull it out of his chest.

The arrow dropped to the ground, and Jack fell to his knees. He looked back up at Alice with dull and empty eyes. The wind ruffled his hair and instantly, Alice's senses came back to her. She ran to Jack in order to meet him on the ground, but he was suddenly and harshly dragged backward by his collar.

Wildfire pulled him away and Alice was left sitting on the blood-stained ground.

"No, no, no, no! Jack! Please, please, don't do this!" she cried.

"It's fair game. I told you all that this would happen. All you had to do was give up and surrender. But you couldn't even do that!"

Wildfire almost seemed taken aback by what was happening. As if she hadn't really expected the arrow to hit one of them. She seemed weary, unsure, and uneasy about what she was doing. It was the first time Alice had seen her behave in this manner.

"It doesn't have to be like this! Let him go!" Alice pleaded. She stood up and prepared herself for a fight. She was the Light Spirit. There had to be something she could do. There was no way she'd let her friend die on her behalf.

"Just stop," Wildfire said, in a sad-like tone as she noticed what Alice was doing. "This fight is over. Give up."

It was only then did Alice realize that the battle around her had come to an end. Fire Kingdom soldiers had banded together to encircle Alice, Wildfire, and Jack. Many of the Flame Cats that had come out to fight lay dead on the ground. Prince Urijah and Fawn had been apprehended. Fire Kingdom warriors held them immobilized. Wesley had been tackled to the ground. Three large men had to sit on top of him in order to keep from slipping out of their grasp.

Wildfire was right, the fight was over.

Alice dropped to her knees. She could see Jack grimacing from his injuries as he laid on the ground. Wildfire stood over him, keeping her gaze locked on Alice.

"Please," Alice began. "Don't do this, don't take him from me! Don't make yourself a killer. You don't want that! I know you don't!"

"Tsk." Wildfire spat as she turned to the side. "You brought this on yourself. What happens next is because of *you*."

"I know that!" Alice cried. "It's my fault! He jumped in to save me! It's because of me that we left our home, that this all happened! Don't you think I know that!"

"Then why did you do it!" Wildfire shouted as if she was angry Alice allowed her to win.

"I . . . I didn't have a choice."

Wildfire picked up Jack by his collar again and started dragging him away toward the vehicles. He coughed and choked on his own blood, gasping for air.

"No!" Alice screamed. "You're not a killer so don't make yourself one! Let me heal him! I can save him!"

"I *am* a killer. I've hurt a lot of people, I've killed many. This time shall be no different," Wildfire said as she continued. She was unemotional, although she did grit her teeth together in discomfort.

"Please listen to me!" Alice begged. "Take me! I'm the one you want! I'll go with you! You can have me. I'll give up. You won't have to chase me or fight me anymore. I'll go wherever you want and do whatever you say! I'm begging you, just please, let me *heal him!*"

Wildfire paused. She closed her eyes and clenched her jaw, deeply thinking about what she should do next. After a long moment of dreadful silence, she sighed and let go of Jack.

"Fine," she whispered, walking a little way away from him.

Alice got up and ran to Jack. She met him on the ground and lifted his head to rest on her lap. She frantically began unbuttoning his shirt with shaky and unsteady hands. If she was going to save him, she needed to act quickly. Alice had never worked on an injury of this magnitude before, nor did she understand how to heal wounds caused by arrows, but she would certainly do her best.

She pressed her hands to the open wound on Jack's chest and a soft white light emitted from her palms. His skin was blazing hot and his cheeks were red. Alice focused the majority of her energy on the arrow wound, but as she looked around, she noticed that there were dozens of smaller cuts, scrapes, and bruises all over him. Not to mention the burn marks on his arms that would most certainly leave scars and his broken wrist.

Alice soon found herself overwhelmed by the damage and pain he had endured. She moved her hands all over him trying to heal everything at once, but it seemed as though she was getting nowhere. Hot tears flowed down her cheeks and dripped onto Jack's warm skin. He grimaced, and slowly opened his eyes that were cloudy with pain.

"A-Alice." He coughed weakly.

She continued trying to heal all the parts of him that were broken but to no avail.

"Alice . . . just stop."

She knew where this was headed and that's why she didn't stop. The thought of what was coming next only made her more frantic to try and save him.

"Alice!" Jack said as loud as his voice would allow him to go. He grabbed Alice's wrist with his good hand to get her attention. She instantly stopped what she was doing to look at him.

"Y-you're gonna be okay . . . Jack. I-I'll heal you . . . and then we'll get out of this . . . a-and everything is gonna go back to the way it was . . . I p-promise," she said in between sobs. So many tears poured out of her eyes that she soon found it hard to see. She whipped her sleeve across her face to try and clear her vision.

"It's okay, Alice," Jack whispered. "You don't have to cry."

Alice looked at him and she couldn't stop sobbing. She took in deep gasps of air every time she got the chance to. She was struggling to breathe, that weird kind of struggle that happens from crying too much.

Jack took his gaze from Alice and stared up at the sky. It was beginning to darken, but many shades of red and yellow still swirled around it. The light from the sky reflected back into his blue eyes. As he looked at the sky filled with tranquility, he took a deep breath, soaking it all in.

Alice held his hand. She was warm.

He closed his eyes and thought back to everything that had led up to this point. He remembered when he had first met Alice. In fact, he still remembered the way he felt when he saw her for the first time. He remembered that feeling because he felt it every day. Every day since then and every time he looked at Alice, it was as if he was seeing her for the first time again.

If he had never met her, he wouldn't be in this situation right now. Jack was very well aware of that, but even still, he wouldn't have had it any other way. If this was when his time came to an end, then so be it. He had a good run. He only wished he could have known Alice for longer.

"Alice, listen to me," he began. "There are things in this life that we may never understand. People come and go into our lives like the wind, but there will always be some who you wish could stay forever. *You* are one of those people, Alice. I want to stay in your life forever and I want you to be in mine forever. Even if it's selfish of me. However, the gods sometimes have other plans in mind for us . . . this seems to be one of those plans."

"Don't you do that," Alice cried. "Don't start saying your goodbyes. You're going to be fine. You'll make it out of this!"

"Oh, Alice." He smiled. "You're so naive, but that's what makes you so special. Do you remember the day we first met? My mom had just found you in the storm and I had just recovered from another cold."

Alice nodded. She thought about that day often.

"When I saw you for the first time . . . I was in awe. Not because of how beautiful you were or because you were the Light Spirit. It wasn't because of any of that. It was because of how strong you were. You had just suffered one of the worst tragedies I had ever seen, yet you still found a way to smile. You still went and played in the forest with Fawn and I. No matter what questions you had or whatever hardships you suffered in your past, you still smiled. You stayed strong and pushed forward . . . which is something I thought I could never do . . . until I met you.

"In the end, I'm just thankful for your existence . . . rather I'm meant to be part of it or not. I hope that your inner strength will help this world the way it helped me."

"N-no, Jack," Alice cried. "Don't go. I'm scared."

He squeezed her hand and smiled at her. "*Never* be afraid. You mustn't let fear decide your fate."

From the corner of his eye, he could see the blood pooling around him. He didn't have much longer.

"Listen to me, Alice. There's been something I've wanted to tell you for a while. It's been bugging me for so long and I just never knew how to tell you." He let go of her hand to reach up to her cheek.

He held the side of her damp face with his hand and whipped away a few of her tears.

Alice held his hand there, beside her cheek. His skin that was blistering hot moments ago had significantly cooled down. He was growing cold and his lips were turning a pale blue color.

"Alice . . ." he whispered so hoarsely it strained his weakening voice. ". . . I love you."

Alice instantly cried out so hard it made her tremble. Her hand shook against Jack and her whole body grew numb. Jack *loved* her. It was a feeling she had never felt for anyone else in her entire life, but in that moment, she felt it for him. The fact that she was only realizing it now made her cry even harder.

She looked down at Jack as she continued to sob. His beautiful blue eyes suddenly turned dull. His hand slipped away from her face as Alice felt the life of the person she cared for the most drift away.

She opened her mouth to tell him how she felt while he could still hear her. "I lov—"

Before Alice could finish, a massive blast of fire landed right on top of her. The heat was unimaginable and she brought her hands to her face. The explosion shot her backward a few feet and there were remnants from the fire burning across her hands. But Alice didn't feel the pain from the fire or the heat. She could only feel the pain of watching Wildfire drag Jack's lifeless body across the stone and onto her vehicle.

"No!" she whined. "No! Don't take him from me! Don't do this! Please! I'm begging you!"

No matter how loud Alice shouted, her screams didn't reach Wildfire's ears. She boarded the vehicle with Jack's body and a completely, utterly, emotionless expression was displayed across her face. Her eyes, on the other hand, were blazing a fire so hot and bright that Alice feared they might explode.

The Fire Kingdom soldiers that had apprehended Fawn, Wesley, and Urijah let go of them to board their vehicles. Both platoons gathered up their men and started their engines. Wildfire's vehicle was the first to leave the scene. The other vehicles soon followed suit, leaving the battlefield nothing more than an empty area stained with blood and fallen bodies.

Wildfire stared right into Alice's eyes as she made her get away with Jack's body at her feet. Everything about her expression inside her eyes was telling Alice: *I win.*

"Don't take him!" Alice yelled so loud it strained her voice. "Don't run away! I'm not done with you, coward! Turn and face *me*! I'm the one you want! Don't forget that we're just kids who are fighting an entire army! Where you have the advantage! We're not like you at all! We don't have the numbers that you do! And when we lose someone, it costs us *everything*! Don't run away you monster! You're a coward, a coward! Jack is stronger than you'll ever hope to be! Much stronger! You didn't win against him! He kept everyone safe! He held out until the end so that no one would die! You're the one who lost! Jack is the true victor!"

Alice screamed out as loud as she could. She had run out onto the sand and parts of it had darkened with some of her tears. She screamed so loud she felt it rumble her chest. But no matter how loud she screamed, it wouldn't stop the horrible feeling inside her heart.

She collapsed to the ground and buried her face in her hands, continuing to sob. Fawn and Wesley came to stand beside her. Both of them were weeping profusely. Wesley bit his bottom lip to stop it from quivering and Fawn ducked her face into her elbow. Her chest heaved up and down as she tried not to make any noise. Large, clumpy tears poured out of their eyes and streamed down their rosy cheeks to no end.

Reezu, Mayday, and Boo came to stand beside the kids. Mayday whined and curled herself into a little ball at Fawn's feet. Boo landed on Wesley's shoulder and spread his tiny arms wide to hug his friend's neck. Reezu laid down behind the kids with his warm feathery side pressed up against them. He curled his long neck around the kids in a hug and closed his eyes.

"I . . ." Alice whispered with her strained voice beginning to crack. ". . . I never got to tell him."

Firelord Ash laid with his head on his desk, asleep. He held a rather small unicorn horn in his bare right hand. His other hand wore one of the long red gloves he preferred to always be dressed in. Beside his head was a pink and gold music box with a fairy slowly spinning around. The music box played a familiar melody, a song he had grown accustomed to as his old friend, from many years ago, used to hum it from time to time.

He breathed slow and shallow breaths, and his eyes moved left and right behind his eyelids as he dreamed. However, it was more than a dream. It was a vision, a memory. A memory that didn't belong to him, but rather to the former owner of the small unicorn horn held in his hand.

Inside the dream world, Ash watched as a tall teenage boy played with a little girl with long blonde hair. The boy had to be fifteen or sixteen and the girl couldn't be more than five. They were in the middle of a dark and mysterious forest. The trees were so big that Ash couldn't see the top of them. Exotic mushrooms grew along the trees and glowing, jellyfish-like creatures floated in the air.

Ash watched the memory play out. Everything was a bit hazy as if he was looking through smudged glass. Because of the haziness, he couldn't see the girl or boy's face. The boy was an old friend of his and Ash remembered him well. He was almost grateful that he couldn't make out his friend's face in fear of being overwhelmed with memories that he'd rather not revisit. As for the little girl, his imagination would have to suffice, concerning what she looked like.

Ash followed behind the boy and girl as they walked through the forest. The boy held the little girl's hand. He had large, black wings sprouting from his back, and brown hair. The girl had a tiny unicorn horn that wouldn't be fully grown for many years.

Eventually, they made their way to a wooden door built into the trunk of one of the massive trees. There was no doorknob, or anything indicating how the door would open.

"We have the keys! We have the keys!" the boy cheered. His voice carried a deep, familiar accent. He lifted his hand and placed it on the door's wooden surface. He lifted the girl's hand to place it on the door as well. As soon as both their hands made contact, the door began to glow a golden hue. A second later, it opened itself. Inside the tree was a pitch-black staircase going down as far as they could see.

While holding onto the girl's hand, the boy took the first step into the doorway, but the little girl hesitated. She peered down the stairs with wide, nervous eyes.

"Don't be afraid, my dear," the boy said. "This is only the beginning of what's to come."

"I know," the girl whispered. "Do we have to?"

The girl was anxious and hesitant to continue, but the boy's teachings were already inside her head. Everything he had taught her was coming alive in a fluttery sensation of confidence that pushed her forward.

"This is our duty to make the world better," the boy said sternly. "*You* are Wonderland. That is your whole. Accept your nature and we can rule our world . . ."

With the girl's hand in his, the boy walked down the secret staircase. There was no light, so the girl began to emit a soft white light from her horn.

As they continued down the staircase, the boy started to hum a familiar tune. It was the same song played on the music box Ash had been listening to, the music box this boy had given the girl.

Ash didn't follow them down the stairs, he already knew what they would do next. He closed his eyes and let the memory drift away.

In an instant, his eyes snapped open and he sat up. He was back in his study, still seated at his desk. The unicorn horn remained in his hand and the music box continued to play its eerie tune. Hearing the song again brought back everything Ash and his friend had been through all those years ago. The music was nostalgic and terrifying at the same time. Ash could almost spell that sweet scent belonging to his friend as if he was in the room with him. That sweet scent that smelled like candy . . . no it was even sweeter than candy. It was more like . . . *vanilla.*

The memory inside the dream upset Ash. It wasn't even one of his own memories, but it sent chills down his spine to see his dear friend again and to see the things he had done. His friend was capable of pulling off many dangerous and exotic feats. In fact, he *lived* for them. But to bring a child into such plans was bizarre to Ash.

Thinking of his friend reminded Ash of the time they had spent together many years ago. It was a time filled with chaos, danger, and wonder. Everything was unpredictable when his friend was around. The two of them had big plans for the world. In fact, they still did, but they had taken a bit of a detour in recent times.

Ash placed the tiny unicorn horn into the music box and closed it so that he wouldn't have to hear that melody play any longer. It reminded him of everything too much. It reminded him about what he was bringing back into the world. For all these years, he had wondered if he was doing the right thing by abiding by his friend's wish to have the world. Each time he came to the conclusion that it didn't matter if taking the world was right or wrong, his friend wanted it done and Ash would do it for him during his absence.

The thought of seeing his friend again soon and allowing him back into the world made Ash excited and nervous. The world would certainly be more interesting in the coming weeks, but things would also get very dark, very quickly.

After all, the chaos brought on by the Dark Spirit was something that not even Ash could handle.

As the desert came to an abrupt end, the Fire Kingdom came into view. Reezu landed at the edge of the sand. For as far left and right as they could see, the sand came to an end and went down a slope into a valley. Inside the endless valley was none other than the Fire Kingdom. There were a few small, grassy slopes but past that, there was a city with bright lights lighting up the night sky.

Alice, Fawn, and Wesley hopped off of Reezu. All of them wore numb and broken expressions on their faces. It had taken them a couple of hours to get here from Medina. Force Captain Wildfire had to be far ahead of them by now, but it didn't matter. There was nothing they could do against her, and it wasn't like Jack was in any immediate danger. He was *dead.* Now they would simply try and retrieve his body in order to give him the burial he deserved.

Alice didn't even want to think about what she would tell Queen Rosenia and the princesses. How would she tell them? How *could* she? Alice would have to find a way soon because their journey was now coming to an end before it had even begun. They weren't going to make it to Etaellaca. There was no way they'd make it without Jack. The plan now was to head to the Fire Kingdom capital to take Jack back and then they would go back home. Everything had been for nothing.

"Well, buddy," Alice said, turning to face Reezu. "I guess this is where we go our separate ways."

Alice had decided that traveling through the Fire Kingdom with Reezu would be far too risky. He was gigantic and very noticeable. With him by their side, or flying in the air, they'd stick out like a sore thumb. Instead, Reezu would fly solo through the desert directly east to the coast. From there, he'd wait on the beach for the kids in the Fire Kingdom capital, Palace City.

Reezu bent his neck down to press his massive head against Alice's. She rubbed his soft feathers and he purred a deep and sad melody.

"It'll probably take us two weeks to get to Palace City from here on foot. We'll be together again soon." She kissed his beak.

"See you later, Reezu," Fawn said as she rubbed the bird's side.

"Bye-bye, birdie," Wesley whispered. He hadn't said much since they left Medina. Alice worried about his mental health. He had been through a lot in such a short period of time, which couldn't be good for a ten-year-old kid.

Reezu took a step back and flapped his enormous wings until his talons lifted from the sand. He flew up into the sky and away to the east. Alice soon lost sight of him.

"Well, we better get going now," she said to the others. "We still need to find somewhere safe to spend the night."

She and Fawn started down the slope. When Alice realized Wesley wasn't behind them, she stopped to turn back at him.

"Come on, Wesley. Let's go."

He held onto the satchel that once held the Sun Stone. He looked at Alice and Fawn with large, sad eyes. He was crying.

"I'm sorry," he began in a hushed voice. "I'm sorry but I have to go back."

"What?" Alice asked, perplexed.

Wesley reached into the satchel and to the others' surprise, pulled out the Sun Stone. "I got this back. One of the soldiers had it. During the fight, I came down from the sky to retrieve it."

"Why didn't you mention that earlier?" Fawn asked.

"This stone," Wesley started. "We stole it from them. We left the Flame Cats defenseless in their own home. They need it, and now we know how to make it strong again. It was weak before because it wasn't exposed to sunlight. The Sun Stone gets its charge from sunlight, and as long as it remains exposed to the sun, it'll create a strong barrier for all of Medina."

"That's right," Alice said. "But we don't have time to take it all the way back. Besides, we need it to protect us from the Fire Kingdom."

"I'm going back to Medina," Wesley said firmly. "I only came this far with it to make sure you guys got through the rest of the desert safely. I'll be taking this home now."

"No," Alice begged. "We can't split up now! We've been through too much together!"

"Alice," Fawn began. "He's right. We were wrong to take the stone. I thought that the Flame Cats deserved it, but I was wrong. They're not evil war criminals like I thought. They're innocent people like us who fell victim to the Fire Kingdom. They need it more than we do."

"But . . ." Alice whispered. She stopped herself because she realized that the others were right. She just wished they didn't have to split up. They had already lost one.

Alice walked back up to the top of the slope to stand beside Wesley. "You sure you can make it there and back on your own?"

He nodded.

"Alright then. Take the Sun Stone home and then meet us in Palace City in two weeks. If you're not there after a while, Fawn and I will assume the worst and come looking for you."

"Okay," Wesley agreed. "And I'll do the same if I can't find you once I get there."

Alice and Fawn hugged Wesley. The three of them stayed there like that, breathing in each other's scent and feeling their warmth, for a long while. Who knew if they'd be able to do this again?

Once they let go, Wesley picked up his staff and twirled it so that the glider opened. "I'll see you in two weeks." A moment later, he floated into the sky and flew off to the north. Alice and Fawn watched him go until he disappeared from sight. And then they headed down the slope.

Alice had always hated saying goodbye. Goodbye always meant going away. At least, in this case, it was goodbye only for a little while. She only wished she could say the same about Jack.

She wasn't sure if this was the next part of their journey or the end of it. Hopefully, things would be clearer in time. One thing was for certain though: their world was changing.

Every aspect of everything they thought they knew about themselves in the range of Infinity was not the same as it was when they had left home.

Alice reached into her pocket and pulled out the Sacred Scroll. She looked at it with a twinkle of curiosity in her eyes. This is what it meant to be a spirit. Always coming and going, sacrificing and suffering. She didn't want to be the hero . . . at least not *alone.* She remembered something important.

There once was a Dark Spirit who roamed Infinity. Someone who'd share her burden and understand her struggle. He may not have been good, and he may have been evil, but he was someone who was similar to her. He was someone Alice had an unusual curiosity in.

Alice found herself thinking more and more about the Dark Spirit in recent times. After all, sometimes, the world needed a little darkness in it to be complete. How else could the light shine through? She tucked the scroll into her pocket and looked up at the moon. It seemed to peer back at her. It always had. It was as if it was watching her intently at all times, studying her every move.

Alice walked closely to Fawn as they made their way down the slope. It would only be a matter of time until they reached Palace City.

They were willingly walking into Wildfire's open arms . . . right into the heart of the Fire Kingdom.

END OF BOOK ONE

The Adventure Continues in
Sunrise, Book Two

www.ingramcontent.com/pod-product-compliance
Lightning Source LLC
Chambersburg PA
CBHW050830190726
48286CB00007B/2036